THE LOST CHILDREN

An absolutely gripping killer thriller with a huge twist

STEVE PARKER

JOFFE BOOKS

Published 2018 by Joffe Books, London.

www.joffebooks.com

This book is a work of fiction. Names, characters, businesses, organizations, places and events are either the product of the author's imagination or are used fictitiously. Any resemblance to actual persons, living or dead, events or locales is entirely coincidental. The spelling is British English.

ISBN-13: 978-1-78931-032-0

For Caz. Your support and understanding are everything.
Thank you.

Grateful thanks to Jasper for taking the chance and pulling me out of the void and Anne for clearing up my mess.

PROLOGUE

Day 1 — Sunday

Up to the moment when his brain erupted through the back of his head in an explosion of blood and bone, Samuel Babatunde's day had been going pretty well.

When Papa Benjamin, his pastor and saviour, had picked him from the flock and given him the honour of carrying out so sacred a task, Samuel's heart had nearly burst out of his chest with pride. Of all the congregation, he was the one who had been trusted with this simple but important mission — to dispose of it now that it had fulfilled its purpose.

He was under no illusion. He had seen it, touched it, washed it clean and blessed it. He knew exactly what it was, what had happened. He understood and approved and would do exactly what had been asked of him. This he would do happily to ensure that the spirits would bless and watch over Papa Benjamin and his work.

Had he been able to, he would no doubt be regretting two things at this point. The first, ever having met "Papa" Benjamin and his good lady wife, Blessing. The second, having been selected by the aforesaid Papa Benjamin and his good lady wife Blessing to carry out this task.

* * *

The man had been watching Samuel for a few minutes now, through a little round window. Whenever he looked through this window, a particular memory always, always crept in, one of the few good ones he had of his family, and his father most of all. It made him smile slightly.

With a few beers inside him, his dad would tell him stories about his own childhood. Drunken ramblings mostly. Nobody really listened. Nobody gave a fuck.

Dad had grown up watching a kiddies' television show called *Play School.* Big in the sixties and seventies, the show featured a couple of presenters who used to dress up, play guitar and sing songs, and generally embarrass themselves for the benefit of the nation's schoolkids. Good of them, really. One of the things the old man rambled on about was the windows — round, square and arch. The famous windows, Dad said. They weren't real windows, of course, merely studio mock-ups. The presenter used to ask the children at home to look through one of the windows with him. His dad's favourite presenter was a bloke called Brian Cant — Uncle Brian, his dad called him. Nobody knew why. Nobody gave a fuck.

Uncle Brian would pick a window and the camera would move toward and then "through" the window, fade out and then show a little film. It was supposed to be something you saw through that window — a trip to the zoo, or a farm or a factory, all sorts of stuff that might be of interest to kids in the seventies. Dad's preferred window was the round one. Said you always saw better things through that one. So now the man smiled to himself. Whenever he looked through his own round window, the one on top of his rifle, something happened. Everything he saw in it died.

From the moment he stepped out of the building, the man kept the crosshairs aligned with Samuel's head. Samuel held the little bundle tight against his body, doing his best to shield it from prying eyes as he moved away from the door. From a forensic point of view that was a mistake, but one that didn't matter so much now that he was dead.

When Samuel reached the industrial waste bins, he stopped and looked all around to see if anybody was watching. But he neglected to look up. Perhaps, in some cases, it's best not to. In Samuel's case, he would no doubt have been surprised to see his old working partner, Death, looking directly at him. Through the work he did in the church, he had called upon Death many times and had stood in the same room when He came to collect. But that was back in Africa and a good few years ago, so they hadn't seen too much of each other lately. He wouldn't have been happy to see him again. He dropped the bundle in the bin and began to cover it up the best he could with bits of cardboard and plastic.

The man, expressionless, checked the wind direction.

Took a deep breath.

Calmed himself.

And squeezed the trigger.

Through the little round window the man watched Samuel fall. He didn't roll or jerk, just dropped as if God himself had stolen his legs away. The man allowed himself a little grin. In a few minutes, when Samuel failed to return, someone from the congregation would come looking for him. They'd find him dead. They would find him and they would raise hell. Then others would come, panicking, screaming, crying, hysterical. His target, Papa Benjamin, would be among them. But today, like all the other days, he would spare Papa Benjamin. The man packed away his weapon, made his way off the roof and casually strolled down the stairs. There was no need to rush.

He reached the ground floor and heard the first shouts of alarm. Quicker than he'd expected, but no matter. He was in time. He stepped out into the street, ducked down behind a car and peeped around the bonnet, watching. Reaching inside his jacket pocket, he unclipped a mini Uzi and waited for them all to come spilling out, weeping and wailing, hysterical. No matter where he carried out his work, the aftermath was always the same. And when Papa Benjamin arrived, he knew he'd try to retrieve the bundle and have it taken away before the police turned up. But that wouldn't happen.

He didn't have long to wait.

From an old brick-built building opposite the dead man, the doors to the Light of Our Lord Deliverance Ministries burst open and several people came out, running anxiously toward the shouting man, to where he was pointing. They saw the body of Samuel Babatunde and the screaming kicked up a notch. They stood around him, weeping, shouting, unsure of what was happening, unsure of what to do.

The man immediately recognised Papa Benjamin in the crowd. He couldn't forget him and never wanted to. His eyes locked on him, watching him carefully. Unmoving as a stone, he watched Papa Benjamin, calm, unflappable, barking orders with just one thing on his mind. Remove the bundle. Fast. Benjamin and several men ran toward the bin, stepping over Babatunde and beginning to rake through the rubbish. The first short burst from the Uzi made everyone drop to their knees. It had them cowering with their hands over their heads before they all went scrabbling in search of safety. Some of the crowd, their grief instantly forgotten, picked themselves up and began to run in all directions, screaming in terror and panic. For some, no doubt, it was a little too much like home.

The man kept them pinned down until he made out the faint sound of wailing sirens in the distance. He estimated he had two, maybe three minutes before they arrived. He fired another short burst. More screaming. Papa and his boys were still down, the bundle still in situ. They wouldn't move. Papa Benjamin wouldn't risk it.

The first of several police cars tore through the entrance gates, tyres squealing on the concrete path, sirens blaring, lights flashing. The man fired one last short burst as the cars screamed toward the crowd, and then he was gone.

CHAPTER ONE

Ray Paterson could feel the butterflies in his stomach rising as he mounted the steps to Tower Bridge Police Station. His first day back at work, and already he was wondering whether he should have agreed to come back at all. He knew that his return could go one of two ways. He'd either be welcomed back into the fold like a conquering hero or else he'd be shunned, like some kind of pariah. He knew the most likely outcome would be a mixture of both. The more pragmatic of the team would understand that he'd been justified in killing Detective Constable Adam Walker for his crimes. Hell, any one of them would have done the same had Walker raped and butchered their wife. The more liberal, woolly leftie types who now flooded the force would never understand his actions and would never forgive him either.

Paterson walked into the foyer and pressed the buzzer on the door frame. He held his warrant card up to the Plexiglas to give the civvy desk jockey behind the counter a good view of it. As soon as the buzzer went, he pushed the door open and said, 'Detective Superintendent Paterson, here to see DI Clocks.'

'Top floor, turn right, blue door. Go straight through the squad room and DI Clocks's office is at the back. He's waiting for you,' said the civvy.

Paterson nodded, pushed the door open and stepped over the threshold. Instantly he was back in the world he knew and where he felt most comfortable. Police stations have their own ambiance and Tower Bridge, being one of the oldest, had ambiance in abundance. Unlike the modern police stations with hard carpeting and dry wall everywhere, Tower Bridge was all lino floors and solid brick walls that had been painted over God knows how many times. They had a smooth, cold feel. The high ceilings, coupled with the solid stone steps, created a cathedral-like resonance. He loved it. His footsteps echoed as he made his way up the old stone stairway, the steps slippery under his leather soles, worn smooth by the passage of time and the feet of countless policemen and civilians.

A wave of nostalgia flooded him and he remembered this station when he walked in for his first day as a police constable. At that time, the station was more or less shut down and officially housed only a few uniformed policemen — the Home Beats — officers with special responsibilities. The top floor contained the near mythical Flying Squad, SO8 — a select band of armed CID officers whose specific concern was armed robbers.

Once filled with policemen going about their business and lairy prisoners who freely donated their blood to help brighten the place up, that station was now a thing of the past. These days it was a relic used to house the Major Incident Room and then only on a temporary basis.

Reaching the top of the stairs, Paterson turned toward the squad room and stopped dead. Standing in front of the door waiting for him, holding a half-drunk, lukewarm mug of coffee was Detective Inspector Johnny Clocks. Paterson could just about make out the legend "Millwall — No one likes us," written in large blue letters on the side of the mug.

'Fuck me blind, guv. You made it then?' Clocks said, a big grin on his face. 'I thought you might bottle it. Glad you never did though. Come on in and meet the team.'

Composing himself, Paterson held out his hand. 'Hi, John. You're looking well. So, this is you in a suit then?'

Clocks nodded. 'Yep. I thought that as they were stupid enough to make me a DI, the least I could do was to chuck out the Levis. Whadya think?'

Paterson gave him a quick up and down. It wasn't a Tom Ford or even close, more like a Dagenham Ford, but at least he'd made the effort and it wasn't too bad. Fitted him well and he could actually carry it off. Old-fashioned, though. 'Yeah, not too bad at all. Looking sharp, John, looking sharp.'

Clocks seemed pleased. After all, if Mr "Savile Row" himself said he was looking good, then he was looking good. 'You're a little flushed, Ray. Didn't catch you doing the old dirty dance when I called, did I?' He smirked.

Paterson smiled. 'Nope. Good boy now. Up early and went training. Came straight from the dojo.'

'From where? Is that anything to do with your kung fu shit?'

'Well, we prefer to call it martial arts, but kung fu shit works just as well.'

'You need to give all that up, Ray, man of your age. It'll play havoc with your bones when you get older.'

Paterson patted Clocks on the stomach as he sidled past. The man himself was over forty and it was beginning to show on him. 'Christ, John, I'm thirty-one. What are you? My mother?'

Paterson stepped into the office, and all heads turned. It felt like he'd walked into a pub where all the locals stare at the new arrival. Friend or foe? Feeling slightly self-conscious, he followed Clocks toward his office, nodding vaguely and muttering the odd "Morning" or "Hello" as he passed.

He was about ten feet away from the door when the applause started. It was slow at first, and shook him slightly. Were they taking the piss? Turned out they weren't, and soon the whole office had joined in, embarrassing him now. He turned to look at them all properly. Some he recognised, most he didn't. But they were all smiling, genuinely pleased to see him back by the look of it, and he smiled back. It would be okay.

'Alright, alright, you shower of shit,' said Clocks, waving his hand, splashing coffee on his new suit. 'Settle down. Anyone would think he's some sort of pin-up hero boy.' He slapped Paterson on the back. 'You'd better say something, Ray, or they'll be doing this all day. Saves 'em having to do any bloody work.'

Paterson grinned at him. Still rough round the edges, suit or not. 'Thank you,' he said. 'I appreciate it, I really do. I never expected this. To be honest, I wasn't sure what I expected, but thank you. It's good to be back at work. It hasn't been easy as I'm sure you know, but what's done is done. I won't let you down, any of you.' He glanced at Clocks. 'DI Clocks has been a rock while I've been off and he's kept me straight. To be honest, working with him was the only reason I came back. It will take me a while to find my feet again but I'll get there. Thank you all for your support.' He did a little half bow, a show of respect, the kind policemen do before a magistrate as they enter and leave the court.

DI Clocks stood aside to let Paterson into his office. 'Right, you big bunch of snivelling tarts! Dab your eyes and put your hankies away now. We've got plenty of shit to sort out.'

* * *

Paterson took a seat on the receiving side of Johnny Clocks's desk. While the man himself plonked his butt down into a soft leather padded chair on the business side, he looked around the office. Fair size, high ceilings, large double-glazed window looking out across the Thames and Tower Bridge. Paterson frowned. 'You look at that every day? Doesn't it bother you?'

Clocks, rummaging around in his drawer, raised his head and looked at Paterson, then out of the window. 'What? The bridge? No. Why should it?'

Paterson looked at him, cocked his head slightly. 'After what happened up there . . .'

Clocks dismissed the bad memories with a shrug. 'Wanna quick drink?'

'What? No. Christ, it's ten o'clock on a Sunday morning. I thought you said you'd eased off a bit.'

'I have,' said Clocks, depositing two glasses on the table. 'I normally start at eight.' Paterson gazed out the window again.

'Besides,' said Clocks, starting to pour, 'wasn't me who shot the wicked fucker, was it? No. That was you.' He sat back, took a gulp and grimaced.

Paterson sighed deeply. 'I know what I did, John, but you covered for me. Bad night for both of us.'

'Dunno what you're talking about, Ray. Way I remember it is exactly what I told everybody who asked, and that's what I'll keep telling anybody who wants to ask in the future.'

'You know nobody believes it, don't you?'

'Don't give a tuppenny toss what people believe. It's what you can prove that counts, and no one can prove any different to what we told 'em. They weren't there, were they? No. Me and you were. That's it. Now can we quit doing all this bollocks again because it's getting on my wick? We've kicked the arse out of it this past year and it don't do no good.'

'Fair enough, John.' Paterson eyed him. For all of Johnny Clocks's bluster and bravado, that night on the bridge had taken a heavy toll on him personally and professionally. He'd gone to bat for him, above and beyond. Hadn't had to do it. Before the rooftop incident, neither man had had much time for the other but for some reason — perhaps it was when he'd found the butchered body of Paterson's estranged wife Lisa lying scattered around her bedroom, or perhaps it was when he'd witnessed DC Walker casually throw Inspector Billy Kingston off the bridge into the Thames — Johnny Clocks had looked at the shaking, white-faced Detective Superintendent Paterson after he had pulled the trigger and decided that he'd go unpunished for shooting Walker in the head.

Paterson knew that Clocks was getting his drinking under control now, perhaps not fully, but he was doing well. And he seemed to be settling down quite nicely with Lindsey Mullins, now an inspector herself but still with SCO19. Considering she once almost knocked Clocks's spark out for running his mouth and disrespecting women, Paterson had never had it down as a match made in heaven, but it seemed to be on the right track, so good luck to them both.

'The decorators are in your office at the moment, Ray,' Clocks said. 'Reckon they'll be another couple of days so you can bunk in here with me. We've got a lot to catch up on. But first . . . you're about to have a very busy day. We have ourselves a shooting. That's why I called you in and why we're all here on a fuckin' Sunday morning instead of tucked up in our beds.'

Paterson stood and made his way over to the water cooler. 'What we got?'

'Male, black, late fifties, early sixties, dressed in his Sunday best. Shot in the nut, according to the uniforms who turned up on scene.' Paterson's brow wrinkled. He remembered what that looked like.

'Should be right up your street,' said Clocks, and grinned at his own poor taste. No response. He moved on. 'No obvious motive at the moment. Doesn't seem like your usual black-on-black crime though, so there's no need to call in the Operation Trident boys at this time.'

'Why is this one unusual? What's different?' said Paterson, ambling back to his chair holding a plastic cup full of water.

Clocks looked at him. Paterson hadn't been the best policeman in the world before the bridge shooting and, having been off for so long, was probably even rustier now. Time would tell. Ease him back in, the commander had said. 'Well, we haven't got much at the moment. Couple of the boys are down there now trying to get to the bottom of it, but from what we've got so far, from the uniforms' description at least, it's not likely gang related, is it?'

Paterson nodded. 'Fair point. Could he have been a dealer? Deal gone bad on him maybe?'

'Hang on, there's more. The scene of the shooting was some kind of industrial estate, lots of old abandoned offices that seem to be heavily populated with these pop-up African churches — y'know, they're every bloody where these days. If there's any empty doorway, they'll open one up.' Paterson frowned. 'Anyway, someone found our man with his toes turned up, had a screaming fit and a load of Africans piled out of one of the buildings to see what was going on. It all kicked off then with the hollering and hooting, and while all that's going on it seems our shooter suddenly strolls around the corner and starts firing a fuckin' machine gun into the air.'

Paterson took a sip of his water. 'What's that about? Anybody hurt?'

'Nope. Seems he just wanted to scatter them. Keep them away from something. Anyway, as soon as someone ventures out, he starts shooting again until he hears the sirens in the background. He then fucks off into the sunset just before the area car shows up. Vanished.'

'CCTV?'

'Nah. Not around that neck of the woods. As I said, mostly abandoned offices. No security on site, no patrol. Nothing.'

'Who's down there now?'

'I've sent DS Chris Sharpe and DC Richie Sole. They're good lads. Know what they're doing.' Clocks put his empty glass back in the drawer and stood up. 'Right, drink up. We're off.'

His mobile rang. DS Sharpe.

'Go on, Chris. What's up?' Clocks nodded a few times, gave a few *huh, huh*s, and then his face hardened. 'Christ. We're on our way.' He ended the call and pushed his chair back hard, catching Paterson by surprise.

'What's happened?' Paterson drank the rest of his water and got to his feet.

Clocks slipped on his jacket, shaking his head. 'The boys on scene have found another body. Well, bits of it, dumped in a skip next to where our man went down.' He threw open the door to the main office and hurried out. Paterson followed.

'Riggs, Hutchings! Sergeant Miller, grab yer coats. With me. Now!' The men scrambled for their coats and notebooks, pleased to get out of the bloody office, a bit of action. 'Rest of you, look alive. If the press call, say nothing to no one. We have a chopped up kiddie too.'

* * *

The crime scene seemed relatively calm. Ahead of them the familiar blue and white plastic tape, strung across the road from drainpipe to drainpipe, flapped gently in the light summer breeze. Behind it, the forensics team in their white paper suits were at work. On the other side, a gaggle of uniformed police, some with clipboards, milled around, busy taking hurried statements and contact details from the assembled crowd, mostly African women all dressed up to the nines in their Sunday best — wrap-around skirts and big headdresses in vivid colours.

'Bollocks! Africans!' said Clocks. 'Won't be easy getting the truth out of that lot anytime soon.' Paterson wasn't happy about the implications but he knew Clocks was likely right. This was a difficult community to talk to. They were mistrustful of whites and mistrustful of white policemen above all.

Paterson noticed the cars — Mercedes, Jags, Lexus. There was money here. This wasn't the poorer end of the African community. Clocks pulled his phone out of his pocket and dialled up DS Sharpe as he walked.

'Chris, we've just turned up. Where are you?' He nodded, looked up, saw Chris Sharpe waving from a top-floor window. 'Top floor,' he said to Paterson, pointing to the building nearest to them. 'Bit of a problem apparently.' Paterson looked up, and the man behind the glass gave a small wave.

'Miller,' said Clocks. He pointed to the crime scene. 'Go liaise with the forensic boys. Tell 'em we'll be over in a minute once we've sorted out whatever this is. Shouldn't be too long.'

'Sure, boss,' said Miller.

They ducked under the tape and made their way up the stairs toward the sound of a deep male voice, heavily accented, arguing with DC Sole and sounding very agitated. The voice stopped for a moment while the two CID officers and three black males looked round at the new arrivals.

'Guv,' said DS Sharpe, 'glad you're here. I think they're witnesses but this bloke is refusing to give his details and says he won't let us in to see his boss in the back room.'

Clocks strode across the room. Sized up the men. Big boys, all suited, all tall, all muscular. Professional heavies and not easily intimidated. They would need telling, not asking. He held his hand out to shake his potential opponent's. The big man eyed him up, took the puny hand and shook it. Clocks tried to hide his grimace but his voice let him down. 'Jesus. That's a grip and a 'alf you got there, mate.' He shook his hand to get the blood going again. 'I'm Detective Inspector Clocks and this,' he turned to Paterson, 'is my senior officer, Detective Superintendent Paterson. What seems to be the problem here?'

The big man eyed Clocks up and down. There was more than a touch of arrogance in his bearing. Not a good start. The big man turned to Paterson, the "superintendent." He'd evidently decided he wouldn't bother with Clocks.

'Officer,' he said, his voice heavily accented. West African? Nigerian? 'This man want to see my pastor.' He turned to DS Sharpe, who was eyeing him up, itching for a ruck. 'I tell him Pastor Atewojaye is in distress. The dead man, the victim, was a personal friend. I say if he want to see him, he can make an appointment.'

Before Paterson could speak, Clocks jumped in. 'Oi! Big boy. Let's get a couple of things straight, shall we? First up, don't ever ignore me when I talk to you.' The big man turned sharply towards Clocks, and Paterson's stomach tightened. 'Second, while I'm gutted for your loss and all that, you don't tell *us* to make appointments with you. I don't know where you're from, mate, but it don't work that way here. Goddit?' Clocks moved closer to the man, staring straight at him. Sharpe and Sole geared themselves up. 'This is a murder enquiry and I'm going to see your boss right now, mate, not when he fancies it. Understood?'

The big man eyed him up, turned and looked at Paterson, who nodded. The heavy looked back at Clocks. 'The pastor is a very distressed man. You must understand this. The pastor has given me instructions to let no one in. You must respect this.'

Clocks held his hand up, gestured for him to wait, and walked over to Paterson. He turned his back on the group. Quietly he said, 'Ray, what's he bangin' on about Italian food for?'

‘What?’ said Paterson.

‘Pasta. What’s he talking about pasta for? I don’t understand.’

Paterson grinned. ‘Pastor,’ he said, and spelled it. ‘P-a-s-t-*o-r*. Think of it like a vicar. He’s in charge of this church.’

Clocks looked around the room. Not his idea of a church. Johnny Clocks was about as religious as Richard Dawkins, but he’d been to the odd wedding in his time and none of the churches had ever looked like this. This was an old office. Dilapidated, paint peeling on the ceiling, damp on the walls, posters sellotaped over the bigger patches. Some were graphic shapes of Africa overlaid with the red, yellow and green of the various flags, most advertised the meetings of different travelling ministries. In one corner over by a window was a podium of sorts, probably where the “pastor” stood when he addressed his congregation. Next to it was an old Korg keyboard. ‘Right. I’ve got it now. Pastor. Couldn’t understand you properly. You’ve got a bit of an accent there, geezer.’ Sharpe and Sole glanced at each other and flashed a quick smile between them. Paterson gently shook his head.

‘Thing is, as I said, I have a dead man out there, and turns out there’s a dead kid to sort out as well. Now, I appreciate your pastor fella is upset but so am I. I don’t like it when dead bodies turn up on my ground and I especially hate it when dead kids turn up. So,’ he stared the man in the eye, ‘big as you and your mates are, we’re going in to see your boss right now and if you make any attempt to stop us, I’ll have a small army up here who will educate you as to the mistake you’re making trying to stop the police from doing their job. Now, do you understand me?’

The big man stood his ground, looking uncertain. The little man was serious, not to be intimidated.

Clocks picked up on the hesitation. ‘Good man. You know it makes sense.’ He walked past the man, prompting the others to join him.

'Don't mind him,' said Paterson to the big man. 'He wasn't given enough cuddles as a child.'

Clocks banged on the door and walked straight in. He found Benjamin Atewojaye, Pastor of the Light of Our Lord Deliverance Ministries, seated behind a large wooden desk and cradling his head in his hands. His wife Blessing looked out of the window at the unfolding scene downstairs, snivelling loudly. Both of them jumped when Clocks barged in through the door.

'Morning,' said Clocks, his voice loaded with sarcasm. He took them both in. Short, expensively dressed and hugely fat, he'd have put them both in their sixties. 'Police from London. So sorry we didn't bother to make an appointment with you like we've been instructed to but — and here's the important bit — you do as we say not the other way round. Goddit?'

DCs Sharpe and Sole came in and closed the door behind them.

Paterson always felt uneasy watching Johnny Clocks at work. He wondered how he kept getting away with being so confrontational. As his senior officer, he was obliged to talk to him about his manner, but as his friend he knew that would be somewhat difficult.

'DI Clocks,' said Paterson, his voice low, 'dial it back a bit, please.'

Clocks didn't deign to respond. His eyes were fixed firmly on the lavishly dressed man in front of him. The man liked a bit of gold — rings on his fingers, couple of teeth, big wristwatch. Surprising that the big square plaster on his cheek wasn't made of gold too.

Pastor Benjamin bridled at the sudden appearance of the police in his sanctum. He was clearly unused to being spoken to in such a brash and disrespectful manner. 'What the hell is dis? Who are you?' He pushed back his chair abruptly. For a man so big, he was fast. 'What is going on?'

Paterson piped up before Clocks had a chance to make things worse. 'Sir, I'm sorry to barge in unannounced but we're investigating the shooting downstairs.' He held up his warrant card. 'Would you mind taking your seat again so we can talk? Please.' He gestured for the pastor to sit back down and, after a few seconds' hesitation, Benjamin did as he was asked. Paterson turned to the woman. They had money, Paterson could tell. Growing up in a moneyed family, he knew all about the world of lavish and often vulgar displays of extravagance and had learned to appreciate the finer things in life. It was the one trait that had made its way over from his childhood. He knew that his own, conspicuous displays of money — the flash cars, expensive suits and watches — were a bone of contention among his much lower-paid colleagues, but he saw little point in trying to hide his wealth. He was probably the most Googled and envied policeman in the Met. Everyone loves an anomaly.

The woman was clearly distressed. She had been crying, and was visibly jumpy. Clocks appeared to be watching her closely, trying to figure her out. Something about her obviously didn't sit right with him.

Introductions out of the way, Clocks picked it back up again. 'I'm sorry we got off on the wrong foot, but your guys outside were a little bit obstructive.'

Benjamin, settling down a bit, nodded. 'I understand. They sometimes take my instructions too . . . literally. They are very protective of me, of us. They should of course have allowed the police in to see me.' He looked across to Blessing. 'Now what is it I can do for you officers?'

'The fella downstairs with a hole in his head, what can you tell me about that?' At Clocks's blunt words, Blessing let out a little cry and began breathing heavily, almost panting.

'My wife,' said Benjamin, agitated again. 'Look what you have done to her. She is very upset and you have not helped the situation. What is wrong wit' you?'

'Hard to tell really,' said Clocks in a throwaway fashion. 'Sorry, luv,' he said, turning to Blessing. 'DC Sole, get the lady a few chairs and go fetch her some water.' Paterson winced at the reference to Blessing's size and hoped that Benjamin hadn't picked up on it. He didn't seem to have done.

'Mr Atewojaye, is it?' said Paterson. Benjamin nodded. 'Did you know the man downstairs? If you did, what can you tell me, please? We're trying to find out how this happened and catch whoever did it.'

Benjamin looked directly at Paterson, and held his gaze. 'He was my friend. We have known each other for years. He has worked for us in the church for so, so long. He was a good man, Mr Paterson, a *good* man.' He squeezed the word "good" for all it was worth.

'Do you know why this happened to him?' Clocks said, shooting a glance at Blessing. She stiffened slightly. Not much, but enough to be noticeable. She knew. And she was putting on a display of grief.

'No, sir. No. He was a good man, a dear friend. He has done no harm to anyone. He was a man of God. He served God. We all serve God.'

'Did you see or hear anything? A shot perhaps?'

'No, sir. We were just closing up our church. The cere . . . ah, sermon was over and we were all singing praise to God.'

Clocks ran his fingers through his hair, glanced at Paterson. Hoped he'd picked up on that slip of the tongue. Paterson interlaced his fingers in front of his crotch, spread his legs a bit, standing firm, nodding rapidly, listening.

'What's the name of the church again?' he said.

Benjamin eyed him quickly, then gave a proud smile. 'It is called the Light of Our Lord Deliverance Ministries.'

'Sounds impressive. Certainly a mouthful. Tell me a bit more about what you do.'

Benjamin looked suddenly irritated and he shifted in his seat. He pulled open one of the drawers in his desk and pulled out a small handful of leaflets. 'Here, sir. Have a look. You can see. We praise God and Jesus and ask that he brings good things upon this world. Good fortune to our brothers and sisters of all races and colours.'

'That's nice,' said Paterson. 'Let's hope he does. And what else do you do?' With her back to them, Blessing Atewojaye looked out of the window again. Clocks's face turned to stone.

Cocking his head to one side, his tone inquisitive but slightly harder, Benjamin said, 'I don't understand you, Mr Paterson. What is it you mean?'

'Well, do you do other church type things here? Weddings, that kind of stuff?' Clocks smiled. Paterson had picked up on it. Good boy.

Benjamin gave a big wide smile, flashing the gold teeth. 'Ah, I see, sir. No, sir, we do not do weddings. We do not have the licence for such things, although I admit I would like to. Love is a very wonderful thing. I would be happy to preside over a wedding, yes, sir. Why do you ask me such a thing?'

'Curious, that's all. It's just that a minute ago, you almost said "ceremony" but you corrected yourself, and so I wondered what ceremonies you carried out here. Nothing more.'

Benjamin shook his head and waved his hands vigorously, still smiling, still showing gold. 'No, sir. It was a mistake, that is all. I meant to say sermon but I was confused. My friend is dead and I was not thinking.'

'Okay, sir,' said Paterson, smiling back at him. 'No worries. I understand. It must be terribly distressing for you.'

'It is terrible.' Benjamin lowered his voice while rising from his chair. 'Now, Mr Paterson, if there is nothing else I can do for you, I would like to take my wife home. She is most upset.'

'Of course she is,' said Paterson. 'I understand. But, just before you go, my officers here,' he pointed over at DS Sharpe and DC Sole, 'will be taking a short statement from you, your wife and your friends outside. Please make sure you cooperate fully and give them what they ask for.' He held out his hand. 'Thank you for your time, Mr Atewojaye. We'll be in touch.' For a preacher man, his grip was pretty strong. Hands felt rough too.

Clocks stepped forward, a thin smile on his lips, hand thrust out. 'Sir,' he said, shaking the pastor's hand before turning away to join Paterson outside.

* * *

They breezed out past the big heavy and his mates, ignoring the hard stares.

'Well done, Ray,' said Clocks. 'You picked up on it then. I thought you'd missed it.'

'Nope,' said Paterson. 'I got it. He's a lying fucker.'

'They both are. How come you didn't mention the dead kid?'

'No point, John. He knows we know about it and he'll be wondering why we didn't say anything. He knows we picked up on the ceremony, so that'll worry them too. I don't know if the two are connected but let's mess with their heads a bit.' They started back down the stairs. 'Let's see what they do.'

'Bloody hell! You've changed, Ray.'

'Haven't we all, John? That said, you're still going in like a bull in the proverbial. You need to take it a bit easier. It winds people up.'

'Fuckin' good job an' all,' Clocks said. 'When you wind people up, they get confused, let their guard down cause they wanna come back at you. They get all puffed up, brain floods with adrenaline or some shit, can't think straight . . . and when they do start talking, they make a slip.'

'I can see that there's a sliver of logic in there somewhere, but you never gave him a chance to breathe before you were on him.'

Clocks pushed the door open and they both squinted in the sunlight. 'He's got "wrong 'un" written all over him. Her too. The whole fuckin' place has. I could smell it as soon as I walked in. That and the damp.'

'Hmm,' said Paterson, looking beyond the plastic tape boundary toward the skip. He recognised the three CID that Clocks had ordered out of the office and they headed over in their direction. On the ground, the dead man lay in a pool of blood. Only horror and bad memories awaited him there.

'We'll talk about it later,' he said. 'Right now, I think our day is about to get double shitty.'

* * *

Paterson and Clocks gave their details to the officer with a tablet PC, and pulled on the white paper shoes they'd been handed. They carefully made their way along a pathway of small metal plates laid by the crime scene manager. The plates provided a clean way in and out of the scene, avoiding as much cross-contamination of evidence as possible. They went across to meet up with DS Miller and the other two.

'What we got then, boys?' Paterson said to no one in particular. In the background, the forensics team were buzzing around the large plastic skip containing the body of the dead child. They'd get to that. One thing at a time.

DS Miller, pen in one hand, notebook in the other, casually pointed to where the top half of the man's skull was missing. 'African male. In his sixties, most likely. I'm no expert but I'd say cause of death was a fucking great bullet to the head.' He turned and gestured to the brick wall behind him. 'Again, no expert, but I'm guessing that gloop running down the wall came out of the back of his head when the bullet went on its merry way. C'mere. Show you something.' He walked Paterson and Clocks nearer to the blood and brain matter clinging to the brickwork, then went down on his haunches. Paterson did the same. Clocks stayed standing.

'What am I looking at?' said Paterson.

'How tall do you reckon our man is? Was?'

Paterson looked at him and shrugged. 'No idea. Five eight, five ten maybe. What's this for?'

'This wasn't done at ground level. Wasn't a walk-up job. Looks to me like the main core of the splatter is about four and half, five feet off the ground, which suggests that our shooter angled down.' He stood up sharply. Paterson got to his feet and turned to look with him at the rooftops of the surrounding buildings. 'Reckon our shooter was likely up there.' DS Miller pointed to a building at the far end of the estate. Straight line of sight, completely unobstructed view.

Paterson eyed him up. 'How do you come to that conclusion?'

DS Miller held out his hand. Paterson shook it automatically. 'Sorry,' he said, belatedly introducing himself. 'Superintendent Paterson.'

Miller nodded at him, looked him in the eyes, scanned his face quickly. 'DS John Miller. I guessed who you were, sir. Welcome aboard. As for this, it's far from a conclusion. It's a guess. A reasonable guess, mind. Before I joined up, I was a marine, started when I was eighteen. Seen this kind of thing a few times out in the field. It's good work, no mistake. Whoever did this knew his onions.'

'Military?' said Clocks, eyeing the building in the distance.

'Maybe. Forensics and ballistics will give us what we need to know for certain but for now, if I were you, I'd arrange a chit-chat with the army. See what they have to say. Me and a few of the boys will make the rounds of the local gun clubs.'

'Good stuff, Miller. If it's not already been done, take a couple of uniforms, get them to block all the entrances and exits. No one in, no one out until we've got some sort of statement and full details from them. You and one of the others, go take a look on the roof for me first. See if you can find anything up there. Give DI Clocks a call if you do, and we'll come over.'

'No worries, boss,' said Miller. He turned on his heel at once, responding to the order given. Old habits.

Clocks was quietly impressed. Paterson giving out direct instruction without hesitation was a good sign as far as he was concerned. Perhaps he had changed after all. 'Right, Ray,' he said, 'time to take a look at this poor little sod.'

His face was sombre now. Gone were the cocky grin and incessant childish quips which had earned him Paterson's disrespect all those months ago. Both men had changed as a result of the Walker affair and, in Clocks's case at least, it seemed to be for the better.

Earlier, as they'd scrambled out of the office, Clocks had made mention of a dead child — or rather bits of one — and Paterson had fought back the memory of his wife, hacked to pieces by Adam Walker, the policeman-cum-prolific serial killer who had worked among them. Detective Constable Adam Walker. One of their own. One of his team had slipped through the net, twisted the system and rampaged through Bermondsey for a month, solely in order to teach Paterson a simple lesson. Walker had carved a word into each of his victims until he'd spelt out his message: 'Don't. Touch. What. Isn't. Yours. Ray.' Everybody had thought Walker was acting out because Paterson had been sleeping with his wife, Trish, but that wasn't the real reason. The real reason, as Walker took great pains to point out to him during their final confrontation on Tower Bridge, was that Paterson had undermined his cover. By sleeping with Trish he'd shaken the façade that Walker had carefully constructed over the years, that of a happily married man, respectable cop and all-round decent member of society. Paterson learned the hard way the dangers of further destabilising what was already unstable.

When he discovered the affair, Walker had toyed with the idea of killing Trish, but realised that would have had the police swarming all over his home. Still, according to his warped way of thinking, Paterson's disrespect couldn't go unpunished. Walker began teaching him a lesson that would cost him everything he held dear: his best friend and mentor, DS Dave Jordan, carved to pieces and left for dead in a disused warehouse, his estranged wife, Lisa, raped and butchered in the home they once shared. And the girls. Slaughtered for no other reason than to act as message boards for Walker. As for his high-flying career, that was under threat from the moment he took up the Walker case. It was in tatters when he shot the unarmed murderer in the head on top of Tower Bridge.

And now, here he was, just about a year later, walking toward another dismembered corpse with Johnny Clocks, a man he'd once despised and who had despised him. He was also the man who'd covered for him and kept him out of prison. Paterson owed him.

As they got closer to the bin, Paterson felt his stomach clench. He breathed in deeply.

Covering his own nerves, Clocks reverted to type. He turned to Paterson and nudged him as they stepped carefully on the metal steps. 'Guv, this bloke all in white with the hood and white mask. What's he remind you of?' No response. 'Don't you think he looks like a negative of one of them Muslim women?' Paterson blanked him. He wasn't in the mood.

He introduced himself to the white suit standing in front of the bin, busy photographing it and its contents. 'Detective Superintendent Paterson. What do we have here?'

The man stopped what he was doing and turned to face him. Paterson spotted the tear in his eye. Bastard of a job but it had to be done. The man lowered the camera, gave a weak smile, quickly dabbed at his eye. 'From what we can see, sir, it's the body — the torso — of a small child. Male. The head, arms, legs and penis are absent.' He choked on the words, and his eyes filled again. Paterson and Clocks stood rigid, shaken. Nothing they were hearing made sense.

Paterson spoke first. His voice was broken. 'What . . .?'

'We've found the head. The eyes and teeth have gone.'

Johnny Clocks turned away. Not again. He couldn't stand this.

'Where was it?' said Paterson.

'In the skip too. Haven't found the rest yet, I'm afraid.'

Paterson edged forward, not wanting to see but knowing that he needed to. All part of the job. He caught sight of a bloody hole where the child's arm should have been, and heaved, quickly and violently. He turned away sharpish, and shook his head. Composing himself, he turned back to the forensics man. 'Did he do this?' he said, pointing toward the dead man.

'I don't know, sir. We won't know until both bodies have been removed and forensically examined. See if there's been an exchange between them.'

'How was the little 'un found?' said Clocks, regaining a modicum of control.

'Apparently a uniformed officer spotted the remains. He was first on scene, realised he was looking at a murder, backed away from the dead man, bumped into the bin, turned and caught sight of something in there. Didn't know what it was but it bothered him enough to not go back because he didn't want to contaminate the scene any further. Told one of your boys when they showed up.'

'Do we know if the body was covered up at all? Seemed to be lying on a cloth of some sort.'

'Again, don't know for sure but it looks like he was loosely wrapped. Likely came undone when he was dumped.'

'Okay,' said Paterson. 'Thanks.' He turned to walk away, then spun back. He'd forgotten something. 'Sorry, who's going to do the post-mortems?'

The man in the white suit had resumed taking his crime scene photographs, and his back was turned to them. 'Doctor Hudson.'

Paterson managed a wry smile. They'd met before. Obnoxious bastard of the Scottish variety, but bloody good at his job.

Clocks's phone rang, breaking Paterson's reverie before it could get a hold. 'Alright,' he said into the phone, 'give us a minute. We'll pop up and see you.' He hung up. 'That was DS Miller. They've found a bullet casing on the roof.'

CHAPTER TWO

There's something about the smell of a mortuary that never quite leaves you. The second you step inside, it assails the nostrils and worms its way deep down into your throat, so deep you can taste it. For days. If asked to put a finger on what exactly the smell is, the layman would be hard pushed to say. Some, those who'd watched too many TV crime shows, would opt for formaldehyde without having the first clue what it smells like, though they have an idea it's not pleasant. The plain old truth is, the smell is death. Death and internal organs mixed with various chemicals. Sometimes, on a bad day, depending on the manner of death, that smell can be horrendous, truly stomach churning. Luckily for Paterson and Clocks, today was a relatively good one.

The freezers were full up. It was a given. The good people of Bermondsey died in all manner of ways — old age, car accidents, building falls and so on — but the one thing you could pretty much always rely on was a good old-fashioned act of violence. Friday and Saturday nights were reserved for stabbings and glassings. You'd get the occasional shooting now and then, but not so much these days. Sunday mornings were exclusively for what they called the "sudden deaths." These were usually your old folk who couldn't be bothered to get up any more and died. Just like that. Someone noticed once that there was a spike in the figures that coincided with the *Strictly Come Dancing* final. Quite a few of the oldies seemed to dodge the coffin for the best part of three months while it was on, and once the final was over they called it a day. Like they were hanging on to see who won and then thought, `Fuck it.' Whether they were disappointed with the result or gutted that they'd have to wait another year for the next series, nobody ever found out.

As Paterson stood under the harsh glare of the overhead lights, for some reason he remembered being introduced to DS Jordan when he first arrived for duty at Tower Bridge Police Station. 'Welcome aboard, son,' the big man said, pumping Paterson's hand so hard he thought his arm would drop off. 'And welcome to "M" district, also known as "Dial M for murder."' He waited for some sort of acknowledgement of what he'd just said. Paterson looked at him blankly, then gave a weak smile. He'd no idea what Jordan was talking about.

'Too bloody young, ain'tcha?' Jordan shook his head in despair. Bloody kids in the job. 'Was a film a good few years back.' Paterson shrugged. 'Anyway, point is this is a rough old hunting ground. Stay awake, pay attention and you'll learn a lot. Now fuck off and get me a cup of tea. White, one sugar, there's a good lad.'

'What have ye been doing wi' yerself, laddie?' "Jock" Hudson, his accent as broad as ever, dragged Paterson back to the here and now.

'Oh, y'know,' said Paterson, 'keeping busy. Waiting for the axe to fall. Usual sort of stuff.'

Hudson nodded. Paterson didn't want to talk about it. Secrets and all that. 'I take it you know I was the examining officer for Adam Walker?'

Paterson looked at him, breathed in, held it. Where was this going? Johnny Clocks tensed, stared hard at the back of Jock's head. He'd worked with Hudson a good few times over the years and didn't have much time for him. He wasn't happy with the doc for piping up like that. 'I did know, yes,' said Paterson.

Hudson held his gaze. 'Just wanted to say good shot, laddie. That's all. Oh, and welcome back. Now, let's go through what you've brought me today.'

Paterson breathed out. Slowly. He knew he'd have to get used to people digging him out here and there. Walker and the way he'd died would follow him around like a ball and chain. Behind him, he could feel Clocks relax.

'First up. Your man. Big old lump. Driving licence identifies him as one Mr Samuel Babatunde, sixty-six years old. Cause of death is the fuckin' great hole in his head. Obviously. We'll stick with that for now as there are no other signs of injury apparent. He is obviously well fed and his stomach contents showed that he had eaten quite a hearty, if not particularly healthy, breakfast. He shows evidence of heart disease but only what you would expect to find in such a fat bastard.'

'Tell us about his nut, Jock,' said Clocks, clearly impatient and wanting to get this over with.

Hudson smiled. Why was it policemen never wanted to get into the nitty-gritty? Always on the hurry-up. 'Not much I can tell you yet, not for sure anyway. I can tell you it's a mess, eh? Whatever he was shot with, it was large. Not your usual thirty-eight or twenty-two that's for sure.'

'Overkill . . .' commented Paterson.

'I'd say so, Superintendent. Whoever shot him down certainly wasn't playing around.'

'We found a bullet casing on top of one of the buildings. John, show him.'

Clocks dug around inside his jacket, pulled out a small plastic evidence bag and handed it to Hudson. For some reason that baffled them he held it up to the light and let out a low whistle. 'This is a big bastard for sure. No need for that. D'ye know what it came from?'

Paterson took the casing off him and handed it back to Clocks. 'Not for certain but one of our boys, ex-army, reckons it could have been a rifle called a . . . hang on.' He pulled out his notebook, flipped over a few pages and said, 'An M2010 enhanced sniper rifle. Apparently, it is accurate up to about thirteen hundred yards.' He slipped the notebook back in his pocket.

'Yeah, same bloke said it could also have been the, ah, Accuracy International AWM rifle — also called the L115A3, whatever the fuck that is. Ballistics will confirm when we run it over there,' Clocks said.

'I would imagine it made a loud bang when it went off. Anyone hear it?' Hudson said.

'Nope,' said Clocks. 'My DS reckons it could have had a suppressor — a silencer to you and me. I'd say probably more like selective deafness on the part of the witnesses.'

Hudson raised his eyebrows, extended out his bottom lip. 'Hmm. Odd. Still, it's your job to figure that out, gents. Have fun with it.' He nodded toward the small bundle, covered in a tiny white sheet, marooned on the large stainless steel table where it lay. Spots of blood stained the bleached cotton. But not many.

'Now for the bit we've all being avoiding, gentlemen.' All three men became instantly and visibly uncomfortable. Dead people are one thing, dead kids are quite another. And what had happened to this poor soul didn't bear thinking about.

Hudson pulled back the sheet quickly, as if whipping a plaster off a wound, and revealed all that remained of what was once a living, breathing child. Somebody's son. Paterson and Clocks clamped their eyes shut, desperate not to look, desperate to fight back their own horrors and forget. 'I would say the poor wee laddie was no more than five or six.' Hudson's voice brought them back into the room. Both breathed deeply as they gazed at what was once a human being, now reminiscent of a side of beef. Both of them closed their eyes again. Hudson spotted them. 'It's okay, gents. I've already done my weeping. You go ahead. I'll talk.'

Paterson suddenly felt hot. His legs buckled ever so slightly and he pulled at his collar to try and breathe more freely. 'Y'okay?' asked Hudson.

'Go on,' said Paterson, 'I'll be fine.' He undid his top button, started pulling his tie open.

Hudson gave a little nod. 'To state the obvious, we can see that his limbs have been removed as has his head. Looking at the cuts involved, they have been completed using an extremely sharp instrument. Not a saw, there are no teeth marks, but something like a large butcher's knife. His penis would have been removed with a smaller, more precise instrument.'

'Christ almighty.' Johnny Clocks was struggling.

'The head,' Hudson nodded toward a freezer, 'has had the eyes and teeth removed. Again, not surgically. Crudely, I would say. Same butcher's knife. I've found something around the eye sockets. It seems to be some kind of juice, although I canna possibly say what it is until the results come back in. The outside of the sockets have a reddish appearance about them and it would appear they have been irritated and that this was done pre-mortem. It's like an irritant was rubbed into them for some reason.'

'What killed the poor little sod?' Johnny Clocks was now supporting himself against a large glass-fronted metal cabinet.

'My best guess at the moment is that his throat was cut. That would have been what initially caused him to bleed out. That alone may have killed him, but I could be wrong and his head might have been removed all in one go. That would most certainly have killed him.' Paterson couldn't decide whether Hudson was making a pathetic attempt at a joke. The senior pathologist was known for his dark humour, which was partly why he and Paterson had failed to hit it off at the first murder they both attended. He let it go. 'He would have bled out quickly. Fear would have accelerated his little heart and forced the blood out of his body even quicker.'

Paterson was thinking out loud. 'Apart from Sammy's brain splatter, there were no obvious traces of blood anywhere. No pools of blood, so . . .'

'He was killed somewhere else, Superintendent.'

'Anything else, Jock?' said Paterson.

'Aye, couple of things. Given the method of death, there is a marked absence of blood on the torso, which would indicate that he was cleaned up after death. Washed, if you will. One other thing. You may have noticed that his body has an . . . unusual pallor.' Paterson and Clocks shook their heads, looked at each other. Hudson leaned forward over the torso, and rested his hands on the cutting table. Paterson hadn't noticed it before, but today he saw that Hudson had a habit of pointing with his chin, punctuating his words. 'As you know, the pigmentation changes after death and a number of things — time, the environment and so on — contribute to that change. But on viewing the young lad, it seemed a strange kind of pale. Unusual.'

Paterson looked at Hudson's face, searching it as he waited for him to get to the point. 'Go on.'

'I'm pretty certain that this child was of albino origin.'

'A what origin?' said Clocks. 'What's an albino?'

Hudson straightened himself. 'Glad you asked, Johnny boy. It's a congenital condition, to do with a recessive gene. People with the condition have a complete or partial absence of pigmentation in the skin, hair and eyes. It's rare in the Western world, where it's reckoned about one in every seventeen thousand have some form of albinism.'

'Where isn't it rare?' Clocks asked, suspecting that he already knew the answer.

Hudson looked across at Samuel Babatunde. 'Africa. Most notably Tanzania. Roughly one in every thirteen hundred or so people have the condition.' Yep, Clocks was right.

'So these two *are* connected?' said Paterson, mostly to himself.

'I'm still awaiting results, and obviously there is more to do to confirm specific evidence traces but I'd have to say the odds are so great that if I bet a penny on them being unconnected and won, I could buy fuckin' Africa.'

Clocks snorted. Sensing they were gearing up to leave, he felt a bit better. 'Well that's not going to happen, is it, Jock? There's more chance of me kissing the Queen than you betting a whole penny.' Hudson frowned. Stereotyping at its worst.

'Thanks, Jock,' said Paterson, signalling to Clocks that it was time to go. 'Keep me updated. Send me a full report as soon as you have it. I'll pick it up on my iPad.' He started for the door, Clocks following. Then he stopped and turned back. 'Jock?' The Scotsman lifted his head. 'Good to see you again. And thank you for what you did for me.'

Hudson eyed him, smiled, and waved him out of his workshop.

* * *

Back in the office Paterson started up a whiteboard, noting down the facts as they had them so far. He blu-tacked two photos onto the board, picked up a blue wipe-dry pen and wrote:

Deceased — Samuel Babatunde — African, mid-sixties.
Cause of death — Single head shot. Major Trauma.
Motive — Unknown.
Weapon — Military-grade sniper rifle???
Awaiting ballistics.
Known to Benjamin and Blessing.

Coming off the picture of Babatunde at a right angle was a blue pen line leading to a photograph of the child's torso.

Deceased — Unknown child. 5—10 years?

Albino descent? African/Albino???

Cause of death — As yet undetermined. Cut throat/decap?

Motive — Unknown.

Body washed?

Above and in the middle of these two pictures, forming the top of a triangular point, were the names of Benjamin and Blessing Atewojaye, Light of Our Lord Deliverance Ministries and the words "Team of heavies." Two blue lines flowed from the lower pictures back up to them.

Clocks shouted to the room of detectives. 'Everybody, listen in. You've seen the pictures. You know by now what we've got, but what we don't have is what the fuck is going on here? We've got a dead man shot by a soldier, possibly, a dismembered albino kiddie, a pretend vicar and his missus who are surrounded by a bunch of leftovers from the Black Panther movement and not much else. So, has anyone got any ideas? Anything at all?'

Most stared at him blankly, but at the back of the room, a single hand went up. Detective Constable Leon Webster spoke up. He was nicknamed "the Crocodile" on account of having far too many teeth for one head. Fifteen years in the job, and from Nigerian parents.

'Witchcraft, sir.' Everyone turned to look at him, not sure if they'd heard him right. The room went silent.

'Sorry?' said Clocks. 'Wanna try that again for me? I thought you said witchcraft for a second. *Did* you say witchcraft?'

Webster lowered his hand, suddenly self-conscious. 'I did, sir. Voodoo if you prefer. Just before I joined up there was a big case in the papers. A member of the public found a child's torso floating in the Thames. Black kid. Turns out that a crazy black lady who was casting spells and driving out demons had sacrificed the poor child to some god or other. A political cock-up allowed her to go free, and no one got nicked for it. I don't know if they ever identified the body, but he was given the name "Adam." Nothing like it had ever been seen in London before, and we were out of our depth to say the least. I think the squad dealing with it at the time called in a civvy expert in African cultures. He confirmed it was most likely witchcraft. From what I can remember, the kid was brought over here and chopped up because believers in that shit think that by chopping up kids they can use their bits and bobs in magical spells.' He shrugged. Not much more to say.

Paterson sat quietly, taking notes in his pocketbook. 'Thanks, Officer. Sorry, I don't know your name yet. That's interesting. We'll talk later.' He stood up and walked over to the whiteboard. 'Anyone ever heard of this church?' he said, tapping at the name. 'Anyone know what they do?' A general shaking of heads.

Webster again. 'Trouble is, sir, there's so many of these churches now. It seems like any empty office or flat or shop is taken over by Africans all holding a Sunday service. There's a lot of money in it.'

'How so?'

'The pastors of these places get their congregations to part with money as a "gift" to help them do God's work. They charge for all sorts of stuff. Blessings, healings — that's a big one, lots of money in a healing.'

'How come you know so much?' said Clocks.

'My mum and dad are very religious people. I grew up with these makeshift churches. Mostly they do no real harm as such, just prey on people's need to believe in God. Didn't matter how much I tried to tell them it was a scam, Mum and Dad wouldn't have it. The religious don't. They're not interested in facts. They have their beliefs. That's all they need.'

‘How many of these churches do we estimate we have on our patch?’ said Paterson.

‘Don’t know, sir, but I don’t think you’d see much change out of five, six hundred maybe.’

‘How many?’ Paterson’s voice went up an octave, shot through with disbelief. ‘Five or six *hundred*?’

‘That’s just the more visible ones, sir,’ said Webster. ‘There’s probably a lot more tucked away out of sight. All sorts of shit goes on in people’s homes.’

‘Do we have a database of these places?’ Paterson asked.

‘No,’ said Webster, and put his head back into his notebook.

‘Well, that’s something we’re going to have to put right. Are these places regulated by anyone?’ Paterson flapped his hand dismissively. ‘I just heard myself. Stupid question.’

‘Okay,’ said Clocks, ‘if we run with this for now, tentatively, does anyone have any ideas about the dead man? DS Miller reckons he was punched out with a military rifle. Let’s assume our shooter was, or is, a soldier of some sort. Why would he gun down Sammy boy in broad daylight? What’s his motive? Let’s bat it around, kids. Nothing’s off the table. Go.’

‘He’s not really a soldier. He’s an American cop practising for the annual “Kill a black man academy awards,”’ said Webster. Clocks was surprised. It was the sort of shit he would have said himself a year ago. He had to grin. The others laughed nervously. It all got a bit tense for a second.

‘Nah,’ said Clocks, breaking it up. ‘Those fuckers only do you face down, mob handed and on video. This took skill.’ The tension dissipated.

DC Carrie Gedmine said, ‘Maybe it’s got something to do with Africa itself? Maybe the dead man was involved with the killer back home.’ Paterson raised his head. He had a personal interest in Detective Constable Gedmine.

'What? Like a domestic?' said Clocks, throwing Carrie one of his boyish grins. He'd always liked her. She hated him — the old him anyway. However much he fantasised about her, though — and fantasise he did — it was a moot point. He was with Lyndsey now. Somehow, he and Lyndsey Mullins had built a relationship out of the ruins of last year's events. Mullins was one of the SCO19 officers that had stormed Adam Walker's home address, searching for his missing wife. Her anger and disgust at Clocks's juvenile quips and remarks came to a head during the search. After he found a bag full of vulvas in a freezer, Clocks made a remark that culminated in her literally punching his lights out. He apologised, she accepted, they made up, but no one could have seen them getting together as a couple. That came from way out of left field.

She'd helped him get straight when he went on the drink. Helped him grow up, to stop making childish comments and arguing with everyone all the time. That one was very much a work in progress. He, of all people, helped iron out some of the aggressiveness in her. Still, he knew that if he went sniffing elsewhere, even so much as thought about it, she'd shoot his face off. She was a no-nonsense kind of a gal and he liked that. You knew where you stood with Lyndsey.

'No,' said Carrie, tossing her long hair around, flirting with him a bit, winding him up a lot. 'Not a domestic. I'm not saying they were lovers. Maybe the gunman had a grudge and tracked him down here. Maybe . . .?'

'Yeah, maybe,' said Clocks, dismissing her, aware that it would wind her up. Two could play that game. 'Anyone else got anything?' A lot of blank faces and shaking heads. 'Right.' He nodded to DC Webster. 'I want you to dig into this church. Find out everything you can about them. Dig bloody deep. DS Miller, get in touch with the nearest army base. I think it's Woolwich?' Miller nodded. 'Find out who's in charge and make me and Mr Paterson an urgent appointment with some big-knob. They can be a bit stroppy if it involves their own so tell 'em if they don't make an appointment for us by tomorrow, we'll be coming anyway. You'll go with us too, to make sure they don't bullshit us with army speak.' DS Miller grinned. *I'll do it, but good luck barging your way into an army base.*

'Me and the guv'nor are going to find out if we really have got some kind of voodoo going on. See if this one fits whatever criteria there are for it. The rest of you, start door knocking, see if you can drum up anything else that might be useful. Go get some more detailed statements from the people that there were there yesterday. Leave the Atewojayes alone. They're ours.' He glanced at Paterson, who gave him a knowing look. 'Back here at six. Debrief. Be safe out there.'

* * *

Less than two hours later, Paterson and Clocks found themselves sitting in the office of Detective Chief Inspector Kim Hardwell. As the officer in charge of SCO5, the Met's Sexual Offences, Exploitation and Child Abuse unit, she was quick to get them in after speaking with Paterson on the phone.

Tucked away on the eighth floor of New Scotland Yard in an office that gave a commanding view over the Thames, she listened intently to Ray Paterson's story. Every so often she would nod her head, almost as if to tick off some kind of checklist she was running through in her mind. Paterson seemed to be hitting a lot of those markers.

Hardwell had been in charge of SCO5 for the past five years, and during her tenure had seen things that would have driven most people over the edge. Fortunately, she had found a way of dealing with it — a full bottle of red every night and a monthly counselling session paid for by the Met. It wasn't perfect, but it was something.

She was a stern-looking woman in her mid-forties, hair scraped back tight and minimal make up. She was married with two young girls, whom she no doubt hugged and kissed every minute of every day that she could when she wasn't out fighting the monsters amongst us, all too often disguised as parents. That was the part she found hardest. How could any parent inflict such damage on their own child? Children ought to be protected at all costs. The thought that anyone, let alone a parent, could or would harm a child drove her out of the door every morning. The story she was hearing now, though shocking, was not new to her. She was familiar with the story of Adam, the boy in the Thames, but she knew that he was not alone. There were now dozens upon dozens of similar cases spread across Europe, each case differing slightly in detail but all having their roots in one thing — witchcraft.

'So, that's what we have so far,' said Paterson. He closed his notebook, reached over for his tea and then scooted back in his chair. 'One of our officers suggested that it could involve witchcraft, African witchcraft, and quite frankly, if it does, we haven't got a bloody clue what to do next.'

'From what you've told me and the pictures you've shown me, I'd have to agree wholeheartedly with your officer's assessment. It has all the hallmarks of a ritual killing. These are carried out primarily in certain African states, but sadly it's becoming increasingly common across the world.'

Paterson and Clocks straightened their backs slightly as they listened to her. Her voice was as no nonsense as the rest of her, and she spoke with a calm authority that commanded respect.

'Why?' said Clocks. 'What's going on?'

'It's difficult to explain it, Mr Clocks, and I don't pretend to be anywhere near an expert on the subject. But, to do so, you have to try to understand the mentality of the people who do this and their motivation.' She hesitated, searching for the right words.

'Go on,' said Clocks. He reached over for his tea, which was now on the lukewarm side. He grimaced slightly as he gulped.

'This is a simplified version. It's not that I don't think you'd understand, but voodoo is a deeply complex belief system that is rooted deep in a nation's psyche and cannot easily be explained to outsiders. What I'm going to say will be uncomfortable to listen to, no doubt, but I'm asking you to not make snap decisions based on what is no more than a thumbnail sketch.'

Clocks's eyes narrowed. *Stop yammering and get the fuck on with it, woman, and don't start making excuses for murder.*

'Africa is not one country. It is a collection of widely disparate states. But the vast majority of these states are officially divided between the Christian and Muslim faiths. Unofficially, some anthropologists estimate that around ninety-three percent of the combined African population hold a deeply rooted belief in spirits, good and bad, and in the old ways of what is commonly known as voodoo. Do you know how many people that is?' She looked back and forth between the two men. Paterson, she thought, might have a clue. Clocks, no chance.

'Nope,' said Clocks, justifying her thought. 'Give us a hint.'

She nodded. 'I will, Inspector. Rounded up, that would be just over one *billion* people.' She paused to let the number sink in. 'I don't know if that's true of course, but even if you halved that number you'd be looking at about half a billion. Half a billion people who hold beliefs so steeped in ritual and sacrifice that we cannot begin to fathom them. Practices have shifted and changed over time and place. Sometimes, they can involve physical abuse: beatings, torture and occasionally, sacrifice. Of course, not every practice involves sacrifice, and even those that do, tend towards chickens and goats.'

'Explain a bit about the sacrifice aspect, please,' said Paterson. 'Why is this done?'

‘So many different reasons. Mostly it’s for medical purposes. A child in a village falls sick. They call in the local witch doctor, he performs a ritual of some kind. It might involve drumming, trances, the burning of herbs, chanting, usually a bit of rolling around on the floor. The chicken gets its head cut off in a sacrifice to whatever god or ancestor they believe is causing the illness and the kid gets better. Or doesn’t.’ She paused again, looked between the two men who were clearly having a hard time with this. ‘All harmless stuff so far. Nonsense to us Westerners, but not to those brought up to believe in it.’

‘And if the kid don’t get better?’ said Clocks.

‘Well, that’s when things usually take a turn for the worse.’ She lowered her eyes. ‘The parents will most likely believe that the bad spirit hasn’t left the child. Often the witch doctor will return and declare the child to be infected with something called “Kindoki.” It means, simply put, witchcraft or possession by bad spirits. It’s a term used primarily in the Congo but it’ll do for our purposes. Ultimately, what it leads to for the supposedly infected child is a period of abuse. This is usually in the form of severe beatings, to drive out the spirits. It’s common for them to have chilli peppers rubbed into the eyes, since chillies are believed to have magical powers. Then there are cuts to the torso to let the demon out. Being held underwater is also common, to drown the evil spirit. These rituals can go on for several days, often ending in the death of the child.’

‘And the parents stand by and let this happen?’ Paterson was aghast.

‘They don’t just stand by, sir, they often take a very active part in it. They believe that they are fighting a devil of some sort, and if it means the death of their child then so be it. The demons must be driven out before they can infect anyone else.’

'Christ,' said Paterson. The nearest thing he'd ever come across was in a film called *The Exorcist*, from back in the seventies.

'A belief in bad spirits pervades the African mind-set and shapes the way they move through the world. They nearly all believe that anything even slightly bad that befalls them is caused by someone else who has used spirits to bring them harm. That someone might be jealous of their success or wealth. The spirits called down might inflict a sickness, a failing business, a bad marriage, children misbehaving, a downturn in finances, the car playing up . . . everything will have a connection to a malignant spirit sent by another person. To combat it, they seek out the witch doctor, who will get rid of the spirit by casting "good" spells. Unfortunately, in some cases a chicken or goat is considered insufficient in terms of an offering, and that's when things turn very dark. There are a number of cases where children have been ritually killed and their body parts used for the making of talismans — good luck charms, if you will — or for medicine. Children's bodies are considered to be particularly useful for medicinal magic. They have strong energy, you see.'

Paterson noted her eyes begin to fill with tears. Talking about the subject was clearly painful to her. 'Look, we get the picture, we can leave it there for the time—'

'Haven't finished yet, sir. I'm okay.' Her voice was flat. She took in a deep breath. 'The child you have. You think he may be an albino, correct?'

''S what the pathologist thought on his prelim,' said Clocks.

Her head dropped slightly. 'Albino children are a special case. In Tanzania, mostly, there have been a number of cases where albino children were forcibly removed from their homes. Albinos are highly prized. They're not white, not black, not mixed, but . . .' she gestured, looking for the right word, 'otherworldly. Yes, that's it. Otherworldly. Albino children are frequently attacked, mostly by groups of men wielding machetes and knives whose job it is to remove parts — hands, arms, legs — to be used in spells or as charms.'

'Oh, come on,' said Paterson. His face was a mix of disbelief and horror. 'Surely it doesn't go on in this day and age?'

'Let me finish, please, sir.' She went on, 'These parts are usually taken to order. A wealthy client will consult with a witch doctor who tells him that such and such a part will bring him luck and riches. The bigger the part, the more the luck and riches for the client. The client pays off the witch doctor who in turn subcontracts out to a few locals to find an albino child.'

'Who are these clients?' said Clocks. 'Why ain't they been nicked?'

'Again, Mr Clocks, different countries, different systems. It is said that nobody knows who these clients are, but I can tell you that whenever there is an election, the rate of attacks goes up.'

'Christ,' said Paterson. 'Politicians can be involved in this?'

She shrugged. 'So it's believed.'

Kim Hardwell pushed her chair back and stood up. She smoothed down her jacket and walked toward the door. Paterson and Clocks both stood automatically. 'I'll introduce you to one of my officers. She's of African birth, brought up in London, hugely experienced in these sorts of matters. She'll work with you on this, reporting to me on a daily basis.'

'Hang on, ma'am,' said Clocks. 'What about our kid who was cut up? What's the story there then? Why has this happened here in England?'

She stopped at the door and stared hard at him. 'As I said, albinos are considered extremely special. My guess is he was brought to this country for a very specific purpose, most likely involving money. Big money. Do you have a full report back from the path lab yet?'

'No.'

'When you do, check the contents of his stomach. It will likely contain a trace of the Calabar bean. It's used as a paralysing agent. And if I'm right about the money aspect, there'll be flecks of pure gold in there as well.'

CHAPTER THREE

Paterson pushed the DB11 in and out of the traffic around Westminster, drumming his fingers on the steering wheel. His driving was a little more aggressive than normal. It's always hard to make any progress in central London, but he felt secure in the knowledge that most drivers would give him space and let him take a few liberties. Very few people would fancy a run-in with an Aston Martin. He doubted they could handle the insurance claim.

'This is a nice motor, sir,' said an upbeat female voice from the back seat. 'These seats are more comfortable than what I've got in my living room.' She shifted around on the soft cream leather. 'Not really built for passengers though, is it?' Her legs were cramped and she finally settled in a sideways position, legs extended over the seat.

Paterson glanced at her in the rear-view mirror. She'd been introduced as Detective Sergeant Abbi Okonkwo, proud owner of a whip-smart mind, a wicked sense of humour and a laugh so filthy it made men blush. Eight years with the Met, she had landed at SCO5 at roughly the same time as DCI Hardwell. They'd inherited some nasty shit from the outgoing team, but had forged a formidable partnership that had been responsible for breaking up a number of child importation gangs. The two of them had sent some very heavy people to prison.

Paterson figured her for mid-thirties at most, although her eyes had the look of someone much older. She'd seen things. 'Thanks,' he said. 'It is a bit tight in the back, that's why I always sit up front. It gets me about though.'

Looking out of the passenger seat window, Johnny Clocks grinned to himself. 'So,' he said, 'nice to have you with us. What's your story then?'

She stopped stroking the leather and looked up at the back of his head. She thought he was going a bit Prince William on the crown but was willing to give him the benefit of the doubt as the light was a bit dull in the back. 'What do you want to know, sir? I'm an open book.'

'Just tell me a bit about yerself,' he said. 'Who you are, what you do, what's your story. That sort of stuff.'

Abbi leaned forward and put her head over the back of his seat, trying to get a better look at his face. She didn't like conversations where she couldn't meet the other person's eyes, but accepted that sitting in the back of a car didn't make it easy.

'Well, my name's Abbi. I'm five foot nine in my stockings, with or without the suspender belt — who wears them these days anyway? They're so out of fashion. My bust size is 34DD and I like my men like my coffee: white, smooth and creamy. I'm single and looking to mingle if you're—'

'Whoah, whoah, whoah! Hold up,' said Clocks, half turning to look at her. 'I didn't mean . . .' And then he saw her expression. A big beaming Cheshire cat of a grin was spread right across her face and then she erupted in a huge roar of laughter.

'Oh, you're a funny cow,' said Clocks, turning his head away. 'Fuckin' winding me up.'

'I'm sorry, I'm sorry. I didn't mean to, it's just that I knew you had a sense of humour. I could see it in your eyes. I'm sorry. I'll behave.'

Paterson was grinning, aware that this would likely be the only time they would have for any bonding banter. Shit was coming. 'Nice one, Abbi. Good to see him put in his place for once. But seriously, what's your deal?'

She pulled herself together. The ice had been broken. Job done. 'Sir,' she said, 'I don't know how much DCI Hardwell has told you, but she would no doubt have given you a precis of voodoo and its background. As you know, there is a huge African community across many parts of the UK and these practices are becoming more and more common. Not to the degree of the case you have here, thank God, but we're currently running to about fifteen hundred child abuse cases involving "faith and belief" every year, and that's probably an underestimate because schools and caregivers miss the signs.'

Paterson's eyes flicked to the rear-view again. The smile was gone.

'What you need to understand is that the vast majority of Africans, despite their underlying belief in witchcraft, are utterly appalled and deeply opposed to the methods used by these so-called witch doctors. They don't condone beating a child and certainly not the murder of one, but witchcraft is a reality nonetheless. They pray that they never have to face a choice, hope they never face misfortune, pray that their children are never badly behaved because, deep down, really deep down, they don't know what they would do. For the witch doctors, it's all about money. Lots of it. The reason why these churches are springing up everywhere has to do with cash. The adherents will happily part with money to ease their way into heaven and keep themselves safe from the evil spirits that roam the earth, and there are hugely unscrupulous people who are happy to prey on their fears and make it all right — for cash.'

'Admission to heaven. Cash only. Always a few quid involved somewhere,' snarked Clocks.

She ignored him. 'For the right amount of money, all kinds of charms and spells will be cast to change a person's fortune. Belief in the spirits is deep seated in Africa, and no amount of Christian or Muslim teaching will eradicate it.'

'Jesus,' said Clocks, 'we're in century twenty-one. How fuckin' backward are these people?'

Abbi folded her arms tight against her chest. 'Be careful in your judgements, sir. A belief in evil spirits is rife across all religions. Certainly Christianity is not without its demons. All across the world there are churches that fight the Devil and drive him and his buddies out of people. It's not just "backward Africans" who—'

'Hold up! That's not what I meant, Abbi, and—'

'That's what it sounded like. Sir.'

'Well, it wasn't. Don't try and twist what I said.'

Paterson weighed out of this one. It looked like Abbi had Clocks on the ropes and he didn't want to be referee for the knockout blow.

'Let's consider the highly civilised Americans, shall we?' she said. 'How many of their little wooden churches tucked away in the backwoods and up in the mountains are doing healings, driving out demons, playing with bloody rattlesnake venom. Fuck's sake, look at all the huge rallies that are held in stadiums around the world and attended by thousands and thousands, all paying a fortune to be cured, to have the Devil cast out.'

'Maybe,' Clocks conceded grudgingly, 'but the Americans don't go cutting kids up as sacrifices to the gods, do they?' Now he folded his arms, not quite sure how or why he'd got himself into a row with her.

'Don't they?' asked Abbi calmly. 'Are you sure of that? Can you really be that confident of knowing what people are capable of?' Clocks looked out of the window, really not wanting to get involved in a losing argument.

'So,' said Paterson, his mind whirring away, 'I get what you've told us and I can see the money angle, so now that we get it, what the hell do we do to stop it?'

'The truth is, sir, nothing. Child sacrifice is rife. An epidemic. And it's global, not just in Africa. Always has been, always will be. If you don't believe me, stick the words "child sacrifice" into Wikipedia. See what it comes back with. Witchcraft is banned in many African states, but you can't stop it. No one can. Even the legislators believe in it on some level.'

'Legislators?' said Paterson. 'How can they? They're educated people, surely?'

She shrugged. 'It's like I said, sir, this is a belief system. Education has nothing to do with belief. Never has done, has it? Educated people all over the world believe in the man with the white beard up there on the fluffy cloud. Some of the most famous thinkers in the world did. So, what's education got to do with that?'

Clocks turned round and craned his neck to look properly at her. 'Maybe you're right. Maybe it can't be stopped,' he said, fixing her with a glare, 'but we can fuckin' stop it here. I need you to do whatever it is you do, get in with the African community leaders on the ground and let's find out what the fuck is going on, who's responsible. Let's get them banged up and off the street. Every last one of these dirty evil bastards.'

He snapped back round and stared ahead. Abbi could see a vein pulse in his temple. Paterson indicated, yanked the car out into the flow of traffic and put up with the abuse yelled at him from white van man who really wasn't used to others cutting him up.

'Any idea why the man would have been shot, Abbi?' Paterson asked, once they'd gone south of Westminster Bridge.

'There have been rumours for a while now, about a man they call the "White Ghost." It seems he has been responsible for the deaths of a great many of these churchgoers all across Europe.'

'Who the fuck's the "White Ghost" when he's at home? More bloody scary witchcraft stories?' Clocks didn't bother with eye contact this time.

Abbi threw him a glare that he neither noticed nor cared about. 'It seems that some white guy with a rifle has been popping off people who're involved in the witchcraft churches.'

'How'd you know he's white?' asked Paterson.

Abbi shrugged again. 'We don't, for sure. That's why it's called a rumour. Although the fact that someone is shooting churchgoers is verifiable.'

'Any idea who he is, or why?'

'Nope,' she said. 'Although it's whispered he's a soldier. Obviously carries a grudge for some reason.'

'Nothing's obvious, love,' said Clocks. 'Certainly not at the moment.'

'Perhaps someone he knows was sacrificed,' Paterson said. 'A son. A relative. Maybe he is carrying a grudge or maybe he's just a plain ol' nutter amusing himself.' Paterson splayed his fingers out across the steering wheel a few times, hoping for some sort of verification from Abbi that his thinking was correct.

'Maybe,' she said, 'but it seems that he's following one man in particular.' Both men tensed slightly. 'The Very Reverend Benjamin Atewojaye.'

Paterson nearly kerbed the car.

* * *

As they walked into the main office, John Miller stepped out in front of them waving a sheet of A4. 'Sir, I've got Mr Hudson's path report here and a note from ballistics.'

'With me,' said Paterson, and headed toward the office at the back of the room.

Miller fell in line behind Paterson and Clocks but made a point of stepping in front of Abbi, relegating her to the back of the line. Grinning, she kept going at the same speed and deliberately clipped his heel with her foot, causing him to stumble awkwardly against Johnny Clocks.

'Oi, you fuckin' idiot,' said Clocks, who himself lost his balance when the bigger man fell against his back. 'Mind what you're doing!'

'Sorry, guv,' Miller said, embarrassed, and turning to glare at Abbi. 'I tripped.'

'Sorry,' she mouthed at him with an expression that was a clever combination of sweetness and light and go fuck yourself.

In the office, they all found a seat and Paterson instructed DS Miller to bring them up to speed. Clocks reached into his bottom drawer, pulled out two tumblers, two old tea-cups and an open bottle of Glenfiddich. 'Sorry, folks, all the good stuff's in the dishwasher. Me and the big guv will have the glasses.'

'No, we won't, John. Nobody's drinking unless it's tea or coffee. You're off it, remember?' Paterson looked straight at his second-in-command.

Clocks hesitated for a second then nodded and put the bottle back in the drawer. 'Fair enough, sir. You're right, of course. Apologies. ' He looked across at Miller. 'What we got then?'

'A couple of things, guv. First off, we did some digging into the Fatewojayes' background—'

'The *who*?' said Abbi.

Miller looked a bit sheepish, but not much. 'Fatewojayes. Atewojayes. It's a piss-take. Because they're so big. Someone thought it would be a giggle if we mashed it up a bit.'

'Got it,' said Abbi, unamused.

Miller went on. 'There's a large number of people in the system with the same name, so until we have a fingerprint or a DNA match, we don't have anything on either of them from their names. Hudson found a fibre trace on the body of the child that matched to Samuel Babatunde's jacket. It was found attached to some clotted blood at the base of the neck, and the thinking is that it transferred when Babatunde picked up the body.'

'Right, so we've got him connected to the child for sure, and we know that he was a friend of Atewojaye and was at the service he held that day. That's enough for us to drag him and the missus in for a bit of questioning.' Clocks was feeling it now. Something for him to get his teeth into, and it corroborated his feeling about Mr and Mrs Atewojaye being "wrong 'uns."

'Go on,' said Paterson, rubbing the back of his neck. He still held most of his tension there.

'The bullet that killed him was sent to ballistics and they've done a sterling job in identifying it so quickly. It's a point three hundred Win Mag.'

'What's one of those then?' said Clocks.

'One of them, guv, is used primarily for hunting. Big in the States and used pretty routinely by military snipers. SCO19 marksmen use them too. Delivers a hell of a lot of stopping power and is accurate over a thousand yards or so, depending on the weapon used for delivery. Travels at about 3,000 feet per second.'

'Fuckin' hell,' said Clocks, his eyes wide. 'You ain't getting out the way of one of them bastards if it's coming at yer, that's for sure.'

'No chance at all, guv, especially as the rifling on the bullet casing shows it was fired from an L115A3, otherwise known as the Lisa Three.' If Paterson was stung by the use of his dead wife's name now attached to a killing device, he didn't show it. Clocks was embarrassed though. He didn't know what Miller was talking about and wanted it clarified but he also didn't want to upset his friend. He knew it must have hurt him.

Miller pressed on, almost excited. 'It's known as the Lisa Three because when you look at it written down it kinda looks like the word "Lisa" — if you squint your eyes. It's a bolt action sniper rifle. This sort of rifle has got no business being on the street, guv. It's a fucking killing machine, bar none. This kind of weapon takes a great deal of skill and knowledge to use properly. I'd say whoever is using it knows exactly what they're doing, and I'd suggest that we're definitely looking for a rogue soldier here with a stolen gun. My best guess is someone's gone on the run and the army have hushed it up. This isn't Joe Public's gun.'

Paterson rubbed his neck harder now. He still had a question to ask and he knew he really wasn't going to like the answer.

'Did we get an appointment with the soldier boys?' said Clocks.

'We did. Ten tomorrow morning, over at Woolwich.' Miller pulled out his notebook and opened it to a page marked with an elastic band. 'A Brigadier Montague Harrison will meet with us. He's a big rank.'

Paterson couldn't wait any more. 'Back to the boy. Do we have a stomach contents report?'

Miller chucked his notebook onto the desk, flicked over to page two of the report and scanned it quickly. 'Yep, we do. First thing to note is that the body was drained of blood. Completely. It would seem that there were a few things present in his stomach, all of which are odd, one thing extremely so. There was a mixture of various plants and traces of a—'

'Calabar bean,' said Abbi. She'd been so quiet they'd forgotten she was there. 'Traditionally used as a paralysing agent.'

Miller double-checked the wording. 'Yep. She's right. And the strangest thing of all, there were shavings of—'

'Gold,' Paterson interrupted. 'Pure gold.'

Miller looked up. 'Yeah, how'd you know that?' Paterson gestured for him to continue.

Miller shrugged. 'Hudson says fourteen grams, which is about half an ounce. That's a fucking lot of metal to have to eat. The poor little sod must have been forced to swallow all of this shit while he was conscious.'

Paterson closed his eyes and tried to fight off the image of a lonely, frightened child being abused, as well as the king-sized headache that was threatening him.

'Money magic,' said Abbi, and stood up, breathing out loudly. 'Whatever else this is about, it's first and foremost about shitloads of money. A spell of this magnitude has been cast by someone who possesses very strong power, so as to ensure the transaction is conducted with the most favourable conditions.'

Miller screwed his face up. He still had no idea who she was or what she was doing here, but he wasn't too keen on all this bullshit talk about magic.

'John,' said Paterson, standing and heading for the door. 'I know you want them nicked but not yet. I want full twenty-four-hour surveillance on them starting tonight, with live updates to you and me.'

'What are you looking for, Ray? Sorry. Sir.'

'What do we actually have? A link between Babatunde and Atewojaye, yes. We already know that exists on Atewojaye's own admission, but there's no direct evidence that the Atewojayes were involved in this child's murder and I don't want to give them any outs. I want to see what they do and where they go in the next twenty-fours. I'll make an operational decision then, but I'm aware the situation could change. In the meantime, we need to get whatever info we can on our shooter.' Paterson glanced at his watch. 'DS Miller, full searches of all databases. I want to know of any other uses this weapon might have in civvy street, gun clubs, sports that sort of thing. I want to know how easy it is to get hold of one and who might have been able to. I want to know if there are any reports of this gun being stolen. I want to know if it's been used in any other murders. Abbi, you said this was going on all over Europe.

Get onto Interpol. See if they have anything. I want to know if any army personnel have gone AWOL. Get the team to lean on their snouts, particularly those that supply weapons. Someone may have heard something about a big-arsed gun like this floating about.'

Miller struggled to jot it all down fast enough.

'Abbi, pair up with a local. Go make yourself busy amongst the African community leaders. I want to know anything you can find out about the Atewojayes. Everybody back here tomorrow at eight in the morning. I want to know what we have, ahead of our meeting with this brigadier . . . whatever he's called.'

* * *

Lying in the dark of his bedroom, Paterson stared up at the ceiling and the shapes thrown in by the light and movement from the street outside. Day one back at work had not been the ease-in he was hoping for. Not by a long shot. Overall though, he was pleased with the way he'd held up, how he'd taken charge of the day's events and the fact that Johnny Clocks had given him respect. Things had definitely changed.

He knew he had to be careful though. His mental state was now a fragile thing that continuously tormented him with a potent cocktail of memories, thoughts and feelings that all conspired to drag him back down.

Since the savage killing of his estranged wife, it had become increasingly easy to take to the sofa, to curl up under a blanket, to coke the day away, to do any and all things necessary to ease the pain. And now, reflecting back on the day, he questioned whether a return to work was going to be as beneficial to his recovery as his psychiatrist had said it would be. The dumb bitch who never had to face the real world. No. She could bang on until the cows came home about the benefits of getting back into the workplace, being amongst like-minded colleagues, sharing the banter and such, but she would never have to see a chopped up kiddie, or a man with his head blown open or any of the things he had seen or was likely to see in his work day. That, Mrs Psychiatrist, tends to fuck you up even more.

To be reasonable though, it had been his decision to go back. He'd already resigned but didn't realise that Wallace Young, now the Commissioner of the Metropolitan Police, had refused his resignation and stuck it in a drawer pending the outcome of the Walker case. Good or bad thing? He didn't much care one way or the other, truth be told, but he did know that, deep inside, his desire to be a good policeman — the kind he'd always wanted to be — was still buried. And even deeper was the desire to catch the wicked bastard who had butchered a small child.

Blinking away the thoughts, he swung his lithe frame out of the bed and plonked his feet onto the floor. He sat in the dark for a moment or two waiting to see if he had disturbed his sort of live-in, live-out lover.

Detective Constable Carrie Gedmine had turned up at the door within about five minutes of his arriving home. How did she always manage to show up inside five or ten minutes of him? It did fleetingly cross his mind that she might, just might, be hiding in the bushes with a pair of binoculars and a packed lunch. Getting a bit too clingy for his liking.

Tonight, she'd turned up saying that she had something he would want to see. She was right. Most people would want to see Carrie Gedmine turning up on their doorstep wearing next to nothing under her coat. Whether they wanted to have sex with her or not, they'd have to at least admire God's handiwork. She was that well put together.

Tired as he was, there was always a little something in the tank for such visits and besides, he could do with the distraction. It would help him sleep. Hopefully. She'd be gone in the morning and at her desk when he arrived for work. They'd be all professional in the office — 'yes, sir, no, sir' — and at night, she'd be relishing their little secret. Truth was, she enjoyed the secrecy, the little touches, the glances, right under the noses of their colleagues, wondering if any of them had guessed, had worked it out. She would tell no one. Well, no one except her best friend, Lyndsey Mullins. Lyndsey wouldn't tell anyone, not even Johnny Clocks.

Carrie stirred slightly and he hung back for a moment or two until she settled back down before padding quietly into the bathroom, careful to lock the door behind him.

Passing his hand to and fro underneath the bathroom cabinet, he switched on a low-level blueish light designed to provide enough of a light to see while resting the eyes. The salesman had said it would help him remain sleepy during a nocturnal bathroom visit and help him to fall back into a gentle, restful sleep when he got back into bed. Like most sales pitches, it was full of shit. Dragging a couple of lines of grade A cocaine up his nostrils wasn't particularly conducive to a good night's sleep either.

He gently popped the "safe" tile in the back of the shower. Blending seamlessly with the rest of the tiles, it was a spring-loaded affair that when pushed inward, popped back out to reveal a small box tray. Rich people used them for stashing those bits of overpriced jewellery that they *really* didn't want the burglars to find but knew they could make an insurance claim against them safe in the knowledge that those bits would never show up on the streets or on a stolen goods database. Paterson's, however, held a small bag of white powder and his ready rolled ten pound note. There are other things than jewellery that you don't want found.

CHAPTER FOUR

Day 2 — Monday

After a fitful five hours' sleep, Paterson was at his makeshift desk in Johnny Clocks's office. He glanced up at the clock that hung, slightly wonky, over the door. Not quite seven thirty and he'd already been in for an hour. He was going back over the paperwork, such as he had, before the morning got off to a start.

A large Starbucks triple espresso in hand, he was trying desperately to shake off the effects of his midnight run at the bathroom coke machine. He slugged the tiny coffee back and screwed his face up at the bitterness. This wasn't the coffee he was used to, not by a long chalk. He lobbed the empty paper cup into the bin just as Johnny Clocks came barrelling through the door arse first, holding three paper cups in a precarious triangle of hot liquid. More coffee.

'Jesus, Ray. How long you been here? I thought I'd be first in with the coffees.'

'Been here a while, Timex,' Paterson said, making no effort to help Clocks with the drinks. It felt odd calling

Clocks by his nickname again. He hadn't used it for the best part of a year now and wondered, briefly, why he just had. He figured it was probably because he was back in the environment. One of the lads again. Hopefully.

'What you got me?'

Clocks carefully set down the three cups on his desk and backhanded a few files out of the way before setting out the cups in a line. 'Let's see if I remembered right. You like a double decaff, soya latte, extra hot, extra foam, no sugar, a dusting of chocolate and vanilla with a touch of cinnamon, right?'

Paterson nodded, amazed. He never expected Clocks to remember all that. It was hard enough for the baristas, let alone a man whose idea of a good coffee was one without lumps in it.

'Thought so. Like I was gonna ask for all that poncey bollocks, I'd have been there all day. I got you a straight black.' He reached into his trousers pocket and chucked half a dozen tubes of white sugar on the desk. 'Might be a drop of milk in the fridge if you want it. Smell it first though. I forgot the little wooden stick things so you'll have to use yer pen to stir it.'

Paterson smiled to himself. 'Who's the other one for?'

'John Miller. He's coming with us to see the army bods, remember? Thought he might come in useful as a military bullshit detector.' Paterson had forgotten but now that he'd been reminded, was glad that he'd asked him. He'd taken a bit of a shine to DS Miller. Seemed to know his stuff, didn't beat around the bush and having an ex-squaddie around certainly couldn't do any harm when it came to punchy time, which he knew, with Johnny Clocks around, probably wouldn't be that far off. He wondered what the punishment would be for smacking a brigadier. Hopefully he'd never find out.

There was a tap on the door and Miller poked his head into the room. Clocks pointed to a coffee and told him to sit down. After the good mornings were out of the way, they set about planning for the visit. 'Right,' said Paterson, 'what can we expect from these army boys, Miller?'

Peeling the lid off his coffee, Miller took a quick sniff, seemed satisfied and said, 'Don't expect them to cooperate. They might seem like they are, but given the weapon that's out there I guarantee that if they know anything about it, and they will, they're going to be dealing with it in-house. If the shooter is one of theirs, they absolutely won't want this being made public. Way too much damage to be done to their reputation.'

'So how do we deal with them?' Paterson said.

'Be polite, civil,' he shot a glance over to Clocks, 'and ask the right questions.'

'Which are?' said Paterson, sipping at his miserable cup of coffee.

'Let them know we know what sort of gun has been used, what sort of ammo. Give him the details, and that we know *only* a military marksman would have access to that kind of gun and the training to go with it.'

'Is that true?' said Clocks.

'Not strictly. Our Olympics team used them but I think it's safe to say it wasn't one of them.'

Clocks smiled. 'Why? Why couldn't it be? Just asking.'

'A gun like this doesn't travel easily across Europe. Masses of paperwork involved in doing it legit so, if it was one of the Olympic squad, he's gonna know the paper trail will lead straight to his door. It's highly unlikely that it could get past airport security, x-rays and all that. Not one of them. My money says military. Might not be now, but I'll bet a pound to a pinch of shit he was trained by them.'

'Can you buy this type of gun here?' said Paterson.

'You can, but you're looking at the best part of twenty odd grand for the gun alone. Another few grand for a suppressor.'

Clocks let out a low whistle. 'Tasty. Whatever happened to the days when a villain used to cart around a double-barrelled sawn-off? You knew where you were with that.'

'That was in the seventies, guv,' said Miller. 'Long before your time.' Clocks scowled at him.

Paterson glanced up at the wonky clock. Nearly eight, and he could hear the office beginning to fill up. Briefing time. Picking up what was left of their drinks, the three men strolled out into the main office and Paterson went over to the board. No time for niceties. He put the cup down on the desk in front of him and turned to face the assembled team. He spotted Abbi scribbling in her notebook.

'Morning,' he said. 'Who's going first?' He scanned the room, an expectant look on his face.

Abbi stopped writing and looked up. 'Sir,' she said. She sounded tired. No doubt she had had a late finish. 'I met with two of the most prominent community leaders last night. It wasn't an easy job, as they're not particularly enamoured of talking to women. Cultural thing. Think women are inferior.' She glanced around the room, as if daring any of the males to agree with that statement. No one did. Times were indeed changing. She pressed on. 'I had to use a bit of leverage, but once I got onto the subject of child sacrifice, they opened up a bit more, and became almost chatty.' Clocks squinted at her.

'To my surprise, they had heard of the Atewojayes' church. They've heard bad things about it, that it's used for witchcraft ceremonies. Rumours mostly, as it hasn't been going that long in this neck of the woods. There are rumours of children being taken there and beaten, but nothing as bad as sacrifice.' She glanced down at her notebook. 'Interestingly, nobody knew them as the Atewojayes,' Paterson and Clocks both turned their heads at the same time. 'The names they had were the Very Reverend Walter Abimbola and his good lady wife, Doris.'

'Doris!' said Clocks, grinning. 'Doris! Really?' Abbi nodded. 'Classic,' said Clocks. 'You couldn't make it up.'

Paterson wrote the names down on the board under the respective photos. 'Isn't the term "reverend" something to do with Catholicism?' he asked of the room. Someone said, 'Just means he's a member of the clergy. A proper vicar.'

Paterson scribbled it down without looking up. 'I'm sure. Question is, why the name change? Abbi, anything on the new names then?'

'Nothing, sir. Again, we have nothing much to put into the system to try to match against.'

'Fair enough. Keep at it. I want something. Next up? DS Miller?' He looked down at Miller, waited, then lifted his head and spoke to the room. 'DS Miller has already apprised myself and DI Clocks of some information that came to light. He'll fill you all in at the end of this briefing.'

'Actually, sir,' Miller said, 'I never got the chance to mention it in your office. I got back a report from Interpol that confirms there's been a spate of assassinations across Europe during an eight-month period. Seven victims. All the dead were Africans. Both sexes. All shot through the head with Lisa and Win Mag bullets. All members of Light of Our Lord Deliverance Ministries.' He paused to let that one sink in.

'Jesus,' said Paterson.

'Indeed,' said Miller. 'And there are reports that Lisa's been busy in Africa itself, but we can't verify this. Reporting out there isn't too good. It would seem that the only known suspect for this spate of shootings is one gentleman by the name of the "White Ghost." That's it, I'm afraid. No one has any idea who he is or what he looks like or why he's doing this.'

'So someone's following Atewojaye around Europe and whacking out his mates for some reason? Must be pretty pissed at him,' said Clocks.

'I guess so,' said Paterson. 'But the question I want answered, among a thousand others, is why hasn't he topped either of the Atewojayes or whatever they call themselves? Why shoot members of the church but leave the leaders alone? Doesn't make any sense.'

'Could be saving them for something?' said Clocks in between sips.

Paterson looked at him. 'Like what?'

'I have no idea, but it seems to me that if our shooter is so bloody good with a gun he could take those two fat bastards out with no trouble, so why hasn't he? Discuss.'

Paterson rubbed his face, the tiredness getting to him. 'He's making a show of it. He's saying that he can get them if he really wants to, but this way he keeps them in fear.'

'Maybe,' said Clocks. 'But why them specifically? We don't know for sure that they're involved in killing this child but I'm wondering if they're doing this all over Europe, a kind of travelling butcher's shop, and this White Ghost fella has got the 'ump about it. It's just a thought.' He turned to DS Miller. 'Do we know if any other kids have been killed the witchcraft way? In Europe?'

Miller flipped casually through the papers, not really looking. 'Nothing in here, but I'll go back to my sources. See if there are any reports of killings or beatings at the time the church was in town.'

'What about the surveillance team? Any news from them?' said Paterson.

'SCO10 report nothing out of the ordinary as yet,' said Miller. 'Seems the Atewojayes do live at the address they gave, although they're not shown on the voters' register. Probably rented. They were seen to enter the house yesterday afternoon, couple of big buggers with them — should imagine they're the ones you bumped up against yesterday — and they haven't been seen since.'

'Okay, let's stay in touch with them. I want a full report from them at the close of play today. Anything happens out of the ordinary, I want to know immediately, understand?' Miller nodded.

'Right,' said Clocks, gesturing for the team to get moving, 'You lot, make yerselves busy. We're gonna go piss off the army.'

* * *

Johnny Clocks was back. As the car made its way through the streets of Woolwich, he could see that little had changed since he was a boy. Surface-wise, there were plenty of shiny new office buildings, mostly underpopulated. Hugely expensive flats lined the banks of the River Thames, all inhabited by people with more money than sense and an inability to carry out even the most basic due diligence tests. Every one of these residents had bought the glossy brochure, but not the actual lifestyle. Tucked away behind wrought iron gates and high brick walls, they kidded themselves that they wanted privacy. Johnny Clocks knew it was to keep the wolves at bay.

The crime stats told him it was still a hole, but he didn't need them to know the place was still run down. He could feel it. However much money the council and private investors throw at a place to shine it up, at its core are people and their mentality cannot be so easily changed. This place was fundamentally the same, but with nicer buildings. *Fuck living here*, he thought to himself as they drove past what was left of the old Woolwich market.

As a kid, he'd drag his skinny little arse out of bed at six every morning, rain or shine, and head off down to the market where he'd put up a few stalls in readiness for the market traders' arrival, usually around seven, seven thirty. He'd come back around six in the evening and take them down again. The easiest thing would have been to leave the stalls up overnight but no trader would have risked doing that. They knew that as soon as the sun went down, the local thieves would nick every last metal bar, nut and screw and sell the lot for scrap. Better to pay Johnny Clocks and a couple of other kids a few quid to put them up, take then down and cart them off to a secure storage facility. On a good day, Clocks could make himself about twelve pounds, which multiplied by six gave this fourteen-year-old boy a tidy little cash sum at the end of the week.

Back then, all markets were thriving. People loved them, the hustle and bustle, the wheeling and dealing, the smell of sausages coming from the food wagons. And they loved, really loved, the fly-pitchers. Cockney wide-boys who would set themselves up with two things — a suitcase on a wooden crate and a "lookout," an accomplice whose job was to spot the police coming the second they ran out of whichever product they were shifting. The key selling spiel was to shout that whatever it was had "fallen off the back of a lorry." People love a bargain, and what better bargain was there than stolen goods? You got them cheap while sticking it to the man at the same time. A right result.

Nowadays, markets everywhere were on their knees. A barely living symbol of a dying economy where they once held sway, they now bent their knee to the proliferation of ninety-nine pence stores. Progress, they called it.

Driving deeper into the heart of the town, Clocks saw it was a long way from the place he grew up in. Everywhere he looked, he saw change. Betting shops were ubiquitous. Tattel's Newsagents was now called DM Patel's. Jones's Fruit 'n' Veg was now a noodle bar and every shop window bar one had a hole cut in it, behind which sat a man whose job it was to flog you an international phone card or a mobile phone case. Wherever he went in London, he was always amused by the number of nail bars that littered the high streets. Even if you couldn't afford to buy a pot to piss in or feed the kids properly, at least you had a decent looking set of nails. Proper priorities. So important.

The faces, though, that's what had changed the most. The white working class were mostly gone now, having bought their council houses for a snip under Margaret

Thatcher's regime and moved themselves upwards thanks to the bloated housing market in the noughties. Those who were left had one foot in the grave or were the sad sons and daughters who had never managed to find a way out. They told themselves that they 'loved it 'ere,' and would never move. Nor would they.

Replacing them on the lower rungs of society was a new working class — Africans, Asians, Chinese, Somalis, Nepalese. Different colours, same grinding poverty.

He closed his eyes and pinched the bridge of his nose.

* * *

The office they found themselves in stank of lemon-scented polish. It was spotless but you'd expect that from the army. Nothing out of place, everything just so. Clocks had once heard that the whole of the military lived in fear of the Queen swinging by on an impromptu visit, which probably hadn't happened since Boudicca's days. It was all about the discipline.

Sitting behind a large oak desk was Brigadier Montague Harrison, dressed in full uniform. Behind him hung a large oil painting of some bigwig soldier. From the style of his uniform, this guy had probably fought in the First World War rather than the second. Harrison was an impressive-looking man in his sixties. His best years were clearly behind him, but he was still lean, tanned and physically fit, and could no doubt be a bit of a handful if he needed to be. He was definitely the kind of guy you wanted around if the wheels came off.

Clocks couldn't help but stare at the array of ribbons and medals that adorned the left side of the man's tunic. He wondered what would happen if he turned that side of his body toward a bullet. Would it bounce off? Perhaps that's what high-ranking officers did in battle if, God forbid, they should happen to accidentally find themselves in the line of fire as opposed to their usual centre of operations twenty miles back.

Despite his musings, Clocks could tell, just by looking at him, that the brigadier had earned his medals. His bearing, his confidence, his whole demeanour was that of someone in complete control. Clocks knew nothing would faze this man. Nothing at all.

They were screwed.

Introductions out of the way, Harrison began. He spoke in a deep, educated voice. 'Gentlemen. Thank you for coming to see me today. I understand from your office that you wanted to speak about a matter of some urgency. Something that possibly involves a member of Her Majesty's Armed Forces?' He raised an eyebrow at Paterson.

'Sir,' Paterson shifted in his chair. 'I appreciate you taking time out of your day to speak to us. We're investigating a murder that took place near Tower Bridge yesterday. Victim took a single shot to the head. Thing is, my officer here, an ex-solider, suspects he may have been taken down by a military sniper.' Harrison's eyes darted toward DS Miller and stayed there. Checks would no doubt be made into his background. Miller shivered. Big brass still made him uncomfortable.

'The initial ballistics report tends to confirm his theory. He was hit by a military-grade weapon, an L115A3 with a point three hundred shot. I was wondering if you could tell me anything about that.'

Harrison turned his attention back to Paterson. 'And what is it you think I can tell you?' Cagey.

'Well, sir,' said Paterson, getting ready to wheel out the tact and diplomacy that would one day have guided him into the commissioner's seat had it not been for Adam Walker's unfortunate demise. 'Given that our murder weapon is essentially a military-grade sniper rifle not easily accessible to the man on the street, it's reasonable to think that our shooter may well be a military man, past or present. I was hoping you'd be able to tell me if you have had such a gun stolen. Or perhaps you have someone, sniper trained, who may not have returned from leave. That sort of thing.' Paterson flashed him a winning smile laced through with a heavy dose of *fuck you* attitude.

Harrison sat back in his chair, interlaced his fingers, rested them on the little pot belly that was beginning to creep up on him now he was in his sixties. He'd done well so far. He shook his head slowly, pretending to think about the question, the way people always do when they're lying. 'I'm certain that we have not had such a weapon stolen. I would know about that, of course. I will double check though, and get back to you. Likewise, any absent man. I have your number.' Harrison stood, signalling the end of a very short meeting. Instinctively, DS Miller stood up, fast, almost to attention. Paterson, though, wasn't quite ready to leave. He and Clocks stayed seated.

'Just so we're clear, sir. This is the murder of a civilian on the streets of London that we're investigating. If it was committed by a member of the armed forces, then jurisdiction lies with the police. Not the army.' He stared Harrison down as best he could. 'Am I clear, sir?'

Harrison bristled, evidently not prepared to tolerate impertinence from this young upstart.

'Mr Paterson,' he said, his tone now clipped, precise, 'I thank you for reminding me about jurisdictional responsibilities. Let me assure you that I am well aware of them. I have told you I will inform you if I find out anything that supports your, ah, theory. Now I'm a very busy man, Inspector.'

'Superintendent,' Paterson said, conscious of the intended slight. '*Detective* Superintendent.'

'Yes, of course. Superintendent. *Detective*. Let me show you to the door.' Slowly, Paterson got to his feet.

'Don't you worry about that, fella,' said Clocks. 'We're all highly trained in the art of detecting things. We should be able to find it ourselves.' He made a show of looking around the room. 'I once managed to find my arse with both hands behind my back. Took me a while, but I never gave up. I should be alright finding a door. Oh, hang on. Got it.' Flashing a big grin, Clocks pointed. 'It's over here, just as it was when we came in.'

Brigadier Harrison didn't do humour and he definitely didn't do piss-taking. He glowered at Clocks, who was making a show of looking all around the door before pulling it open. Paterson grinned. Miller was mortified. This wasn't how you treated a man of such high rank. Unless you were Johnny Clocks, for whom rank was just a word that rhymed with "wank."

'Thank you for your time, Colonel,' said Paterson descending to the same level. 'I look forward to hearing from you later today.' Just as he reached the door, he stopped and turned back.

'Sorry, just a couple of things I'm curious about.'

'And what would they be, Detective Superintendent?'

'Who's the White Ghost?'

Clocks caught it. The split-second change of expression that showed the bigwig was rattled. But just a split-second.

Harrison shook his head. 'I have absolutely no idea. Should I?'

'Not necessarily,' said Paterson. 'I just wondered.' He grinned.

'And the other thing?' said Harrison.

'Why on earth would the army bother to send someone of your rank and standing to a little preliminary meeting like this? I'm sure a sergeant would have done. Maybe even a captain. I'd have been happy with that, but a brigadier . . . makes me wonder.'

Harrison stared hard at Paterson and gently closed the door.

* * *

'You shouldn't have taken the piss out of him, sir,' said DS Miller as they got into the car.

'Fuck him. Jumped up prick!' said Clocks, half turning in his seat to look at his DS. He spotted him about to write in his notebook.

'What you writing there? A sorry note?'

Miller shifted forward in his seat, held the notebook up so Clocks could see it. 'No. No sorry note. Just doing my job and jotting a few reminders down. Not that he said much but still, professionalism and all that. Ever thought about trying it yourself, sir?'

Clocks hit Miller with a thousand-yard death stare. 'Watch yourself, Miller. Remember who you're fuckin' talkin' to.'

Clocks turned away, and watched the shops and the people whizz by as Paterson weaved through the traffic toward the relative safety of Bermondsey. He shuffled about in his seat, adjusting his balls, choked by jeans that were a bit too tight for a man of his age. 'Fuck, that's better,' he said managing to release one of them. He settled back down.

'Question is, Miller,' said Paterson, eyes on the road ahead. 'Why *did* they wheel out such a big knob? Is that normal?'

'No, not normal. Not as far as I'm aware.'

'Did anyone mention to them on the phone that we had concerns over the shooter being one of them?'

'Probably got mentioned but only very briefly. Certainly not enough to warrant anyone of his rank showing up.'

'That's what I thought. Seems odd. Given that they knew very little, wouldn't they have sent a junior officer to report up the chain?'

'I'd have thought so,' said Miller.

'Did you catch the look on his face when you mentioned the White Ghost? Wasn't happy, was he?' said Clocks.

Paterson suddenly braked hard to avoid the idiot stepping off the pavement. 'Miller,' he said casually, unfazed by the near miss, 'get on the phone and find out if we've got anything else on the Atewojayes yet. They have to be doing something now.' Clocks glared at the idiot, now sauntering across in front of them. The man stared back and stuck two fingers up at Clocks. In a flash, the door was open and he was half out of the car before Paterson hauled him back in.

'No, John. What have we said about playing nicely with the fuckwits?'

Clocks stared at him, half angered, half bemused. 'You said I mustn't keep trying to punch sense into them. It's a waste of police resources because it's not their fault they're all fuckin' snot-gobbling inbreds.' He took small comfort in the fact that the idiot had started to run the second the door flew open.

'I don't remember using those exact words,' said Paterson and glanced in the rear-view before he pulled away again. 'But the sentiment is accurate.'

'Sir,' said Miller, holding his mobile phone against his chest, blocking out their side of any conversation. 'Speaking to the eyeball squad now and they say they've followed the Atewojayes to a house over in Deptford. Small terrace. Door was opened by a black woman. Crying. Seemed distressed. The heavy boys sat outside in the car while he and she went in. The crying lady seemed to be dead pleased to see them. They've been inside for about a couple of hours now and there's movement behind the street door. Looks like they may be getting ready to leave.'

'What else they got?' said Clocks, interrupting. 'What can they see? What's in the front garden?'

Miller looked at him quizzically. 'Sir? I don't understand . . .'

'Gimme the phone,' said Clocks, leaning back and snapping his fingers in the air. Miller handed it over.

'Hello. This is DI Clocks. This place got a front garden, mate?' A pause, listening. 'What can you see in it? Anything?' DS Miller looked perplexed, while Paterson just let him get on with it. Clocks's instincts were kicking in. 'Kiddies' toys. A little red sit-on bus and a bike, trainer wheels.'

Paterson smiled to himself. DS Miller cottoned on.

'Alright,' Clocks said. 'Make sure you keep eyes on. The second our targets come out, follow them. I want to know where they go but listen, if anything happens in that house and you think you need to go in, do it. My authority. Understood?' He waited a second or two, nodded and hit the "end call" button. 'Well, we know there's at least one child in the household and given there's a little sit-on bus in the garden and trainers on the bike, I'd say it's no older than — what? — seven, eight tops.'

'So what's the play, John?' said Paterson, pulling up at a red light.

'Ain't got one at the moment, guv, but what's the pastor and his missus doing over at a house in Deptford, eh? And it bothers me that there's a kiddie in there. Worries me that they might be going to beat the Devil out of the poor little sod. Mum was all snotty and teary and over the moon when they showed up. Bet she never invited them over for tea and yams.' Paterson winced at the remark. The light turned green and he accelerated away.

'So why not just go in and find out what they're up to?' said Miller.

'On what evidence? No one's actually seen a kid in there,' said Paterson. 'We have no grounds. For all we know, they might *well* have been invited over for tea and, er, biscuits.'

'Like I fuckin' need grounds,' Clocks snorted, then thought it through for a few seconds. 'Trouble is, we can't say we saw a kiddie in there because we've got the eyeball squad looking at it. Can't trust them to back us up if the shit hits. We're gonna have to bite the bullet then an' see what happens.' His mobile rang.

‘DI Clocks,’ he snapped. ‘What’s happening?’ He pressed the phone tight to one ear, his finger jammed into the other. He needed to hear this properly. Paterson sensed something was or was about to happen. His jaw clenched.

Clocks listened intently, with the odd nod and shake of the head in silent answer to the caller. ‘Right. Let them get out of sight and then put that front door in. Not before. Don’t fuckin’ lose ’em. We’re on our way now!’

Paterson flicked on the two-tones and floored the car so hard it forced the others back into their seats. ‘What we got, John?’

‘They’re both out and away in the car. Benjamin was beaming all over his face. Missus Benjamin looked weird, whatever that means, and Mum and Dad were both having a weep and wail while somehow managing to look grateful. I dunno. Anyway, bottom line is, one of the watchers spotted a kiddie, a girl, moving about in front of one of the upstairs windows. Said the poor little bastard looked terrified, snivelling hard, couldn’t catch her breath. And he thought her eyes were bleeding.’

CHAPTER FIVE

Less than twenty minutes after receiving the phone call, all three men were standing inside the tiny, two-bedroom house. Paterson was in the hallway with lead officer DS Reynolds, trying to get the gist of the story through the pandemonium that had broken out. From somewhere at the back of the house, toward the garden, came the sound of a screaming, hysterical woman. Officers, male and female, were trying to bring her down from whatever plateau she'd worked herself up to.

In the kitchen, Clocks and Miller had the male occupant face down on the kitchen floor. The man was onto a loser, shouting and struggling furiously and getting nowhere fast. Miller had him in a straight arm lock, knee wedged firmly into his shoulder socket increasing the man's pain with every wrench. With his free hand, he was trying desperately to get the handcuffs on. No easy task when any man, big or small, is doing his utmost to wriggle free.

Clocks was on one knee beside him, pressing the man's head down into the floor with both hands, shouting at him to stop struggling, yelling that they were police, and threatening to knock him out. Getting no response, Clocks made good on his threat. He stood up and suddenly brought his full weight down onto the man's head. It stunned him long enough for Miller to get the cuffs on him and drag him up onto his knees. A good place to have him. Miller stood to the side and just behind him, ready. If the man suddenly tried to stand, he could kick him forward, pull him backward or push him sideways, depending on which way he moved. Whichever way he tried, he'd be restrained.

Paterson walked into the kitchen, took in Clocks, Miller, the handcuffed prisoner. 'All sorted, John?'

Clocks nodded. 'It is now, guv.'

'Lovely,' said Paterson. 'Why did he kick off?'

Clocks wiped a bead of sweat off his forehead, ran his fingers through his hair, shook his head. 'Got the 'ump when I told 'im he was nicked for assaulting a child. Got the wig-outs when I told him the kid was going to hospital and then into care. He started showing off, so we laid him down.'

'Fair enough. Listen up. Miller, get him back to the nick. John, with me, upstairs. The kid, a little girl, is up there in a bedroom. Paramedics are with her now. I want to find out what the fuck's going on here.'

With one hand, DS Miller grabbed his prisoner by the collar and hauled him to his feet. He then pulled him backward and forward quickly, to disorient him slightly, show him who was in charge, and bundled him out the door, banging him into furniture as they went, so as to keep him off-balance.

Paterson and Clocks hit the stairs two at a time and made their way along a small hallway. They saw a couple of plain clothes milling around in the bedroom doorway and edged past them into the room. Two paramedics, male and female, were gently tending to a small girl, lying on her bed. She was naked underneath a thin blanket. No more than six or seven years old, Paterson guessed. From where he stood, he could see she was in considerable distress, in shock. She grizzled loudly while the female paramedic talked to her calmly, gently trying to hold her still, and her male colleague poured a clear fluid into her eyes. She began to cry in fear and pain. Paterson could see that the whole of her skinny body was covered in welt marks, cuts and scratches. His stomach lurched.

'It's okay, sweetheart, it's okay,' said the female paramedic, dabbing the excess fluid from around the girl's eyes. 'We've got you now, sweetie. You're safe. You'll be fine.' The girl wailed pitifully and began calling for her mother. It reminded Paterson of the sound a small, wounded animal might make. In a strange place, scared and alone. *What the fuck are we dealing with here?* he thought, feeling tears begin to form. He wasn't expecting tears, and his response threw him a bit.

The paramedic patted the girl's eyes dry and lightly taped two thick pads of cotton wool over them. She then wrapped the child's battered body in a silver foil blanket and carefully picked her up and laid her gently onto a padded carry crib. The two paramedics settled her in, gently pulled the restraint straps across her body, picked up the crib and moved out, fast. Clocks looked across at Paterson. His face was like thunder, and rage burned in his eyes, while his fists balled tight.

'I know, John,' said Paterson. 'I know.'

Downstairs, the mother was still hollering. Clocks turned, and stormed toward the door, moving fast. He yanked it open, slammed it shut behind him and barged past the two plain clothes. Paterson went after him, but he'd lost a couple of seconds. 'John!' he shouted. 'John, come here! Don't!' He wrenched the door open but Clocks was already downstairs and storming toward the kitchen. He barged in and stood contemplating the scene. A black woman, arms flailing, intimidating, shouting abuse at two white females, police. The policewomen looked agitated, unsure of what to do with this ball of fury.

The woman suddenly stopped shouting and turned to the man now bearing down on her. He'd figured out how to calm her down. With an almighty backhander he cracked her across the face, and sent her spinning around. He grabbed the startled woman by the back of the neck and forced her head down, hard, onto the kitchen counter. The police girls froze, now totally out of their depth.

'You fuckin' wicked bitch!' Clocks screamed at her, gripping her tighter as she struggled to free herself. Paterson ran into the room, and over to his deputy. He pulled at him, shouted at him to get off her. Clocks held tight. 'Fuck's wrong with you? Call yerself a fuckin' mother? Should be fuckin' ashamed of yerself, you useless, no-good bitch.'

More police piled into the room, having heard the commotion. Two plain clothes helped Paterson drag Johnny Clocks off the woman. He really wasn't in the mood to let her go. Finally, he did — with a last defiant push of her head into the counter top. He turned, shoved at the plain-clothes men, told them to fuck off out of it. He then turned on the two female cops and jabbed his finger in their direction. 'Stop fuckin' around with her and get her down the nick. Do it!'

Clocks moved to the far side of the room — a safe distance away. Paterson followed and interposed himself between Clocks and the woman. She'd calmed down a bit by now. He turned to the officers. One of them, a female, was busy handcuffing the woman.

'None of you saw anything. Understood?' In an uneasy silence, all of them exchanged looks. '*Understood?*' he repeated. His tone was firm, authoritative. Reluctantly, they all nodded. 'Thank you,' he said as the prisoner was led out of the room. 'I appreciate it.'

When it was just the two of them left, Paterson turned to Clocks, still angry but no longer boiling. 'What the hell were you thinking of, John? Fucking attacking a woman.

In front of strangers. Jeezus.' Paterson shook his head slowly, unsure of how to process what he'd just witnessed.

'Fuck her,' said Clocks. 'She fuckin' deserved it. No-good piece of shit.'

'Maybe she did, but it's not for you to go dishing it out—'

Clocks darted a look at him, found his eyes. Snorted in derision. 'Know what you just said? Dishin' out punishment! Best you don't go there, Ray. Hmmm?'

Paterson stared at him. He'd never escape it, would he? You murder one lousy serial killer . . .

Clocks looked away. 'Ray, I'm sorry. That was low. I never meant . . .'

'It's alright. I know. Look, I've got your back too. But, John — witnesses, mate. I know they're on our firm but you've put them in a real shitty position. If that bitch complains, then we'd better hope they play ball.'

Clocks looked sheepish. He'd made a ricket, he knew. These people weren't part of his team, they had no personal loyalty to him, and he'd just knocked a few bells out of a woman right in front of them. Not good. Not even by his standards. 'Yeah, I ballsed up. I'm sorry. I just can't get my head around this shit, Ray. Anything to do with kiddies and I just lose it. You're not supposed to bash kids. You're just not.'

Paterson put his arm around Clocks's shoulders, and led him out of the room. 'I know, mate. All the more reason we have to stop these sick bastards. And when we do, I want you right there next to me. We'll stop them together.'

Clocks nodded, and gave Paterson a weak grin. 'Thanks, Ray, I 'preciate it. Now, get yer fuckin' arm off me, yer big nancy boy before everyone thinks we're in love. Let's go find out what Mr and Mrs Baby Butcher have been up to.'

Paterson grinned. 'We'll start right here in the kitchen.'

‘Ok,’ said Clocks. ‘First off, kitchen counter. There’s a few chillies for a start.’ He pointed to the counter, next to the sink. Remnants of red and green chillies were lying in a small pool of their own juices, and a sharp kitchen knife lay close by. ‘There’s fluid on it. Used that to cut them up, I guess.’ Paterson bent forward and peered closely at the objects. He nodded. ‘We both know that these fuckers have rubbed chillies in the kid’s eyes but we’ll have a job proving it forensically. Paramedic has probably washed it all out.’

‘What would you do if you’d had chillies rubbed in your eyes, John?’ Paterson said.

Clocks looked at him. ‘What? I’d scream the place down. Wouldn’t you?’

‘Yes, I would. But I’d also rub my eyes. Try to stop the burning.’

Clocks nodded. ‘Bloody good point.’ He headed toward the kitchen door and called to the nearest CID officer. ‘Go stop that ambulance, the one with the kid in it. Tell the paramedics not to wash that kid’s hands under any circumstances. There’s likely some forensic evidence on them that we need. Go do it. Now.’

The young CID officer, part of the surveillance team, eyed him up and down. He wasn’t in the habit of taking orders from a stranger, but then something about Clocks’s manner sent him scurrying out the front door.

Clocks walked back into the kitchen. ‘I’ll get someone over there to take a swab. We’ll go back upstairs in a minute. Check for any trace up there. I’ll get a full on search team in here too. We’ll rip this place apart.’

Both men looked around the kitchen. It seemed a bit too large, given the size of the house. The old owners must have dug deep to make it bigger for their growing children who, having done their growing, now had families of their own. The house was bought by an investor. That’s the way it went for most houses in these parts anyway.

'There you go,' said Paterson. He pulled a small magnet from the fridge door and took the business card it was holding in place. After a quick read, he handed it to Clocks who glanced at the writing on the front, and flipped it over and back again. Cheap card, cheap printing, shit colours. In one corner was a squashed-up picture of Blessing. He read the text.

"Blessing Atewojaye. Born gifted!!!

ARE YOU UNDER:

Witchcraft attack? Ancestral spirit attack? Mermaid spirit attack?

Whatever your problem that is not solved by anyone else in the world and you think it impossible to solve, ring BLESSING immediately.

Your problem will be solved in SEVEN days.

Blessing is traditional spiritual doctor, fortune teller, charms and

spells to fix marriage, get husband back. Remove all bad luck, chase evil spirits. Banish child bedwetting, bad at school. Bad luck in bussiness progress? Much debt?

Then you must call me, Blessing: the one true and gifted healer of all bad things."

Clocks shook his head.

'What do you make of that?' said Paterson.

'Well, for a starter her fuckin' English is shockin',' Paterson grinned. 'That's embarrassing, it really is. And mermaid attack? Is she bleedin' serious? Mermaids! Who gets attacked by mermaids? Ain't got no fuckin' legs for a starter. Ain't gonna kick you to death are they?' He paused. 'Might splash you to death, I s'pose. Still, how many mermaids are there in Africa? There's no bloody water there, is there? Little Kofi on the adverts is always asking for a few quid so he can have a tap fitted. Fuckin' mermaids. She's off her bonce, Ray, right off it.'

Paterson let him rant. He knew Clocks would go on about the mermaids all afternoon now. When they got back to the office, he'd tell everyone and anyone who would listen.

'So, now she's over here, is she saying the Thames is full of mermaids? That'll please my little niece if it is. She loves mermaids. What's that red-headed one? You know, Disney.'

Paterson pulled a piece of paper off the fridge. 'Ariel?' he said.

'That's it. That's the one. Loves her, she does. She'll be made up if she thinks Ariel's splashing about in the Thames. Won't be too chuffed if she finds out Mrs Benjamin wants to kill her though.'

'I'm sure we'll find a way to stop her, John. That aside,' said Paterson, trying to coax him off the subject, 'she also claims to sort out evil spirits and business problems. That I find interesting.'

'Yeah, you're right. Seems to tally with what we've been told so far. You found anything else on that fridge?'

'Oh yes,' said Paterson, waving a Barclays Bank mini-statement around. 'Seems they drew nine thousand pounds out of the account yesterday. Let's see if we can't find that lying around the house.'

'Jesus. You think they used it to weigh 'em off, the Atewojayes?'

'I don't know, but all they have left in there now is fifteen quid and a few pennies. Looking around this flat, they clearly don't have much, so my best guess is they're blaming the kid for their bad luck in life and called in Blessing to do a good luck dance in exchange for everything they had in their bank account.'

'And torture the poor little sod at the same time,' said Clocks, his face growing dark again.

'I want them interviewed separately. But not by us.' Paterson stared at his DI, who stared right back, his expression saying, *why not?* 'You know it's not a good idea. I've got previous for assaulting a suspect and you . . . well, you've got previous for assaulting everyone within a five-mile radius. DS Miller can do the man — it's his prisoner. We'll get Abbi to do the woman. Right now I want to get an update on where the Atewojayes are. I might be wrong but I'm guessing they've gone to stick nine grand in the bank.'

* * *

Paterson parked on a double yellow outside Barclays Bank in Tower Bridge Road. His hunch was right. The surveillance team, SCD10, had called it in. Mr and Mrs Atewojaye had gone straight to the bank.

Clocks popped the glove box and pulled out a laminated sign bearing the Met Police crest and a few words stating that the driver was on police business. He wondered if the Met would ever bother forking out for leather cases similar to the blue badge covers you could buy. He doubted it. No point wasting money on looking professional, was there?

'John, when we go in, we go in light but firm. The manager isn't going to be happy with our request, but I'll get him to see sense. Behave yourself. Understood?' Paterson buttoned up the jacket of his three-grand suit.

Johnny Clocks shrugged and got out. 'You're the boss,' he said. He headed toward the door, already pulling out his warrant card.

Five minutes later, in a packed lobby, Paterson shook hands with the manager. Now in his late fifties, David Facey was the epitome of a seventies bank manager. Not that Paterson had been around in those days but he'd seen the odd *Carry On* film. Cheap blue suit, shiny on the arse from years of sitting, a navy coloured woollen tie, shirt collar slightly worn and not quite flat enough. His hair was salt and pepper — mostly salt — and looked like it could do with a run under the tap. He'd started working behind the counter as a sixteen-year-old and worked his way up through the company to the dizzying heights of branch manager. On his say-so, many a business either stood or fell. He'd foreclosed on a number of homes when customers failed to make their payments, and he'd done so with relish. It was the bank's money. He worked for the bank, therefore he considered the money his. *You can't pay, you can't stay* was a motto that had served him well on his heady rise to the lower levels of management. If you cut him open like a stick of Blackpool rock, David Facey had banker written all the way through him. His staff thought so too.

'Mr Facey, thank you for talking to us.'

Johnny Clocks stood behind Paterson, hands behind his back. Catching the eye of the young blonde behind the counter, he threw her his best cheeky grin. She caught it and threw it straight back. Some you win . . .

Introductions out of the way, Paterson said, 'I need some information please as a matter of urgency, and I'm hoping you can help us.'

Facey eyed Paterson up and down and wondered how the hell a policeman could afford a suit that was worth a couple of month's pay for him. Judging by his own suit, the other one seemed more normal. Suit wasn't that dissimilar to his own. 'Of course, Mr Paterson. What can I do for you?'

Paterson glanced around the lobby. 'Could we perhaps speak in your office? This is a sensitive request involving two of your customers.'

'Of course. How rude of me. Please, this way.' Facey gestured for the two of them to follow him to his office, a small box-shaped room behind a glass door overlooking the main office. No natural light could get in and the ceiling had an artificial light and an air-con vent. Broken.

Inside, he took his seat behind a desk crammed with papers, a computer and a couple of old, well-worn calculators. 'Please, take a seat.'

They sat. 'I'll get straight to the point, Mr Facey,' Paterson said. 'What I'm about to tell you is to be kept in the strictest confidence, you understand?'

David Facey was a tad insulted. He was a bank manager. Bank managers understand all about confidentiality. 'Of course I understand, Mr Paterson,' he said defensively.

'You've just had two customers come in, a Mr and Mrs Atewojaye, Africans. I believe they have made a deposit of nine thousand pounds cash, possibly more, but I need you to confirm their details and the sum deposited.'

Facey shifted uncomfortably in his seat. This was unusual. 'Ah . . . I'm sorry, Mr Paterson. I'm not at liberty to divulge that kind of information. I'm sure you can understand my position.' Johnny Clocks stiffened, stared at him. *Don't be a problem, Mister Facey. Don't be.*

Paterson smiled his best smile, made himself all amenable. 'I do, sir, and believe me, I wouldn't be here and putting you in this position if it wasn't a matter of extreme urgency. DI Clocks and I have just come from a house not far from here and we have found evidence of a crime, a very serious one, and it is our belief that the Atewojayes received a substantial sum of money for carrying out that crime. My officers have followed them from that house directly to your bank. In order to substantiate my evidence, I need to know how much they deposited and I need to know now.' Clocks carried on staring, making Facey even more uncomfortable than he already was. But he wasn't easily intimidated.

Scraping back his chair on the cheap nylon carpet, he stood up. 'I'm sorry, Mr Paterson, but to get that kind of information you will need to go through the proper channels. I'm sure you understand.'

Making no attempt to get up, Paterson leaned forward in his chair, put both elbows on the desk and rubbed his face and his eyes. Tiredness was catching up with him in this stuffy little office. He did this for about thirty seconds, leaving Facey standing, looking awkward, unsure of what to do or say.

‘Mr Paterson,’ Facey said eventually, ‘I’m afraid I can’t help you on this occasion. If you would like to make an app—’

Paterson pushed his chair back and stood. He stared directly at him. ‘Mr Facey, much as I would like to, I just don’t have the time to apply. I appreciate your position and the position I’m putting you in. I promise you I will take full responsibility should there be any repercussions. You need to understand that these two people are suspected of a serious assault on at least one child that I can confirm. There are possibly dozens more children involved. They are also strongly suspected of the brutal killing of a child. A *child*, Mr Facey. I’m following a trail of evidence, and you and your bank are the last stop on that trail. Do you understand?’

Facey looked a bit rattled by the sudden change of demeanour but stuck by his guns. Policy. ‘I’m sorry, truly sorry, Mr Paterson, but I have a duty to the bank and you must understand my position. If I were to give you what you’re requesting without the correct procedure being appli—’

‘Alright, I tried. DI Clocks. Would you be good enough to educate Mr Facey for me, please?’

Johnny Clocks pulled his chair back slowly. He stood up. Slowly. Facey backed himself up against the wall, looked at Clocks, then back to Paterson, who shrugged.

‘We all understand your position, sir. You’re a company man, a rules man, getting near gold watch time by the looks of yer, and don’t wanna do anything to nuts up your piddly little pension. I get that. Now, my guv’nor just explained things but perhaps you didn’t quite get the gist of it, so let me have a go. We know that those two are heavily involved in hurting children — really hurting them. We also strongly suspect they’ve just received a shitload of money for hurting another little kiddie a little while ago — she’s just been taken to hospital by the way, and we think they’ve just put that money in their account. Now, we could apply for access like you want us to, but that will take time we haven't got. Not time we're prepared to waste.'

Facey pulled at his collar. 'So the way I see it is, you tell us what we want to know, or I will sling you over that desk, whack a set of handcuffs on you, nick you for obstructing police in the execution of their duty and drag you out of here, through that packed lobby and show you up for the piss-ante little jobsworth you are. I will also let it slip, in a very loud voice, that you've been arrested under Operation Yewtree and on top of that, I will make sure you spend a bit of time on remand.' Paterson grinned. He shrugged when Facey looked at him with pleading eyes. *Yewtree. Really?*

Operation Yewtree had been set up by the Metropolitan Police to investigate allegations of sexual abuse against predominantly young children by the now dead predatory paedophile, Jimmy Savile, and various other media personalities. The enquiry had three strands to it: claims against Savile, claims against Savile and others, and claims against others. Facey was about to be lumped in with the claims against others category. Nobody in their right mind wanted that.

Clocks pushed on while that thought sunk home. 'I honestly don't think you'll make it to trial. You'll either have a heart attack brought on by the fear or you'll get fucked to death by some very lonely but unpleasant gentlemen. Up to you, of course, but you might wanna rethink our request. Time's tickin' on.'

Facey blanched. He visibly shook as Clocks's words bounced around in his brain. He pulled his handkerchief out of his pocket and wiped at the sweat breaking out on his forehead. Clocks kept up the stare. Paterson gave him a "serves you right" kind of look.

Facey nodded, resigned. 'It is highly unusual, officers, but now that it has been explained with such clarity, I understand your need for speed. Please sit back down and I'll get you the information you require.'

'Thank you for being so understanding, Mr Facey,' said Clocks, settling back into his chair. 'And while you're at it, we're gonna need a little peek at your CCTV as well.'

CHAPTER SIX

'SCD10 from DI Clocks, update for us please.' Clocks spoke quickly into the radio and took it away from his face when he'd spoken, listening.

'DI Clocks, DI Clocks from DC Baines SCD10, we have targets back at home address. Tucked up inside. Bodyguards also inside. Been there for best part of thirty minutes.' There was sudden silence as Baines finished his broadcast. Then his voice crackled back into life. 'Stand by, stand by. Movement at the front door. Stand by.' A couple of seconds passed. 'Front door open, targets leaving address. Bodyguards front and rear. Targets are eyes everywhere.' Paterson flicked on the blues and twos and gunned the DB11 into life.

'All units from DI Clocks. Allow, repeat, allow them to leave the perimeter of the house. Once on the pavement, take them down. Repeat. Take them down. We have our evidence.' Clocks glanced at the white A4 envelope resting on his lap. Inside, he had a copy of a paying in slip signed by Blessing Atewojaye for the sum of nine thousand pounds, a signed statement from the cashier who took the money over the counter, copies of the couple's bank statements for the last twelve months and a shiny off-the-record DVD copy of the security camera, showing Benjamin and Blessing at the counter, pulling the cash out of a holdall and paying it in.

'DI Clocks. Understood. All units stand by.' A beat. Another. 'All units! Go! Go! Go!' The radio went silent. Paterson floored the car so hard he felt the front lift. Clocks held the radio against his ear, drowning out the muffled sounds of the siren, listening intently for updates while Paterson weaved in and out of the traffic towards the Atewojayes' home address. Given the traffic conditions, Paterson reckoned it would be five, seven minutes tops before they arrived.

Staring intently through the windscreen, Paterson kept his eyes firmly on the road ahead, but his mouth was moving. 'Why did you want them off premises?'

'Easier,' said Clocks, looking all around him, for idiot drivers who might pull out from a side road, idiots who might step in front of them. Idiots in general. Two sets of eyes on the road were better than one. 'If the eyeballs had moved in while the Atewojayes were walking up the garden path, there'd have been a ruck with the bodyguards, and they might have managed to turn around and wobble themselves back indoors. Might even have had long enough to dump anything incriminating. This way the scene is under our control.' He pointed to the left. 'Watch that bike wanker, Ray.' Clocks had spotted a middle-aged man, top to toe in Day-Glo orange Lycra, dodging in and out of the traffic. He could see the white wire running down from inside his plastic helmet to the iPod on his waist and knew the daft old fucker was probably back somewhere in the seventies and likely couldn't hear the siren. He had him down for a Roxy Music kind of man

'Good thinking, John.'

'Isn't it?' said Clocks, half hoping Paterson would pass close enough to bike wanker so that he could give him a gentle nudge into the stationary traffic. He knew Paterson wouldn't do that. 'That's why I'm a detective inspector and you're detective superintendent. I know how to think.' Paterson smiled. The man had a point.

'Urgent assistance! Urgent assistance!' a panicked voice screamed over the radio.

'Fuck!' shouted Clocks. He sat up sharply, lifted the radio and calmly dialled in another channel. He informed the local controller that uniform presence was urgently required and gave the address, then dialled back to his original channel. The shit had hit the fan out there on the street and the bodyguards had decided to earn their keep.

Like a dog busting to play catch, Johnny Clocks was desperate to get to the fight. Paterson pushed the car that bit harder. They were close now.

'I wanna nick that big lump, Ray. That Benjamin. He's an arrogant prick.'

'All yours, John. When we get in the house, though, I want to have a quick look around before the search squads.'

'You looking for anything in particular?' Clocks scanned the street, hyper alert now.

'The boy had gold scrapings in his gut,' Paterson said. 'I want to find anything in that house that might give me an idea as to how and why.'

'I doubt you're gonna find any gold bars floating around, Ray. They're dumb, but I doubt they're that dumb.' Paterson took his foot off the gas.

'What the bloody hell you doing?' said Clocks. 'They need fuckin' help!' Paterson sat quietly for a second, still driving, still watching the road, but Clocks could see he'd gone onto some kind of autopilot, cogs working overtime in his head.

'That's it, John. That's it!' Paterson glanced quickly toward his partner.

'What's it? What's what?' Clocks was confused, and he didn't like that. Plus he was desperate for a ruck with someone. He liked that.

'Looking at those bank statements, John, these two are making a small fortune, yes?'

'By your standards, no. By mine, yes'

Paterson snorted. 'Always gets a big laugh, John. Take the piss out of the poor young billionaire—'

'Billionaire? What? I didn't know that. Last time we spoke, you were a plain old multi-millionaire. Where'd the extra come from?' He stared at his boss. The fight would wait. He held his hand up. 'Don't tell me. Your old man's companies suddenly farted out another huge dividend all at the same time.'

Paterson tapped the brakes and turned into the Atewojayes' road. Ahead, he could see vans and cars parked any which way across the street. A couple of plain clothes were struggling to pull down a huge black man. Another was already face down and cuffed. 'Nope. Self-made, John. I got fed up watching *Judge Rinder* while I was suspended, so I bought a couple dozen more houses in Kensington and Chelsea, had a few little gambles on the stock market — options, that sort of thing. I learned to play poker, high stakes poker. Texas Hold 'Em. Five thousand, ten thousand starting blinds. That's an easy game, isn't it? Topped the old account up good and proper.'

Clocks stared at Paterson's profile, trying to work out if he was winding him up. 'Are you for real?'

Paterson swung the car violently to one side and shot between two parked cars. 'Don't be a dick. 'Course not. It was a wind up.'

'I fuckin' hate you sometimes,' Clocks said, only half joking.

Paterson slammed on the brakes and they both bailed out of the car. They ran headlong toward the pandemonium in front of them, making a beeline for the house. Clocks pulled out his small friction lock baton and flicked it open. In front of him, the huge man had managed to shake off one of the CID officers and was about to start on the other.

Running fast, Clocks slid across the bonnet of a police car, landed awkwardly, wobbled himself upright and with a bone-snapping crunch brought the baton down onto the man's shoulder. He shrieked as his clavicle broke in two and he fell to the ground writhing in pain. Clocks carried on running toward the house like nothing had happened. The DC, more shaken by the sight of the Met's own version of Conan the Barbarian than he'd been from the fight, just stared after him. Somewhere in the distance, the reassuring sound of sirens told Paterson and Clocks that back-up was on its way. In truth, it wasn't needed. And not particularly wanted either.

At the entrance to the front garden, Blessing was sitting on the floor in handcuffs, weeping and wailing. Two female officers stood over her. In front of them, two more CID men were fighting hard with another of the bodyguards and losing badly. One of them had blood on his face and his eye was already beginning to swell. The bodyguard was holding the other by the throat, pushed up against a tree.

Paterson jumped the low garden wall and ran full-tilt toward the big boy. Without stopping, he ran past and behind the man, grabbing him as he ran. The man instantly lost his grip on the CID officer as he was dragged violently sideways. He crashed to the ground. Hard. But many years of training had taught him what to do next, and he rolled expertly and sprang instantly to his feet. Paterson's momentum carried him on a bit further before he stopped, turned and saw a man of about six foot seven, built like a brick shithouse, staring murderously at him.

The man began to run toward Paterson, like an angry, wounded bull determined to take down yet another upstart matador intent on sticking pins into him. Paterson waited until the man was nearly on him, then dropped to one knee. He drove his right hand forward, hitting the man square in the solar plexus. He heard the grunt as he punched the air out of the bull's gut. The man dropped again, and rolled onto his back. This time he stayed down, clutching his stomach and gasping for breath.

Paterson stood up and walked over to him. The last thing the big bull saw before he lost consciousness was the red cape of Paterson's Louboutin brogue about to stamp on his face.

Paterson and Clocks reached the front door together, slowing down only to allow the other in. They heard shouting inside, a man's voice, angry, agitated. Both of them recognised Benjamin's dulcet tones. There was little agitation from the police voices, other than the one telling Benjamin to shut the fuck up. But Benjamin wasn't the quiet type.

'As I was saying in the car,' said Paterson as they headed toward the voices at the back of the house, 'they've been banking money, and a fair amount, but I have a feeling they've been laundering the big bucks.'

'Laundering? Into what? Gold? Property?' asked Clocks.

'Probably both. Have a look for any documentation that relates to bullion dealers, private banks, that kind of stuff.'

'Will do,' Clocks said, 'right after I nick this bastard.' Clocks strolled into the living room, king of the heap, top of the hill. Benjamin Atewojaye stared hard at him. He was cuffed, his hands behind his back. Johnny Clocks had been hoping the man might have been stupid enough to take a swing at him but the handcuffs had put that little dream to bed.

'Benjamin Atewojaye. Also known as Walter Abimbola. You're under arrest for assaulting a child, on suspicion of assaulting loads more, murdering another one brutally, chopping him up and a lot of other stuff I haven't found out yet. You've also been cautioned. Okay?'

Paterson stood behind Clocks in the doorway, shaking his head. A technicality. Right there. Failing to inform him properly and clearly of the reasons for his arrest, failing to issue a proper caution. Either of which could set him free. The detectives in the room just looked at Clocks. These were older men, not the kids that pervaded the job these days. Old school. A dying breed. They understood what he meant. If need be, they would swear that Clocks had arrested and cautioned Atewojaye correctly.

'Thanks, gents,' Clocks said to them. 'Do me a favour and chuck him in the van for me. I'm gonna poke around here for a bit.'

Benjamin, struggling, shouted, 'You cannot go searching my house without a warrant! I want to see your warrant!'

'Hang on,' said Clocks, and put his hand inside his jacket pocket. 'Let's have a look. Oh, here it is, mate.' He pulled out his extended middle finger. 'It's been signed by Lord Gofuckyerselfyadumbprick.' The CID men loved it. Proper old school, this one. 'Get him out of here.' Benjamin was bundled, hollering and hooting, out of the room.

'I quite like the look of that old briefcase poorly hidden and half exposed under the sofa there, Ray,' said Clocks. Paterson saw the corner of a black case, just as Clocks had said. *Doesn't miss a trick*, he thought, and pulled the case out from under the sofa. It was old and tatty, well worn, black, with two little gold combination locks holding it closed. Paterson placed it on a table and pressed at the catches. To their surprise it popped open, no fiddling required.

Inside were papers. Lots and lots of them. Household bills, mobile phone contracts, vehicle hire agreements, general shit that might come in useful after a good sift through. Tucked into one of the pockets was a little silver case — business cards. Paterson popped it open and there it was. A single card, cream, premium stock, that read: "*Leming's. Private Bank. Bullion Dealers. Harold Odonte.*"

There was a phone number and an address in Bond Street. Paterson held the card up for Clocks to take a look at, like some kind of magnificent prize.

Clocks squinted at it. 'Nice one.'

'Come on,' Paterson said, 'I have a hunch.'

'Care to share?'

'No. Not yet. I may be well wide of the mark and if I am, I don't think I could handle your piss-taking.'

'Fair enough. I totally respect that. Where we off to then?' Clocks knew full well they were off to Bond Street. But they weren't. Not yet.

'We're going to see a man about depositing some of my hard earned money,' said Paterson, pulling out his mobile phone.

Soon the car was speeding its way through the streets of Bermondsey. 'What are you up to, Ray?' Clocks asked.

'We have to move fast here, John. Listen up and tell me where I've gone wrong in my thinking, okay?'

'Go on then,' said Clocks, intrigued. What was coming next? Whatever it was, Paterson was thinking like a policeman now, and that was no bad thing. 'DCI Hardwell told us the dead boy was probably sacrificed because of something to do with money. Abbi confirmed it, reckons some kind of luck ritual, money spell. We know the Atewojayes are involved in some sort of magic. We know the kid had gold leaf in his stomach. And we found a card in the Atewojayes' house for a private bank that's also a bullion dealer.' The light was slowly growing brighter in Clocks's head.

'Right,' said Paterson, turning onto the Old Kent Road. 'I don't know, I have no way of knowing, but what if, what if the Atewojayes killed that child in this bank vault as some kind of good luck spell?'

'Good luck for what?'

'I don't know, John, but suppose they have cash or gold, lots of it, and they want to make sure they don't get caught or something. I really don't know. I know I'm reaching but you have to ask why a preacher man has the business card of a bullion dealer, don't you?'

'Yeah, alright, I can see that, but how did the poor little sod end up in a waste bin on an industrial estate? If they killed him in a bank, what's the church connection and why bring him all the way to Bermondsey?'

Paterson paused, thought it through. 'It's not that far, John. Early hours of a Sunday morning. Wouldn't take that long.'

Clocks shrugged. 'S'pose not.'

'Remember what was said about most Africans being Christians?'

'Or Muslims,' said Clocks.

'Or Muslims, yes.' He glanced across. 'Maybe they felt the need to, I don't know, bless the child perhaps. Some sort of atonement. The Christian bit lying on top of the old religion bit. Squaring it up with God or something. As I said, I'm reaching.'

Clocks waited a second or two, thinking, then said, 'I dunno, Ray. None it makes any bastard sense to me. None of it.'

* * *

Their first stop was Paterson's home address. During his period of suspension, Paterson had moved to a neo-Georgian mansion on the outskirts of West Dulwich. He had needed to get away from his old place in Beckenham and make a fresh start. This seemed to be the place to do it.

On the drive over, he made three calls, the first to DS John Miller. He asked him to pick something up for him urgently. Then he called Harold Odonte, asking him if he would be open to a very lucrative business transaction. Finally, he rang his tailor, with instructions to bring over a collection of suits, shirts, ties and shoes in different sizes. They'd find something for Clocks eventually. If they were going to meet with the owner of a private bank, they needed to look the part. For the first time in his life, Clocks was about to become the owner of a suit that cost more than his car.

* * *

Three hours later, they pulled up outside Leming's in Bond Street in a Bentley Mulsanne, one of the most expensive saloon cars in the world. At just under a quarter of a million, it was not the most expensive car in Paterson's collection — that was the Aston Martin Valkyrie he had on order. Nonetheless, it looked like something the gods had dropped on two mere mortals. Among its impressive list of features — enough to make multi-millionaires and petrol heads alike go weak at the knees — was the uncanny ability to get women out of their underwear faster than the car itself went from zero to sixty. Not mentioned in the brochure, it was a bonus that went with the whole package.

'What's going on with this bloody suit, Ray? Couldn't you have found me a better one? It's too tight, and I can see me socks. It's too short.' They were being ushered into the underground car park by a large security guard.

Paterson rolled his eyes. 'That's a Tom Ford, very upmarket. Thin is in, John.'

'Is it? Fuckin' stupid wearing a suit like this. I can't move in it. Whatever happened to the good old double-breasted?'

'They all got killed in a car crash back in the late eighties, John, and good riddance to them and the flannel they were made out of.'

'Bit harsh, Ray. Mine was a polyester blend.'

Paterson faked a dry heave. 'Dear God, man . . .'

'I feel like I should be in a naughty schoolboy contest in this fuckin' thing. You *sure* it fits me?'

'Yes. Now stop moaning and make sure you check how you speak in there.' Clocks frowned.

The security guards approached the car. Paterson nudged him. 'Jesus! Look at the size of them. They make Atewojayes' boys look like pre-schoolers.'

Clocks stopped fiddling with his suit and looked up. 'Christ Almighty! Best you give Middle Earth a call — tell 'em a couple of their monsters have got out.'

Two black mountains rolled toward them. Both looked to be in their early thirties, at least six foot five and three feet wide. Absolute peak condition. Either one of them could have walked away with the prize in a Mr Universe contest. Clocks was fascinated by their heads, completely bald and looking far too small for their bulked up frames, a sure sign of bodybuilders gone too far.

'They look like a pair of really dangerous Cadbury's Creme Eggs,' said Clocks.

Paterson smiled and gave a half laugh. 'Best not to mention it, though, in case they don't have a sense of humour.'

'Fair point, guv.'

'Listen. In a few seconds we're going to be invited to step out of the car, be subjected to a body search and asked to state our business.' Clocks frowned deeper.

'If you start getting lairy with them, giving it the "cor blimey, missus, apples and pears" or whatever it is you cockney chaps say, we'll never make it through the doors. Looking at these two, we'll probably end up embedded in them.'

Clocks mixed in a smile with his frown. 'Apples and pears? Who'd you think I am? The pearly king of Bermondsey?'

'I was thinking more Bert from *Mary Poppins*,' said Paterson as the first guard reached the door.

'Out of order, Ray. That fucker was an American doing a piss-poor English accent. The worst. More strangled Australian than English.'

The guard smiled, showing a full set of gold teeth top and bottom. Paterson thought it perhaps a little ostentatious. The guard gestured for the two of them to get out of the car. They stepped into the cool air of the garage.

Clocks really wasn't happy with his suit at all. It rode up around his ankles, and it felt to him like the sleeves had crawled all the way up to his elbows. That sort of look had been fashionable in the eighties perhaps, but not now. Surely not. Under the watchful eye of the second security guard, he pulled at the suit until he felt as comfortable as he was going to get. Just as Paterson had predicted, they were both patted down and asked the reason for their visit.

'My name is Paterson, Ray Paterson. I have an appointment with Mr Odonte to discuss business. He is expecting me.' The guard eyed him up and down briefly before looking over at Clocks. 'My associate, Mr Clocks. He, er, keeps an eye on me.' He looked into the guard's eyes, and saw that he understood and that he wasn't in the least bit concerned about Clocks's implied fighting prowess.

'This way please, Mr Paterson. Mr Odonte is expecting you. My colleague will park your car.' Paterson and Clocks followed the man to the private elevator that in a matter of seconds would take them direct to Harold Odonte's private office.

The elevator doors slid open to reveal a man with a smile more dazzling than the sun itself. He stood waiting, his hand outstretched. 'Mr Paterson,' he said. His educated voice bore little trace of his African roots. 'It is so good to meet you.' He shook Paterson's hand so hard he worried that it might come off. 'And you must be Mr Clocks. Please, please, come into my office.'

The sunny smile dimmed slightly as he bowed his head and gestured for them to be seated. The roof of the office was high, the walls a long way apart. Johnny Clocks didn't have overly particular tastes but he knew what he liked, and a glut of black and gold wasn't it. The place was covered in it. Walls, desks, paintings, everything. Even the carpet was black and gold. Floor to ceiling glass, bulletproof, naturally, lined one entire wall, giving a spectacular view of the city of London. In front of it, a large wooden desk took centre stage. Chairs had already been set up for them, and Odonte slid behind the desk and into his.

'Thank you, Hercules,' he said to the guard.

Paterson and Clocks shot each other a look. Hercules. *Really*? Made sense. A name like that gives a boy an incentive to bulk up if he doesn't want the shit kicked out of him at school.

'May I offer you gentlemen a drink?' said Odonte. He pointed to a small bottle on his desk. Paterson knew that the Johnnie Walker, an exclusive bottling named after the founder John Walker, came in at just under two grand a bottle. 'Or are you on duty?' He flashed the beams again.

Clocks unbuttoned his jacket. 'That would be lovely. We're on our lunch break. I'll have a large one, please. Thank you.' He tried to return the big smile but his teeth were just a little bit on the yellow side to have any impact.

'Same for me, please,' said Paterson. He shot Clocks a look — *told you to be quiet.*

Odonte pulled the three glasses, already set out and waiting, toward him. He began to pour. 'Let us get to business, Mr Paterson. On the phone, you said that you were looking to make a substantial deposit with us. I believe you mentioned fifty million pounds.' The flashlight grin took over again. For a second, Clocks froze at the number. Belatedly, he realised he should have asked more questions and listened a bit more closely to Paterson's plan on the drive over, instead of whining about the suit. Odonte handed them their drinks.

'For now,' said Paterson, 'but that rather depends on two things. Your discretion and your security. This money is, shall we say, surplus to requirements, and I would like to rest it somewhere. If it rests well and safely, then I shall be visiting you again. And again. On my future visits, I may well have turned the cash into a more . . . substantial form.'

'Metal or stones, Mr Paterson?' said Odonte. His eyes flickered. Paterson saw. This was what got him off and also what put him on the hook. He'd seen that look in men's eyes many times before, and they all had their thing. Odonte was no different. His thing happened to be yellow metal.

'Gold, Mr Odonte.'

'I see. Well, I'm sure you'll be very satisfied with our arrangements here. We have been based in London since the turn of the century.'

'I've done my homework, Mr Odonte, and I'm satisfied as to your credentials and your reputation. I'm also sure you have done your homework too. You know roughly my financial standing. Does my being a policeman bother you?'

Odonte leaned back in his chair. The smile was gone. He placed his elbows on the desk, steepled the forefingers and touched them to his bottom lip. 'It intrigues me, Mr Paterson. Knowing your net worth, I don't understand why you choose to be a policeman.'

'You don't know my net worth, Mr Odonte. You know what you see printed in the financial reports. Financial reports that are, well, controlled. I'm a businessman first and foremost, Mr Odonte. I learned at my father's knee, listened carefully and learned quickly. Grew up watching an empire being built. Other people take care of the businesses.'

'Your sister?' said Odonte.

'She oversees, yes. She's one of many. I thought that my becoming a high-ranking police officer would open up certain . . . opportunities for me, and allow me to mingle with people that only such a position would afford.'

Odonte nodded slowly. It made sense and fitted with what he knew. 'And what is the deal with Mr Clocks?' he said, and looked across at him.

Clocks sat, stony-faced, his eyes fixed on Odonte. 'The pay and the pension are shit,' he said.

The grin came back to Odonte's face, followed by a deep, raucous laugh. 'I like you, Mr Paterson, I really do. You too, Mr Clocks.' He tapped at his temple. 'You think as I think. That is a good thing.'

The laughter stopped. 'You have killed a man, Mr Paterson. It was in the papers.' This was the bit he'd been waiting for. If he played this right, Odonte would give him anything he wanted. And he wanted one thing. Access to the vault.

Odonte, like many, had read the story and suspected that Paterson had murdered Adam Walker in an act of revenge. He just hadn't been convicted of it. That, and the allusions Paterson had just made, put him in the game as a criminal. A rich criminal, and one Odonte could do business with.

Paterson gave him the slow nod. 'I'd be hard pressed to call him a man, Mr Odonte. I did kill him. Not by choice. By necessity. He was trying to kill me and Mr Clocks and as I'm sure you know, he had already killed many people. We believe it was close to forty by the end.'

'One of them was your wife. Correct?'

Paterson stiffened. 'Correct.'

'So, was it an act of revenge?'

Paterson looked him straight in the eye. No point lying. 'Yes. That helped me pull the trigger but he *was* threatening us and had to be put down. I won't lie. His killing my wife made it an easier decision.'

'Would you have shot him even if he had not killed your wife?'

'Yes. Why do you ask?'

'Just trying to see how you think. Do you regret it, Mr Paterson?' Odonte watched him closely for his reaction.

Paterson never missed a beat. 'Not in the slightest. He was a dangerous psychopath who butchered people. He would have killed me or John. I killed him. I don't lose sleep over it.'

Back with the beaming grin. 'Nor would I. You did the right thing.'

'So now we've got that out of the way, I want to look at your security here at the bank. I want to know that my money is safe. I'm hoping that this place will not disappoint me.'

Odonte hesitated for a few seconds, and then pressed a button underneath his desk. He rose to his feet. Paterson and Clocks followed suit. 'Of course. It would be my pleasure. Please.' He gestured toward the far wall where another elevator was already making its way up to them. 'This will take us directly into the vault.'

* * *

Paterson had to admit that the security was impressive. The lift had taken them five storeys underground. As they stepped out of the lift into a brightly lit corridor, they found themselves flanked by four security guards, each as big as the ones they had met earlier. Clocks noticed the Tasers and CS sprays attached to their belts.

The corridor itself was nine feet high and seven feet wide. The walls, floor and ceiling were lined with what seemed to be heavy steel plates with no obvious sign of a join anywhere. It looked like they were standing in a solid steel coffin some fifty feet long, broken up by security doors every ten feet.

Giving a running commentary as he walked, Harold Odonte obviously took great delight in boasting that the steel was almost eighteen inches thick and behind that, the concrete wall surrounding the oblong was another two feet wide. Buried in the concrete and running at criss-cross angles, forming six-inch diamond shapes, were bars forged of pure titanium. Heat sensitive, night vision CCTV cameras were fixed strategically along the corridor. Four at head level, four up high. The cameras sent securely encrypted 8K digital footage to a secure off-site monitoring station whose computers ran state-of-the-art facial and body recognition software.

Every now and then Odonte stopped showing off for just long enough to give a face and handprint scan before the security doors would open. On the last one, he was also required to give his broadest smile. This layer of security required a dental scan to be taken.

Having made it through security and reached the end of the corridor, the group found themselves standing inside a large, climate controlled room. The floor and ceiling were solid steel as before, but the walls were different. On one side of the room were the usual safe-deposit boxes you would normally find in a bank vault, but on the other was a vault door so large it could have been the entrance to another universe — a genuine *Stargate*.

CCTV cameras were discreetly embedded all around the walls of this room, almost impossible to spot and just as impossible to remove. The unseen eyes followed the men, quietly recording and storing their every movement. At the opposite end of the vault a titanium barred door was the only other way in and out of this room. This was the one they would have to come through later, and Paterson didn't have a clue how they'd manage it.

'As you can see, Mr Paterson, your money will be very safe here,' said Odonte, flashing the smile and twirling around on the spot, his hands raised to the ceiling like he was Indiana Jones and he'd stumbled upon the hidden treasures of the Knights Templar. Clocks already hated him with a passion.

'This is wildly impressive. I had no idea about this place,' said Paterson, in genuine awe.

'Very few people do. You are now one of the privileged few.'

Paterson turned to look at him. 'Has this place always been here?'

'The history books tell us that there has been a bank of some kind on this site for five hundred years or more, but as the city grew in wealth, so it was, ah, upgraded in line with developments.'

'It's just incredible,' Paterson said, turning back to look at the vault. 'I take it my money would be stored inside the vault?'

'Of course, of course, Mr Paterson.' Harold Odonte's eyes flashed like a naughty schoolboy's. 'Would you like to look inside? To see where your money will be . . . resting.'

Paterson nodded. 'I would indeed, Mr Odonte.'

With a smile, Odonte made his way over to the gigantic door and stood in front of the control pad. This time he blocked out their view while he fished something out of his trouser pocket and appeared to place it on the pad. Paterson couldn't tell, but he assumed it was some kind of digitally encrypted pass. Given all the security they'd gone through to get here, this seemed to be the least difficult part of the process.

Seconds later the door began to swing open, slowly and silently, stopping after a further twenty seconds or so. Odonte made a flourish like a waiter at an upmarket restaurant, indicating that the two men should enter.

'Dear God Almighty,' said Paterson. His jaw dropped. He was inside a room about the size of a three-bedroomed terraced house and face to face with five stainless steel pallets piled high with gold bars. Behind those was a huge block of cash. All fifty pound notes. Johnny Clocks just stared. He wondered if this was what the inside of Paterson's wallet looked like.

'Five tons of gold, Mr Paterson. Five. Do you know what that is worth?'

Paterson did a quick back-of-a-fag-packet calculation in his head and came up with an approximate value. 'That's — what? Just under two hundred and fifty million pounds? Give or take.'

'More or less. The cash you see amounts to seven hundred million.'

Paterson looked around the room, still reeling but his mind in overdrive. 'There's only so much gold in the world, Mr Odonte, and only so much gold in this country. How did—?'

'Ah, Mr Paterson, sir, let me enlighten you. It is commonly believed that your Bank of England stores almost two hundred and fifty billion pounds worth of gold. It does not. Think of it like the famous paintings in museums. What you see hanging up are not the originals. Uh, uh.' He waggled his finger. 'Those are stored safely away, split up in vaults all around the country. What the people see are superb fakes, and the illusion of so much security surrounding them fools the viewer into thinking that what they are seeing is priceless treasure. Do you really think that a country's gold reserves are stored all in one place? Of course not. It too is split up and moved around, distributed to banks all over the country. This is done so that, should the unthinkable ever happen and the Bank of England is breached, the country will still retain most of its wealth.'

'Really? I didn't know that, Mr Odonte.'

'We not only look after this country's money, we also look after that of a number of smaller countries whose security is not so . . . robust.'

'I guess that makes sense,' said Paterson, knowing that it didn't. Countries do not voluntarily hand their gold over to another country for safekeeping. That would be a dangerous and foolish move indeed. If the gold did come from other countries, then Paterson knew it was for quite another reason. His eyes swept the room again. Overwhelmed by what he'd seen in the last half hour or so, his mind was off the job, but something was wrong here, he knew it. Clocks did too. Conscious of the cameras, both remained impassive.

Yet Clocks couldn't help himself. 'None of my business, but can I just ask about the cash? Where'd all that come from?' Paterson frowned. Odonte did too. If he'd wanted to tell them, he would have.

Smiling pleasantly, he said, 'You are right, Mr Clocks. I do not wish to offend, but it is indeed none of your business. Discretion. Remember?'

'Sorry,' said Clocks. 'Just wondered if this is where you keep the EuroMillions cash.' He half grinned. Odonte gave a full smile. He had warmed to Clocks, he really did like him.

'Mr Odonte,' said Paterson, 'I'm extremely grateful to you for taking the time to show us around. I am hugely impressed with what I've seen here today.'

Harold Odonte beamed. He was just about to close another customer. The tour always did it for them.

'I will start to make the necessary arrangements and be in touch soon. Tonight, in fact. If you're available this evening, I will make reservations and we can work out the finer details over dinner. I'll send a car, of course. Shall we say nine?'

Odonte eyed him warily but the smile remained. 'That would be most kind of you, Mr Paterson. I look forward to it very much. Now, if you will excuse me, I too have arrangements to put in place. My security team will see you back to your car. I look forward to our future collaboration.'

Paterson and Clocks both smiled warmly, said their goodbyes, shook Odonte's hand and made their way back to the car through some equally impressive security. Two minutes later, Paterson pulled out of the garage and into the city traffic. Immediately they were out, his phone beeped — a text. The screen flashed "Miller." He tapped the screen and glanced at the message. 'Got the ticket.'

'Fuckin' hell, Ray. Di—?'

Paterson raised a finger to his lips, shook his head slightly. Clocks shut up at once. 'I think it went well, John. Very well indeed. I'm happy with that, and Mr Odonte's set-up there. You?'

Clocks played along. 'Very impressive. This could be good for us, Ray.'

For the next two or three minutes they kicked it around and made small talk about their meeting, arrangements to be made, transfers to arrange. Clocks was getting a bit antsy, he wanted to know what was going on and he wanted to tell Paterson something too.

'I don't know about you, but I could murder a pie and a pint,' said Paterson. 'Let's get back over the river and find a pub with a car park. I can't afford a parking ticket.' Both men laughed.

Sitting in his office behind his desk, and listening in on a speaker, Harold Odonte laughed too.

CHAPTER SEVEN

Clocks squirted a big dollop of tomato ketchup into his cheeseburger. 'What's going on, Ray? Why weren't we talking in the car?'

Paterson handed over a twenty to the young girl behind the counter of Mary's Burger Bar and told her to keep the change. Her name was Chrissy. She smiled and thanked him as she always did. He'd known her and her mum, Mary Flanagan, since he joined the force as a youngster of eighteen. He used to chat with Mary and her little daughter, who would frequently be found playing on the floor of the wagon. He used to worry that she'd get hurt — hot fat, hot tea — but Mary would have none of it. She couldn't afford child care and when the kid wasn't at school, she was with her mum.

Like all good young coppers he'd spent time getting to know the locals and ingratiating himself with them, and Mary's was on his beat. Mary was a good woman, kind. She'd do anything for you but, Lord, she took no shit off you.

Chrissy was six months old when Mary chucked her old man out, after she came home unexpectedly to find him in bed with the next-door neighbour. She heard them before she saw anything, and armed herself with the biggest frying pan in the drawer. Creeping upstairs, she opened the bedroom door as quietly as she could. Not that it mattered much since the racket the pair of them were making would have drowned out a crashing jumbo jet.

'So, Ray, I opens the door and there she is. Fuckin' great big old lump goin' up 'n' down on my Shaney's knob. All I could see were her back tits going up 'n' down. Couldn't take me eyes off 'em.' Paterson had had no idea what "back tits" were. He'd never slept with anyone who weighed over eight and a half stone. Never. Bemused, he'd asked her to explain.

'Y'know,' she said, 'big rolls of fat where her shoulder blades should be. Perhaps that's why my Shaney did 'er. A woman with four tits is different, eh?' She cackled like a fairy-tale witch, straight from the brothers Grimm. It was loud but infectious. 'So anyway, I thought "fuck this," and clumped 'er with the frying pan so 'ard she literally flew off Shaney's knob an' landed on the floor like a sack of spanners. Shaney sat bolt upright. He couldn't figure out where the fat cow had gone to and I clumped him as well before he knew what was going on. I broke 'is jaw and knocked out two of his teeth and told him to fuck off out of it and take Jabba the Hutt with him. I knew it was a bit of an ask that. He had no chance of lifting 'er up, the skinny little prick!' She cackled again.

There was no shame in Mary's telling of the story, and she never regretted what had happened. She was happy to tell anyone anything, and saw the lot as part of her big, colourful life story. 'Makes us what we are, luv,' she used to say to him.

Paterson stopped by from time to time and bought the odd sandwich and cup of tea. He had watched the girl grow up over the years. She was probably sixteen now, left school with no qualifications and no hope of a bright future. She'd most likely play out her days on the burger bar until she fell pregnant.

Carrying a tea and a bacon sandwich, Paterson wandered off behind the burger wagon out of earshot and sat himself down on a low brick wall. Armed with a double egg burger, Clocks followed him.

As he sat down he noticed a dog sit and raise its leg, licking at its balls. ''Ave a look, Ray.' He nudged Paterson, and pointed toward the dog with his chin. 'I wish I could do that.'

Paterson looked at the dog and then he looked at Clocks. 'Do you? Well, he don't look the fussy type, John. Pop over and ask him. He's already got his lipstick out, so you're halfway there. Might have to give him a bit of your burger first as a sweetener though. He doesn't look like the sort to go for a bunch of flowers.'

'Well, ha-de-fuckin' ha,' said Clocks. 'You're a real comedian ain'tcha?'

'I have my moments.' Paterson grinned. 'And don't try kissing him. His breath'll be a bit iffy now.'

'Anyway, enough of the hilarity. C'mon, what's going on?'

'I've got a feeling the car's been bugged.'

'What?' said Clocks, just about to sip his tea. 'Bugged? Why? When?'

'The when would have been when the big fella parked it up for us. The why? Think about it, John. I've approached him out of the blue with a proposal to dump fifty million into his bank. He suspects it's bent money but his greed has kicked in. He can't help himself. He's verified that I have money but he's wary because I'm police. You don't get to his position in life without knowing things, and he wants to know whether we're genuine. He wants to know whether we're a couple of bent cops that he can do business with, or whether we're on to him.' He sipped carefully at his scalding tea. 'My killing Adam Walker has only helped our credibility, so another win for shooting the bastard in the head.'

'Wow,' said Clocks. 'This is all a bit heavy, isn't it?'

'Yeah, it is. All this aside, answer me this. What was wrong down there, John, in the vault?' He didn't wait for an answer. 'First thing that struck me was the smell, only faint, but I swear it was some sort of cleaning fluid. Did you smell it?'

Clocks wrinkled his forehead, thinking. 'Cleaning fluid? Is that what it was? I smelt something down there but I thought it was because the air was stale. Some sort of humidifier maybe.'

'Maybe,' said Paterson, shrugging. 'It could have been. But if it is cleaning fluid, why would you need it in a vault that is, for all intents and purposes, locked up tighter than a duck's arse? Can't be too dirty down there, can it?'

'Alright. Wild guess, I'd say you'd be needing something cleaned up.'

'Exactly. Blood maybe? The boy was butchered and drained. Lot of blood that, even in a child. That's going to need cleaning up. I didn't see any drainage in the flooring, so it would have pooled. Difficult to get rid of. Notice anything else?'

'No, I don't think so. Go on.' It was beginning to irk him that Paterson was spotting things he had missed. That had never been the case before, and his mind raced to find something before Paterson spoke. He failed.

'One of the pallets. Toward the back wall. One of the bars was skew-whiff. Not much, but it was out of alignment,' Paterson said.

Clocks snorted. One bar slightly on the wonk. 'Oh fuck off, Ray, that's a bit thin, isn't it?' He bit into his egg burger, grimacing slightly as the yolk ran down through his fingers and onto the side of his hand. 'Bollocks! That's fuckin' 'ot,' he said, licking it off. 'I thought I was one for trying it on, but I think you're stretching it there. That could just have been the way someone piled it up. Or it could be Odonte picked it up to look at it. Maybe he held it up to the light, see if he could see a watermark. Like a five-pound note.'

A bemused look crossed Paterson's face. Surely he was joking? Surely. 'You're joking, right?'

'Of course I'm joking, Ray. Jeezus.' He paused as Clocks shook his head and bit into his burger. 'Or maybe someone picked it up and scraped some of the gold off the bar and fed it to the kiddie.' Paterson left that one out there for a second. He took a last bite of his sandwich before chucking it and the tea into the bin next to him. He stood up.

'Let me tell you what I think, John. I think we've stumbled onto something else. I think that gold and that cash is stolen. From another country. Probably Africa. I think the Atewojayes have something to do with it. I think they are in bed with Odonte, and I think all three of them were involved in the child's murder in some kind of magic ritual to bless the transaction.'

'Yeah, I can see that. Actually makes sense,' said Clocks. 'So, what's the score with the kid getting beaten today? Where does she fit in?'

'Don't honestly know. They both seem to be running a so-called church, so maybe that's their front. Maybe it's legit, if this sort of thing can be called legit. Blessing does seem to run a business driving out demons and mermaids, so maybe that's her day job. At nine grand a throw you only need to do a few of them three times a day, six days a week and you're raking it in. Greed is greed.'

'What about the White Ghost fella? And the army?'

'Christ, John,' said Paterson. 'One thing at a time. Again, I don't know, but let's assume Benjamin has nicked the money from somewhere in Africa. That amount of gold has to be government money. It's way too much even for the most powerful dictators to have. The Ghost could be a private contractor hired to whack him out. I don't know why he hasn't, but there must be a reason.' Paterson shrugged. 'Genuinely don't know yet, but if that is government money, then maybe our government knows about it too.'

And then another thought suddenly hit him. 'Maybe they're involved in it.'

'Say what?' said Clocks. This was now all getting a bit too much like a conspiracy theory for him. He was a straight-up old-fashioned copper, built for instinct not deep thinking.

'Why else did they wheel out a brigadier to talk to us? Miller said it was unusual. It's like the Commissioner of the Met talking to a manager from McDonalds. It wouldn't happen, and certainly not at a first meet.'

'Bloody hell, guv,' said Clocks. 'What the 'ell were you up to while you were on suspension? It seems like you've grown a brain. No good will ever come of that in a senior officer.' Paterson threw him a wry smile. 'Alright, we'll go with that. So, what's the plan?' Clocks was buying a bit of time before he too had to dump his food.

Paterson threw a quick wave to Chrissy and they headed back to the car. 'Back to the nick. Get all the troops in. Miller's got a warrant. I sent him to get one in case we needed it. We do. We're meeting Odonte for dinner tonight. We'll arrest him then and take him back to the bank. SCO19 will be with us en-route and we'll gain entry into the bank one way or another. If need be, the guards will be dealt with but I have a feeling they'll let us in. The big one with the gold teeth didn't seem too comfortable around Odonte. Did you get that from him?'

'Dunno. True, he didn't seem too keen on him, but whether he'll play ball is another matter.'

'Maybe. We'll see. We'll have a full team of forensic officers with us and a metallurgist who specialises in mechanical fits. He'll be able to tell us definitively if the gold in the boy's gut came from one of those bars. My money's on the skew-whiff one. The forensics will do their thing and look for any form of trace evidence to tie the

Atewojayes to the scene. They'll be setting up a makeshift lab for in-situ analysis. It's not ideal, but all I want is enough to bring the bastards in, hold them and charge them.'

Clocks looked impressed.

'We'll also be taking some seriously clever tech boys. I want a month's worth of footage from every CCTV camera in there, and it's my guess they'll be heavily encrypted. I don't have a clue what to do about that, so they can sort it out.'

'Who authorised all this, Ray?' said Clocks, fitting himself into the car.

'Commissioner Young. I called him earlier today and told him my hunch.' Paterson started up the car and pulled out into the traffic.

'Wallace Young? Fuck me. I'm surprised he went for that.'

'Think of the big picture, John. Once the press get hold of this, we won't be able to contain it. There'll be outrage across the country, if not the whole of the Western world. He wants to be in a position to say that we're all over it. That we already have one suspect, Odonte, in custody and hopefully a total of three if the lab boys can prove Benjamin and the wife were involved.'

Clocks grinned. 'Oh, look at you. My little boy's grown up and become a policeman.'

* * *

Paterson and Clocks stood in the middle of the packed Major Incident Room. Every detective on the squad had been called back in, with instructions to ready themselves for a long night. A plain-clothes team from SCO19, led by Inspector Lyndsey Mullins, occupied the back of the room, having been briefed on their way over.

Clocks had unbuttoned the suit jacket but still felt self-conscious. He kept pulling at the sleeves and rolling the trousers back down his leg with his foot. Nobody dared mention it. Lyndsey gave him an evil grin.

'Abbi,' said Paterson, 'the couple brought in from the house. What did you get from the interview?'

'They both coughed, sir. It seems that the husband had a couple of businesses that were doing reasonably well until about a year ago. Apparently, the little girl, Rochelle, had been in school since she was two. When she was five, she was in what they call "reception." It's basically a precursor to starting infants at age six. Upshot is, she became anxious, played up a little bit and started wetting the bed. Around about that time, Dad's businesses went on the slide and they thought the girl was infected with Kindoki. They searched the net, found Blessing. Couldn't believe their luck when they found out she was in the UK. They gave her a call.'

'What happened in there?' said Clocks.

'Mum said they stripped the girl, washed her from head to toe and when they'd done that, they started hitting her, hard, around the face and head. Both of them kept shouting at her, screaming at her, in order to drive out the demons. Poor little mite lost control of her bladder with fear but that just egged Blessing on. Bitch told them it was the spirits leaving her body. When she stopped urinating, they thought it a was good sign but by that time she couldn't stop crying and shaking. They went at her again, thinking that she had another bad spirit inside her, one they'd missed.'

'What role did the parents play in it all?' said DC Sole.

'Active,' said Abbi. 'Both parents helped beat her. They were told it was important. Bloodlines and all that. Anyway, Dad was instructed to rub chilli peppers in her eyes so the spirits couldn't see them, and then the kid went stratospheric with pain. You know where I'm going with this?'

'Yeah,' said Clocks, 'the crazy bastards dished out even more pain.' Abbi nodded, truly distressed.

'Did they pay off the Atewojayes?' said Clocks.

Abbi flipped through her notebook. 'They did. Nine grand. Cash.'

'Charge them both,' said Paterson through gritted teeth, his anger palpable. 'Anything and everything you can throw at them. Get the child into care. She is not to be given to anyone. Anyone. I don't give a shit who comes forward and says they're family. I'm concerned that she's in danger. On my authority, she remains in the care of social services until she can be removed to a permanent place of safety. DS Miller?' Paterson scanned the room until he spotted him sitting at the back with the firearms team — a sight that brought back memories. 'Good job with the warrant. Any problems getting it?'

'No, sir. I went to see Mrs Frost. She's very pro-police and always half pissed anyway. I said that, as a thank you, you'd be calling to take her out for lunch. Signed it straight away, then slid off her chair and banged her head on the floor.'

Paterson smiled, just enough to acknowledge the quip but not enough to let things descend into levity. 'What's happening with the Atewojayes?'

'Both are downstairs in the cells pending interview. Both have had their fingerprints taken and they've been sent up for identification as a matter of urgency. Mr Young has authorised express delivery.'

'Good stuff. What's their mood like?'

'She's clammed up tighter than a duck's arse. Won't say a word. Just sitting in the cell, staring. Gives me the creeps that one. Him? He don't give a fuck. Not in the slightest. He has an air about him, sir. Sheer arrogance.'

'Ok,' said Paterson, 'you and Abbi go do a preliminary interview with him. Find out what you can. When the prints identify them, call me and we'll try to come back for a more in-depth interview. DI Clocks and I have another line of enquiry to follow this evening. We expect to make an arrest at around nine tonight. We'll then be going to

Leming's Bank in Bond Street, and we won't be back until the morning. I want six of you to meet us outside Leming's. If we make our arrest as planned, I strongly suspect we will be nicking a few security guards. These are big bastards. They have Tasers for a start, hence SCO19 are here with us tonight. We will all take our instructions from Inspector Lyndsey Mullins until the building is secure.' Clocks smiled at her, proud of his girl.

'DI Clocks and I will remain on site, the chosen six will bring the bodies back here, put them in separate cells. No interviews.' His face grew stern. 'This place is riddled with CCTV, so everybody play the game. Professional at all times. Understood?'

All nodded, except for SCO19. They would do what they considered necessary. End of.

* * *

Paterson settled into his seat, his back to the wall, with a clear view of the entrance to the restaurant. Johnny Clocks sat himself in a booth with his back to the door so Odonte wouldn't see him when he walked in. Seated at the bar in plain clothes were Lyndsey Mullins and three male officers. They'd strategically left just one seat, knowing Odonte's bodyguard, should he bring one, would likely sit himself there, nestled comfortably between PCs Lenny Gent and Paul Griggs. Next to Mullins was Sergeant Ronnie Smith. They would all make their move, along with Clocks, the second Paterson did what he had to.

Through his earpiece, Paterson got the nod that Odonte and a bodyguard had just stepped out of the car Paterson had sent, and were on their way inside. He took a quick glance at his Rolex — 9:04 p.m. Four minutes late. Paterson couldn't stand tardiness.

The maître d' walked a beaming Odonte and the guard through the packed restaurant and settled him in his chair. The guard veered off and took up the empty seat at the bar.

Odonte thanked the man and turned to Paterson. 'Mr Paterson, it is so good to see you again.' He held out his hand for a shake that never came. Instead, Paterson slid a piece of paper across the table. The warrant. Odonte unfolded it, and his eyes widened.

'Harold Odonte,' said Paterson, 'I'm arresting you on suspicion of murder. You do not have to sa—'

Odonte dropped the smile, fast. He sprang to his feet, sending his chair flying. The guard was up instantly, and slipped his hand inside his jacket. PC Gent was quicker, and introduced him to his Glock. The guard glared at him murderously, weighing up his options, which took a sudden further dive south when he felt the muzzle of PC Griggs's gun dig into the base of his neck. A hand on either shoulder forced him back into his seat.

Lyndsey Mullins was standing behind them all, a few feet away, coat swished back, hand resting lightly on the butt of her gun. Odonte quickly took in the scene, caught a glimpse of Mullins in the mirror that hung above the table and realised there was little point in fighting. His eyes locked on Paterson. He shook his head slowly.

'Mr Paterson,' he said. 'What have you done?'

Paterson didn't answer. 'You do not have to say anything. But it may harm your defen—'

Odonte's voice overrode him. 'You have done a foolish thing, Mr Paterson. A very foolish thing.'

'If you do not mention when questioned something which you later rely on in court—'

'You will regret your actions here this evening. Whatever it is you think I have done—'

'Anything you do say may be given in evidence.' Paterson stood up, handcuffs at the ready. 'Turn around. Put your hands behind your back.' PC Smith spun him around. None too gently. Clocks beat him to it and snapped on a set of cuffs.

They began to push Odonte back the way he'd come. He resisted, his feet digging into the carpet, cursing them all. The crowd of diners had by now stopped eating and were anxiously watching the scene unfolding in front of them. Those closest to the table began to push back their chairs, ready to run if necessary.

'We're going back to your bank, Odonte. Search time,' said Paterson.

Odonte dropped the resistance. He shrugged off the two men, turned slightly to look at Paterson. 'It doesn't matter what you do, Mr rich-boy Paterson. You will not keep me chained.'

'We'll see,' said Paterson, indicating to Clocks and Smith to take him outside, by force if necessary. Lyndsey Mullins took a few steps further back. 'But in the meantime, you'll be giving us full access to your bank.'

PC Gent began to push Odonte toward the door. Clocks moved ahead to ensure no one got in the way. Paterson took a quick swig of his Chateau Margaux and headed out. Shame to leave it. As he swallowed, he caught sight of the diners' nervous faces. The rich were never keen on overt violence, even less so when it meant their expensive dinners being interrupted by a bunch of ruffians.

'Ladies and gentlemen,' said Paterson, 'I do apologise for disrupting your evening. I'm afraid it was necessary. Please allow me to take care of your bills this evening.' He flashed them his most charming smile, turned and said to the maître d'. 'My account please, Andre.'

As he reached the door, he heard the diners begin to break into applause. He smirked to himself. Bunch of wankers.

* * *

Hercules, watching from the CCTV control room, checked his watch — 9:30 p.m. He knew that his boss, Harold Odonte, liked to show off the bank and its vault to his more highly placed customers but he'd already shown two guys around earlier today, so he found it odd that he was back with one of them, the younger one. Two blacks had been booked on Saturday evening, a man and a woman with their small child, hugging a little orange teddy bear. New. Freaky-looking kid, he thought, an awful lot whiter than his parents. Some kind of disease, maybe genetic, but he wasn't going to ask. Not polite and not his place. He just worked the security.

Odonte told him the husband and wife were potential clients leaving the country in the morning, so they had to be shown around there and then. Although it concerned him, he signed Mr and Mrs Abimbola in. It concerned him a lot more when Odonte instructed him to turn off the CCTV. Hercules was charged with the security of the buildings, a role he took very seriously, and he wasn't happy to turn off the cameras for anyone. Even less so as earlier in the day they had only just taken possession of five pallets of gold and a huge amount of cash. This wasn't right.

In hushed tones, he began to question Odonte, embarrassed to challenge his boss that way in front of guests, potential investors, but it was the right thing to do. He could see no good reason for the instruction.

Odonte's temper flared and he gave Hercules a dressing down. He wasn't in the habit of being questioned by security guards, and certainly not in his own bank. Hercules, for his part, wasn't in the habit of being shouted at by anyone, certainly not by a slimy man like Odonte and, boss or no boss, for a second or two he considered the outcome of landing one on Odonte's chin. But in that second or two he remembered he had a mortgage to pay, a wife and kids to feed, and decided it wasn't worth losing his job over. It was his bank, his money, the man could do what he liked. He stood down from the confrontation, flicked off the cameras, showed Odonte they were off and excused himself.

Grinning, Odonte had turned his attention back to his guests and apologised for the misunderstanding with his guard. They headed off toward the vault, the small child walking between the adults and holding Blessing's hand. The child glanced back at Hercules, just for a second, then turned away.

Once they'd left the lobby, Hercules had walked back to his desk and flicked the CCTV back on. He knew something wasn't right and he wasn't being dragged down with his boss . . .

And now Odonte was back, with the young policeman and several others. These policemen, he could see, were wearing chequered baseball caps and armbands, were armed to the teeth and clearly weren't fucking about. He went to the door and allowed them in, much to the disgust and anger of Odonte.

SCO19 entered the building in their usual style, guns swinging, lots of shouting. The second the door opened, Hercules dropped to his knees and put his hands behind his head. He knew, before they even shouted their commands, that he'd be told to lie face down and spread his arms wide, palms twisted up and toes touching the floor. He'd been here before as a young man, a really piss-poor bank robber who'd gotten caught in the act. That was a long time and a whole false identity ago.

Cuffed and secured, Hercules was pulled to his feet and stood flanked by two armed policemen. He wasn't going to be a problem, had no intention of being, but the police were taking no chances with a man of this size. Satisfied it was safe to enter, policemen streamed into the bank and began to crowd the lobby. Hercules caught a glimpse of the street outside, and saw a lot of vehicles, flashing blue lights and more policemen rushing around. Whatever they wanted, it was serious.

Paterson, followed closely by Clocks, ushered Odonte past Hercules and the two men eyed each other. Odonte knew that he was about to be betrayed. He sucked at his teeth, and spat.

Paterson shoved him forward. 'Vault. Now! Move it.' The crowd began to break up and follow after him like an uncertain, disorganised snake.

'Who is in charge, please?' said Hercules, his voice surprisingly quiet for a man of his size.

Paterson stopped abruptly. 'I am,' he said. 'What's up?' Odonte glared at Hercules, trying to will him into silence.

'Please. Take me to the control room. I have something I think you must see.'

Paterson looked at him. He seemed serious. He handed Odonte over to DS Sharpe, with instructions to move him out of earshot. Paterson walked back over to the man mountain with the gentle voice. 'What is it?' Behind them, he noticed another two security guards being walked into the lobby, SCO19 tamed.

'Mr Odonte came to the bank on Saturday night. He had a man, a woman and a child with him. A small child. Mr Odonte said they were very important people, and he wanted to show them the vault.' Paterson and Clocks glanced at each other. 'He told me to turn off the cameras. I did not want to do this but he threatened to fire me, told me it'd lose me my job. We argued. I switched them off but I wasn't happy. When they went to the vault, I turned them back on. I haven't seen it. I didn't want to look but I know you must. You must.'

'What did the child look like?' said Paterson.

'He was small, young, maybe five or six and he had a strange look.'

'What do you mean, "look?"'

'He was different. Very pale skin, eyes, white hair.'

'Did the child come out with them?'

Hercules shook his head. 'I did not see him.'

Paterson's shoulders sagged but at the same time he knew they had Odonte now.

'And that didn't strike you as odd?' said Clocks.

'I mean, I wasn't there when they came out. I was doing my rounds. I did not see.'

'Come on then,' said Clocks. 'Show us where we're going.' Speaking into his radio, he instructed DS Sharpe to move on down to the vault with Odonte and make a start in gaining access.

Paterson's phone rang. Miller again. He debated whether or not to answer it, wanting to get this bit sorted out first, as things had just gotten very interesting. He decided he couldn't ignore the call. He stabbed the answer button and growled, 'Paterson.'

'Guv,' said Miller, his voice edgy. He sounded distressed. 'Sorry to call you, but there's a problem. We need you back here — like, yesterday.'

'Why?' said Paterson. 'What is it?'

'Benjamin Atewojaye's prints have come back. His name isn't Atewojaye or Abimbola. His name is actually Benjamin Kamwelu. We did some checking, and it would seem — no, it's confirmed — that Mr Kamwelu was a *Jenerali*, a general in the Tanzanian Army.'

'Oh, fuck,' said Paterson, sounding as if the word had been punched out of him.

'Fuck indeed, sir. Turns out our General Kamwelu was a thoroughly unpleasant man. Responsible for a number of mass murders apparently, without the sanction or knowledge of the Tanzanian Army. Google has him down as having gone off the rails in later life when he took to murdering whole villages. Killed more people than cancer.'

'Jesus!'

Clocks frowned. 'What's going on, Ray?'

Paterson looked at him. It was a desperate look that said the whole thing had just gone seriously tits up on them. 'From what we can gather, he was, at some point, arrested by the Tanzanian authorities and shipped off somewhere, presumably to be dealt with. We're running it past MI5 as we speak. They should be able to give us the real lowdown on him.'

'Have you mentioned this to him yet?'

'We have. When we confronted him with his name he grinned at us and said just two words.'

'And they were?' said Paterson, a knot the size of a grapefruit working its way into his stomach.

'Diplomatic immunity.'

CHAPTER EIGHT

Day 3 — Tuesday

Paterson had heard of Assistant Commissioner Tony Watson, and what he'd heard he didn't like. Cold, arrogant, selfish, ruthless were a few of the nicer terms that had been used to describe the man who now sat opposite him and next to Commissioner Young. Mid- to late fifties, bit of a tan, cropped dark hair, Watson had the air of a military man. Paterson looked around at the other people in the room. He had no idea who three of them were, but they looked pretty serious. The young man and woman he pegged as intelligence agency, the older man he wasn't sure. He recognised Kayleigh Winters, Young's PA. He'd met her a few times before on his numerous trips to the Yard to be interviewed about his role in the shooting of Adam Walker. She was the note-taker for today's meeting, although he wasn't going to let her see what was coming.

Hands behind his back, Johnny Clocks was looking out of the plate-glass window, taking in the view of Westminster from the eleventh floor of New Scotland Yard. He watched the cars below taking people on their daily commutes to and from whichever office they were working in and thanked his lucky stars he'd chosen policing as a career. Gets you out in the fresh air. He returned to his seat beside Paterson.

Paterson had a few bits of paper in front of him. Notes on the case, what had happened so far and where they were with it, a number of photos of the dead child and Samuel Babatunde, plus a copy of the recovered CCTV that Hercules had willingly handed over to them.

Commissioner Young shuffled a few papers on his desk and glanced up at the clock above the office door. He cleared his throat. 'Good morning, everyone. Thank you all for coming.' Heads nodded around the table. 'It seems we have ourselves a serious problem that we are here today to try to resolve. Before we begin, I'll go around the table and make the introductions. On my right is Deputy Commissioner Watson. To his right are Mr White and Ms Black, both with MI5. Detective Superintendent Paterson, the senior investigating officer for this case and his second in command, Detective Inspector John Clocks. Next to him is Mr Millington from the Foreign Office and, last but not least, Mr Mangu. Mr Mangu is from the Tanzanian Embassy and has been sent here by his government to secure the release of Mr and Mrs Kamwelu and, it seems, Mr Odonte.'

Paterson followed the names around as they were introduced. He wasn't happy with the two spooks at the table with their pretend names and he certainly wasn't happy with the presence of either the Foreign Office bod or Mr Mangu. He couldn't quite understand how what should have been a relatively straightforward murder enquiry had turned, in the blink of an eye, into a diplomatic incident. Clocks just wasn't happy with any of it.

'Mr Paterson, please bring us up to speed with the events that have brought us here this morning,' said Young.

Paterson opened his notes and recounted the whole story for the benefit of the attendees. He lifted his head from time to time to glance at their faces. All poker-faced. No one was giving away a thing. Having recapped the events thus far, he ended with, 'When DS Miller informed me that Kamwelu had claimed diplomatic immunity, we left the bank immediately and returned to the station. On our arrival, we were informed that enquiries were in hand to verify his claim to diplomatic immunity. Those enquiries confirmed his status as an ambassador and that he, his wife and Mr Odonte were afforded diplomatic protection. I was informed that Mr Mangu was on his way to the station and that all contact with Kamwelu should cease, on the orders of the Tanzanian authorities. When Mr Mangu arrived, he produced official documentation from the Tanzanian government demanding the Kamwelus' immediate release from custody.'

'And where are they now, Mr Paterson?' said Commissioner Young.

'Cells three, seven and nine, Tower Bridge Police Station.' Paterson deadpanned him. Young half smiled — missed by all, their eyes fixed on Paterson. Mr Mangu started to protest, but was silenced by Young, who knew what he was going to ask.

'Why have they not been released, Superintendent? You know the rules governing diplomatic immunity, do you not?'

'I do, sir, but I'm not in the habit of releasing sick, sadistic bastards who murder and dismember small children. It just doesn't seem right somehow.' He turned his head toward Mangu, hoping he'd pushed a few buttons. From the look on the man's face, he had. 'I have a job to do,' he said turning back to his senior officer.

'Mr Young,' said Mangu, 'Mr and Mrs Kamwelu and Mr Odonte are all afforded the status of diplomatic immunity. To detain them further is a gross violation of the Vienna Convention. My government demands their immediate release.'

Clocks shifted in his seat, agitated, antsy. He wasn't in the mood for this — not after what he'd seen.

'I'm sure they do, Mr Mangu,' said Wallace Young, his face hard and unforgiving. Commissioner Young was very much a man of the law and if you broke it, you paid for it. Not a man to buckle under threats either. 'But I'm not releasing anybody at this stage, until I have a lot more information to hand. This has all happened very quickly and I will not be pushed into making a rash decision. Understood?' He stared hard at Mangu, who, eventually, nodded. He wasn't finished yet though.

'Commissioner,' said Mangu, 'with respect, this is not a decision that requires thought. It is one that demands action. You must release them, or you will risk a serious diplomatic incident with my country.'

Young eyed the man carefully, and evidently decided he didn't like what he saw. 'A risk I'm more than happy to take, Mr Mangu.' He threw him a *go fuck yourself* smile. 'Mr Paterson,' he continued, 'you have provided us with evidence of an assault on a child, the young girl, but I understand you have other evidence linking the Kamwelus to the murdered boy. Correct?'

'Correct. It's from CCTV footage taken at the bank. The on-duty security guard was instructed to turn the camera off but fortunately he had the presence of mind to switch it back on when Odonte and the Kamwelus left the lobby. When you're ready, sir, I'll play the video footage.'

'From what you tell me, I'm not sure any of us are ready, Superintendent, but go ahead.' Young rose from his seat and went to switch off the lights.

'Before we begin, sir, may I request that Kayleigh leave the room? It's for her own benefit. Inspector Clocks and I have already watched this video, and we are sure she really doesn't need to see it.' Young nodded. Kayleigh Winters left the room, grateful that Paterson had had the decency to spare her from seeing the atrocity she had heard about that morning as she prepared to take the notes.

'There is little to the soundtrack, sir. It seems they had no real need for discussion, but you will hear some sort of murmuring. We're trying to get the tech boys to pull it up, see if we can make it out.' Young nodded.

The silent images that flickered to life on the screen were remarkably clear and bright. They showed General Kamwelu and Blessing, somewhat overdressed for a late night visit to a bank, carrying a holdall. Mr Odonte and the small albino child entered the vault. Teddy came too, the child clutching it tight.

In the vault, the pallets of gold, the bricks of money and a small fold-up table were set out, waiting. Blessing placed her bag on the table and began to remove a number of items. Several small plastic bags containing what appeared to be herbs, a flask, a cup, a sheet, a boning knife and a machete. They watched, transfixed, as Blessing first laid out the sheet and then began to mix the herbs and water in the cup. They shifted uncomfortably when Benjamin smacked the boy, who was crying now and shaking with fear, around the head before pulling roughly at his clothes. He seemed eager to remove them, to expose the child's nakedness. The little boy was a bleached, living skeleton. Paterson clenched his fists, tight. He'd already seen this once. More than enough to add to his nightmares.

After a few moments, Odonte walked toward a pile of gold bars and removed a brick, the one Paterson had noticed. From inside his jacket, he took out what appeared to be a chisel and returned to the table. Once Blessing had finished her ritual, he began to scrape off some gold into the cup. A minute or so later, Blessing nodded to him. Enough. She began to stir the mixture while Odonte returned the brick to its position. Paterson knew he wasn't going to straighten it up properly.

Benjamin dragged the naked crying child over to her and forced him to drink from the cup. The boy coughed and spat, grimaced in protest at the foul taste. Oblivious to the child's distress, Benjamin held his neck with one meaty hand, forced the cup to his mouth with the other and held it there, making him drink. They watched as the child coughed, choked and shook.

A few seconds later the drink was gone and the child desperately wiped at the strands of spittle that hung from his mouth. Confused and frightened, he began to retch but not enough to vomit the concoction out of him. Benjamin grinned. The biggest grin in his arsenal.

Within minutes the little boy began to stagger around the room, swiping at things only his drugged brain could see. Blessing began to dance. Commissioner Young wondered if there was actual music being played somewhere, music they couldn't hear, or whether it was only in her head? And then he caught sight of a thin wire running down from her headdress. Headphones. He'd missed her putting them in.

Blessing's dance became more frenzied. She spun around in a kind of counterclockwise circle dance, with rhythmic stamping, flailing arms, until suddenly her head went back as if some unseen spirit had grabbed a fistful of hair and yanked down hard. She began to shake violently. The camera showed that her eyes had rolled up. They were now two small white balls straining to pierce into the dark of some unseen demon world. At the same moment, the child's legs gave out and he staggered before crashing to the floor.

Blessing stopped. Her breathing slowed, her eyes were wide.

Benjamin picked up the boy — a small, white pile of spindly bones — and dropped him on his back, onto the sheet that covered the table.

Paterson began to shift around in his chair, looking around the room at the walls, at the ceiling — anywhere but at the screen. Johnny Clocks dropped his head down, looking at his feet. He began wringing his hands, his eyes tearing up.

The tension in the room was now palpable as they watched what were to be the final moments of a small boy's life. A security tape snuff movie.

Odonte walked to the end of the table and looked down at the child. He took the tiny head in his hands and stared deep into the sleepy, uncomprehending eyes. His and the child's mouths moved, but nobody would ever know what was said. Benjamin snatched the teddy bear away and threw it to the floor. The boy, uncomprehending, reached for it. He wanted it back. Desperately. His tiny white fingers snatched at air. He needed it. It was his only comfort.

Now the viewers in the room knew what was coming. This was it, they could feel it. This is what it had all been leading up to. Everybody went taut. Young closed his eyes for a second. His heart, made of granite according to some, banged in his chest.

Benjamin moved to the opposite end of the table. His grin was now wider than ever.

Whatever they expected to happen next, it wasn't that Blessing would pick up the machete. Holding it with both hands, she raised it high above her head as the two men began pulling at the child, stretching him out to expose his neck. The lady spook gasped. Mr Millington of the Foreign Office let out an involuntary 'Dear God!'

Blessing took the child's head.

* * *

The lights came back up and showed a room full of ashen faces. Paterson waited until Kayleigh had returned and opened her notepad before speaking. 'I'll be formally charging all three of them with murder, and Benjamin and Blessing with GBH on the young girl in the house.'

Everyone in the room was silent for a long moment.

Deputy Commissioner Watson was the first to speak. His voice faltered. 'Mr Paterson, I . . . have no words, truly. But . . .' Paterson and Clocks looked daggers at him. *But?* '. . . we have to comply with the request from the Tanzanian government.'

Clocks shot up, his chair crashing backwards, startling everybody. 'Do we fuck! Did you not just see that? Were you not lookin'? Is there something wrong with you?'

Watson blanched and stuttered, 'Inspector Clocks! Who do you thin—'

'I'm talking to you, Mr Watson. You've just sat and watched three people butcher a kiddie, but because his government says so,' he stabbed an angry finger at Mangu, 'you just want to hand them over. I don't think so.' He glared at Watson.

'Mr Clocks,' said Commissioner Young, 'please rein it in and sit back—'

'With all due respect, sir, I'm not reining anything in until Mr Watson here grows a pair and stands up for this kid. We're talking murder here, and not just yer run-of-the-mill type of murder. God knows how many more kids these two mental cases have killed.'

'I'm well aware of the law, John,' said Young, his tone calm, reasonable, trying to bring Clocks down. He should have known better.

'Mr Clocks, what we have just seen is a terrible, terrible thing,' said Mangu, 'but it does not change the fact that they are under diplomatic immunity and must be released. I can assure you they will both be dealt with when they arrive back home.'

'Oh, you can fuck right off, mate.' Clocks spat the words out. 'Deal with them? You won't do Jack, and we both know it.'

Watson raised his voice, clearly infuriated by Clocks's lack of respect. 'For God's sake, man. If you carry on like this I'll have you removed and suspended from duty.'

Commissioner Young stared at him, about to say something when Clocks waded back in. 'Do it then. Get me off the case. That'll save you having to behave like a policeman and stand up to people.' By now, Clocks was clearly hoping to goad the man into a full-blown fight. He needed to take his anger out on someone, and a deputy commissioner was as good a target as any.

Young, his voice loaded with anger, said, 'Just so we understand each other, Mr Watson, I make the decisions about suspensions. Not you.' The two men glared at each other, two pit bulls squaring up, until, within seconds, Watson exposed his underbelly to the alpha dog.

'Sir.'

'Mr Millington,' said Young. 'What's the view of the FO on this?' Clocks went quiet, listened.

The civil servant took a deep breath. 'First of all, I have to say that I'm deeply shocked by what I've just seen.' He coughed, paused for a moment, trying to think while fighting back the anger he felt at the position he'd been put in. 'I'm sure anyone from the Office would be appalled at what we've seen, but we still have to look at the implications. Quite apart from the enormous damage if we fail to abide by the Vienna Convention, there are cultural and racial sensitivities to be taken into consideration here.'

Clocks looked out of the window. Sighed deeply. *Christ, not another spineless knob*. 'Look, what's your name? Millington? I don't give a fuck about cultural and racial sensitivities and all this politically correct shit that has you lot picking up yer skirts and running for the hills. I'm a copper, plain and simple. We've caught two murderers bang to rights. On film. Job done, so all I care about now is making sure these pieces of shit go away for a very, very long time. You can all sit there wringing your hands about the implications but while you're doing that, me and DS Paterson will be cracking on with our murder investigation. Sorry to piss on your shoes an' all that but my advice is, if you don't wanna get yer feet wet, go stand in the corner out of the way or make sure you're wearing wellies.' His outburst silenced the room for a second time.

Young cleared his throat. 'Thank you, Mr Clocks. Sound advice I'm sure.' He turned to Paterson. 'Mr Paterson. You've been very quiet. What are your thoughts on the matter?' Young was aware that Paterson was less volatile than his partner. He'd most likely be mulling over the options, such as they were.

Paterson shifted in his chair. Sat up straighter. 'I'm with DI Clocks on this one, sir, all the way. I know that everybody in this room is here for a reason. I know that we are obliged to follow the rules governing diplomacy and I respect that. I also know that diplomatic immunity can be, and is, abused by all nations. I also know that that abuse can, and has, involved murderers escaping justice — Yvonne Fletcher and the Libyans being a case in point. But what I want to know is, how far are you going to take this one, sir?' Young rested his chin on his hand, listening hard and frowning.

Paterson went on. 'This situation is unprecedented. We have irrefutable evidence that these people, two high-ranking diplomats, murdered and dismembered a child. Not only do we have the murder and the assault but the gold and the cash as well. I'll bet that the money came in along with the boy on a diplomatic cargo plane. There's abuse and there's abuse. I don't know the rules well enough but I understand that for certain crimes, including murder, their status can be revoked?'

Paterson didn't wait for an answer. Instead, he rounded on Mangu. 'Your government can allow them to be arrested and tried. Am I right? In cases where a serious crime has been committed, governments can waive a suspect's diplomatic immunity. They want to be seen to be cooperating with the host government.' Mangu said nothing. 'So my question to you is, why won't your government allow it? Why do you want them back so badly that you won't even let us question them? If it was the other way around, we'd be cooperating fully with your people. I have to wonder if there isn't something being hidden?'

He watched Mangu closely for his reaction. He obviously wasn't taking well to this line of questioning. 'Now, here's something I really don't get. Kamwelu's a general who apparently went off the rails, killing people for the fun of it from what I gather, but once he's captured, instead of being dealt with in the proper way, he disappears for a while and then pops up as a full-blown ambassador for the country.' Mangu took a deep breath. He clenched his fists. Paterson steamrollered on. 'Now the question I have is simple — sorry, *questions* plural. What bright spark decided to make him an ambassador? Why? Man's a complete head case. So I get to thinking that maybe, just maybe, someone's making money out of this. Am I right, Mr Mangu? Is someone back home doing alright? Financially, I mean. Someone back home arrange for all this money to get here, did they? Work something up with Benjamin, arrange for him to bring the money in? Did they?'

Mangu banged his fist on the table. 'Superintendent, I do not like the tone you are using. These are serious allegations you are making. You will choose your words wisely when you talk to me.'

Paterson smiled. 'Actually, they *were* chosen wisely. And I think I have my answer. And for the record, you'd do well not to shout at me again. Diplomat or not, I will put you on your fucking arse end.' He stared hard at Mangu who, murder in his eyes, stared straight back. Without breaking eye contact, Paterson said, 'Best not put that last bit in the minutes, Kayleigh.'

Watson intervened. 'Mr Paterson, I don't think you quite understand what's at stake here. We are talking about a major diplomatic incident if we do not return them t—'

'You know what, sir? I've just asked Mr Mangu some perfectly legitimate questions, before witnesses — the very questions you, as a policeman, should really be asking him. I'm getting fed up with your apologist attitude and total lack of spine. Now, the way I see it, it's your job to support your officers and it's your duty as a police officer — no, as a human being — to help bring these people to book. These animals butchered a kiddie. You've just watched them do it. It's not acceptable. Not here, not in Africa. Nowhere. So we are going to fight for that child. We are going to put this scum away, and we are going to make them pay for what they did. Someone has to, because, clearly, none of you lot will.' He looked around the table accusingly, daring one of them to speak, to challenge him. All were silent.

'Now, unless you suddenly grow a pair of bollocks and have something supportive to say, shut the fuck up.'

Young gave a sly little half smile, and allowed Paterson the floor. Watson went red again. Embarrassment? Anger? Probably both.

Paterson turned away. 'I'm also concerned about this "White Ghost," and the army's involvement there. I strongly suspect they know about him and who he is, and they're covering up. Why, I'm not sure yet, but I'll find out. I'm guessing that's why the silent twins are here.' He looked over to Mr White and Ms Black. 'How about it, guys? Want to join in?' They remained mute. Ms Black pulled a Blackberry out of her briefcase and began texting. 'No? Okay then. Well, whoever you're texting, best let them know we'll be going back to see Brigadier Harrison and if he doesn't change his tune and stop with the bullshit, he'll find himself under arrest for obstructing a murder enquiry. I want, and expect, answers.'

Ms Black went white and her fingers sped up. Paterson grinned.

'Mr Millington,' said Paterson, turning his attention to the FO man. 'Would you like a copy of the recording for the Prime Minister? Might help her make a half-decent decision for a change.' Millington looked down at his feet, embarrassed and terrified at the prospect of having to report back on the defiant mood he'd met with from two senior officers — three, if you counted Commissioner Young.

'Thank you for your input, Superintendent Paterson,' said Young, interlocking his fingers and resting them on his stomach. He sat back in his chair, thinking.

Everyone in the room remained silent, waiting for him to continue. He leaned forward quickly, elbows on desk, hands under his chin. 'Superintendent Paterson, Inspector Clocks,' he said. 'If it helps, I have quite big bollocks and I'm with you all the way on this. I will authorise their continued detention in order to allow your enquiries to continue. Mr Mangu, please inform your government that their subjects will remain under arrest and will not be allowed to leave this country any time soon. Mr Millington, I would advise you to speak to the PM and inform her of my decision. I will not be swayed from it, and am more than happy to argue the point, in person if necessary. As Mr Paterson has already suggested, perhaps she should look at the security tape to help her make a decision.'

'Sir, I really think—'

'Unfortunately, *Mr* Watson,' said Young, 'I'm aware of what you think. And unfortunately for you, we think differently. Now, my officers have a job to do and I strongly suggest that you assist them by giving them your full support. Go with Mr Millington and assist him with the PM. I expect you to argue strongly in favour of the suspects' continued detention. This meeting is over. Mr Paterson, Mr Clocks, this is my fight now. Go home, get some rest. I will call you this afternoon with an update.'

* * *

Paterson rested his head on the steering wheel and breathed deeply. He needed a minute to collect his thoughts before he drove away. 'Thank Christ Mr Young is on our side.'

Next to him, Clocks nodded. He turned to look at Paterson. 'They're gonna let them go, though, aren't they?' He sounded resigned to the fact.

'Honestly, John, I don't know,' said Paterson without lifting his head. 'But Young will put up a hell of a fight before he gives in. I'd bet my house he's onto the Met's legal team right now.'

'The fuckin' CPS? Jesus! They'll all be set free in a second.'

'Proper lawyers, John, not that lot. He's going to need to wheel out the big brains for this one. He's going to be looking for something, anything, to hold them, and he's going to blow the budget on it.'

'I hope you're right, Ray. This is so fuckin' wrong. How can we even think of letting 'em go? The bastards should be shot.' He turned his head and looked out the window. Nothing about the scene in front of him registered. He spoke more quietly now. 'I can't have those bastards getting on a plane and laughin' at us. There has to be something we can do, Ray. We can't let 'em get away with it. We just can't.'

Paterson lifted his head, looked at his friend. He knew what he was likely thinking and it worried him. Badly. 'We're not planning on doing anything stupid — are we, John?'

'I can't speak for you, guv,' said Clocks, a little grin creeping into the corners of his mouth. 'But it's a racing certainty that I will. We both know that.'

'Yeah,' said Paterson turning the key in the ignition. The roar of the car's engine echoed around the underground car park. 'And it's a racing certainty I will too.'

As they pulled out into the morning traffic, Clocks dropped his window, flooding the car with cool air. It felt better than any air-conditioning unit and he pushed his head closer to the opening. He closed his eyes and felt the breeze play on his face. It calmed him down a bit.

'What's the story with the Dep Comm then, guv?' he said, pulling his head back slightly. 'Clearly there's no love lost between him and Young.'

'No idea, John, but he certainly got Young wound up. I don't know if there's history between them, but I don't think he was too keen on Watson's lack of solidarity. He was the only one fighting our corner and it pissed him off big time that his number two wasn't backing him up.'

'Yeah, that bothered me too. Even if you don't necessarily agree, you stand by your guv'nor. It's the law.' He looked at Paterson and winked.

'Exactly.' Paterson picked up Clocks's meaning and chose to move on. 'So now I'm thinking, if Watson's not part of the solution, perhaps he's part of the problem?'

Clocks glanced over at his colleague. Paterson looked rough. Dog tired, stubble sprouting on his chin, hair a bit greasy, although that was most likely some kind of expensive gel he'd slapped on yesterday. His clothing was rumpled. 'Are you gonna tell me he's got something to do with all of this?' He didn't wait for an answer. 'If you are, don't. The man's a cowardly cock for sure but leave it at that, Ray. We've got enough shit to deal with as it is without you seeing Reds under the bed.'

Paterson threw him a quick glance. Clocks looked even worse for wear than he did. 'Okay, fair enough, John. You're right. I'm tired, not thinking straight. I need my bed.'

'Amen to that, bruv. I'm knackered meself.'

As they drove around the corner, Clocks spotted something worth investigating. 'Find a parking space, Ray. There.' He pointed. 'Over there.'

Paterson turned his head, trying to see what Clocks had spotted. Nothing stood out. 'What's the matter?'

'I'm knackered, but I'm also starving. Some grub at Wetherspoon's breakfast emporium is seriously required.'

Paterson spotted a car pulling away from the only parking space in the street and lined up the Bentley for a reverse park. 'What's a Wetherspoon's?' he asked, putting the car in reverse.

Clocks looked at him aghast. 'Fuck off. You're jokin', right?' Paterson's face told him he really wasn't. 'Bloody hell, guv. Have you never eaten proper food in your life? You can have a full on English breakfast in here with a cup of tea for about four quid if they're 'avin' a deal. None of that poncey organic shit you always eat. You're in for a right old treat.'

Paterson stepped out of the car. 'One doubts it.'

CHAPTER NINE

The White Ghost parked his motorcycle a few cars behind them, took off his crash helmet and sat watching the two men make their way through the pub doors. From inside his jacket he pulled out a mobile phone and found one of the only two numbers in its contacts list before dropping it back in his pocket.

After a minute or two, he got off the bike and walked over to the big glass windows that ran all around the building. He opened a pack of cigarettes, pocketed the cellophane and lit one up before mingling with the little crowd of early drinkers that stood outside the front door, smoking and pissing away their benefit money before midday. He chatted with them a while. He knew that people don't really look at faces, not people like these anyway. But they looked at his. Everybody did. He was the one most likely to be picked out in an identity parade. But whatever he looked like, they knew one of their own and because of that, they wouldn't talk to the police.

They would say very little about him when they were asked later, and they wouldn't ID him for the life of them. He talked like them, moaned about the weather, moaned about the fucking price of beer and asked who they'd bet on at Goodwood later that day. And all the while he chatted to his newfound friends, he watched Paterson and Clocks at the bar, saw them order their food and take their seats. He noticed Clocks looking around the room, guessed he was looking for the toilets and grinned when he headed off to find them. He wouldn't have long.

Taking the cellophane and the phone out of his pocket, he dialled the number and watched Paterson pull out his phone from inside his jacket. 'Hello, is this Detective Superintendent Pat . . .?' he crackled the cellophane in front of the phone, masking out his voice, making it sound like static.

'My name is Ron . . .' Crackle. 'Jones and I have som . . .' Crackle.

Inside the pub, Paterson was struggling to hear. Head down, he plugged a finger into his free ear, straining to make out what was being said. 'Hello? I can't hear you. The line is—'

'I have information that . . .' Crackle. '. . . With the kid who was killed.'

That got Paterson's attention. He stood up quickly, caught the table with his leg, slopping tea over his side of the table. 'I can't hear you. The line is really bad. Hold on, hold on.' Paterson went toward the door, hoping for a better signal.

The White Ghost watched him make his way towards him. The simple tricks are often the most effective.

Paterson pushed through the door and walked out into the street, straight toward the White Ghost. 'Hello. Hello! Can you hear me now?'

The White Ghost dropped the cellophane. He pulled out a gun and strode rapidly toward Paterson. He pushed him to one side, away from the drinkers, catching him off balance. He stuck the barrel of the gun into Paterson's ribs. 'Loud and clear, Mr Paterson, much better reception out here. Do exactly as I say or you'll be dead before you hit the ground.' Paterson did as he was ordered. 'I understand you've been looking for me. Well, we're going for a ride, Mr P, and I'll tell you everything you want to know. The truth needs to be told.'

Keeping Paterson close to him, he steered him toward the Bentley. 'This is a stupid move,' said Paterson, a hint of panic in his voice. 'I'm with a few colleagues. It won't take them long to figure out I've gone, and that I've been taken. They'll find the car in ten minutes flat.'

'You're with one colleague, DI John Clocks. And you can travel a long way in ten minutes. Besides, we're not going far.'

* * *

Johnny Clocks came out of the toilet, still doing up his flies. As he walked back down the dingy corridor toward the main bar area he lifted his leg and cracked out a little fart followed by an amused smile. *Funny. But where was Paterson?* Straight away, he spotted the spilt tea.

He turned and scanned the room, looking for him — bar, no, fruit machine, nope, big-screen TV, nada. No policeman. His stomach lurched, and he pulled his phone out of his jeans' back pocket and speed dialled his boss while he walked round the room, looking out through the windows to the street beyond. Paterson's phone went to voicemail.

'Fuck!' he said aloud, lurching stomach now congealing fast to ice. He scanned the room again one last time and pushed through the doors. He redialled, half listening to the ringing tone as he looked frantically up and down the street. Then he saw that the Bentley had gone. 'Oh shit!' He turned to the little crowd of smokers.

'Anyone seen a man in a suit come out here?' he said, his voice just loud enough to get the men's attention. 'Anyone? A young man, thirties, dark suit, got in a big Bentley. Probably with another bloke. It was parked over there.' He pointed toward the space that was soon to be the home of a Fiat 500 if the driver, a lady in her eighties, could manage to manoeuvre it in. He pulled out his warrant card and held it up for them to see.

The men all shook their heads awkwardly. *Didn't see a thing, fella. Minding me own business. I fuckin' hate coppers, y'know. Wouldn't piss on you if you was on fire.*

Shaking his head in despair, Clocks hit another number on his phone. 'This is DI Clocks,' he said. 'The guv'nor's gone missing. I think someone's snatched him. Get onto the Yard and get the chopper up in the air quickly. He's in his Bentley—'

He stopped and listened to the voice on the other end. 'I don't know the fuckin' reg number. It's a fuckin' big black Bentley in the middle of Lambeth. Find it!' He hung up and turned back to the men, pointing his finger towards them, scanning across.

'Last chance. If anything happens to him, I'll come back and fit up each and every one of you snot-gobbling, pisshead pricks. Understood?'

The men looked at one another.

'They drove off that way. Two of 'em. The bloke in the suit didn't look too pleased and the other fella, big bloke, was pushing 'im across the road.'

'What'd he look like, this big bloke?'

'Odd-looking geezer. He stood chatting for a minute or two, then 'e got on his phone, your mate came out and the big fella started pushing him away from us.'

Clocks stared at the man. Was he telling the truth? Clocks decided he believed him. 'What was he wearing?'

'A motorbike jacket,' said another man. 'I think so anyway. Black, padded.'

Clocks looked around him, missed the bike first time, caught it the second. 'Is that it?' he said, pointing at it with his phone.

'Dunno, mate. Never saw him get off it.'

'Anything else? Anything distinctive about him? Scars? Bald?'

The men shrugged at first then the one that had spoken first said, 'He was white as a sheet, white hair, eyebrows, the lot. Looked like 'e was a fuckin' corpse. Frightened the shit out of me, to be truthful.'

Of course! The White Ghost. An albino.

'Fuck didn't you mention that earlier?' said Clocks, annoyed. He knew they were old-school London and wouldn't want to help his kind unless they really had to. It pissed him off that this sort of person was so anti-police and obstructive, but was quick enough to call the police if they got burgled.

'So you saw him get pushed across the road, and no one bothered to do anything?' said Clocks, dialling again. Now he had a description. Okay, it was sketchy, but he figured an albino man with a head of snow-white hair riding in a black car shouldn't be too difficult to spot.

The men looked genuinely baffled. It had never occurred to them to get involved. None of their business. Not their problem, so nothing to do with them.

'Anythin' else?' said Clocks as he waited for his call to be answered.

'Yes,' said the man, 'he had a big fuck-off hand gun.'

* * *

The White Ghost told Paterson to park up under a set of railway arches. He checked his watch, knew they wouldn't have had time to scramble any units yet. They were safe.

'Pull the car close to the wall. As close as you can get it. Mind you don't scuff it.' Paterson did as he was told and realised that any hope of a swift exit from the car was now blocked by a brick wall. He'd never make it across the car to the other door. He switched the engine off and sat back.

'Keep your hands on the steering wheel, Mr Paterson, and turn your head to look at me. Do you understand?'

'Yes,' said Paterson, and looked straight at his captor. Full on albinism. A few more pieces began to fall into place. Maybe he was doing it because he was albino too.

'Are you surprised at my appearance, Mr Paterson? Most people are. Bet you weren't expecting this, am I right?'

Paterson tilted his head. 'Yeah, you're right, I am, and no, I wasn't expecting this at all.'

The White Ghost grinned. 'Now you know why the name, eh?'

'Figures, I suppose. Are you doing this because the boy was albino too?'

Now the White Ghost cocked his head. 'Nope. I can see why you might think that but no, it's not my primary reason. It just happened to work out this way. Coincidence.'

'I don't believe in coincidences,' said Paterson.

'You should in this case.'

'Listen,' Paterson said, 'I can't harm you. I'm unarmed, there's no way for me to get out of this car, you're sitting in the back and you have a gun pointed at me. Clearly you want to talk, otherwise we wouldn't be here. What do you want with me?'

The White Ghost smiled. 'I've been digging into your past, Mr P. And that of your colleague, DI Clocks. An interesting story. I, of course, know about the incident on Tower Bridge, but what came across for me is that you both seem to be decent men. You're both moral, both passionate about serving justice. You both have a passion for, shall we say, doing the right thing. What I am doing is also the right thing.'

Paterson frowned. He searched the man's face. How did he consider himself to be acting virtuously? The White Ghost seemed to know what he was thinking. 'My name is Corporal Liam Bailey. Until about a year ago, I was a sniper with the British Army. Until I quit.' He was silent for a second.

Paterson heard the accent — English. Educated, but behind it was working-class London. Family probably had a military background and Junior here had followed in their footsteps. 'You quit,' he said. 'Did they let you keep your rifle as a going-away present?'

The White Ghost grinned at the thought. 'Allow me to clarify. When I say quit, what I actually mean is I went on the run, AWOL. Y'see, I came across a problem that needed to be resolved and my superiors wouldn't let me go ahead with it. So, given the army's obstructiveness, I thought it best to bypass the system and resolve it myself.'

'Let me guess,' said Paterson. 'That problem consisted of General Kamwelu and his lady wife, yes?'

Bailey ignored him. 'I was on patrol with my unit in Tanzania. We were busy minding our own business when we suddenly came under attack from what we thought were rebels. Turns out it was Kamwelu's soldiers. It all went crazy for a while. Both sides lost men. They lost about thirty, and we lost two. One dead and one captured. We lost him in the skirmish. Had no idea where he went. Of course, we were never going to leave him but we couldn't chance being drawn into a trap, so we withdrew. Tactical retreat, y'know? Anyway, our intelligence boys did their bit, they got all over it, tracked him to a small village deep inside a forest, jungle, whatever you want to call it. The plan was to hit it at night, take out any resistance and bring our boy back.' Paterson slowly dropped his hands. Maybe he'd get away with it. He did. He turned a bit more.

'At oh-three hundred, we went in. We didn't know exactly what hut he was in, but we had a rough idea. We had a satellite downlink giving us heat readings. One hut had about five guards outside of it, and some inside, so that looked like a good bet. They were taken care of and I went in, weapon free and suppressed. We wanted speed and stealth.' The White Ghost stared into the distance. He was back there, in the dark, stepping through the door of the hut to be met with a sight that changed his life forever.

'In a situation like that, when you enter a confined space, you take in as much as you can as quick as you can. You look ahead first, step in, check corners, but for the first time in my career, I didn't do that. Two things hit me at the same time. One was the smell. It was heavy, like some sort of incense, herbs and a smell like copper — blood — but they were all mixed together. It was strange. And right in front of me I saw a big man, black, just looking at me, eyes full of hate. General Kamwelu. He must have heard the guards fall, I don't know. Then he started shouting and, it's funny, because it must have all happened in just a few seconds, but it all slowed down, like a slow-mo film. You know what I mean?' He looked at Paterson, not seeing him, still lost in the memory. 'I saw his arms smothered in blood up to the elbows. Fucking smothered they were. He had a small machete in one hand, covered in blood. I raised my weapon. He was a dead man, understand? Then I saw them . . .'

'What?' said Paterson, lost in the images and the story unfolding in his own head. 'What did you see?'

The White Ghost's eyes welled up. 'Children. Five children. Dead. Hanging upside down. Two had had their heads cut off and their blood was draining, still dripping onto the dust. One, a little girl, had had her arms cut off as well. I mean . . .' He shrugged, still unable to make any sense of it. 'Anyway, Kamwelu had kicked off by now and I knew I had to take him. As I raised my weapon, some fucker hit me on the back of the head. Hard. I shoulda checked the corners properly. I staggered, fell forward and I figured I was about to die when I heard the sound of someone falling to the ground. My oppo was right behind me. He'd seen the big bastard hit me and popped him in the head.

'Then he stopped dead in his tracks when he saw what was in the hut. Neither of us were prepared for it. As I stood up, I saw that Kamwelu had been busy chopping up a small kiddie.' His tears were now streaming down his cheeks, unchecked. 'God in heaven, this poor little mite was still alive. Just, but she was alive. How could anyone do that, Mr Paterson?' He looked up, trance broken, and stared into the policeman's eyes seeking an answer that, like all the counsellors before him, Paterson would not be able to give him.

'The sat had only picked up two inside — Kamwelu and the guard. Of course, it didn't register the kids. The girl was dying, so I guess her light was weak, literally fading.'

'Jesus.' It was all Paterson could offer. He had no words.

'Anyway, it all went tits up, big time. More of Kamwelu's guards stormed in and there was a big firefight. My oppo got shot — he lived. Kamwelu got away, we got our boy back, killed a few more of the bastards for good measure and took a shitload of photos and videos of the whole thing. Upshot is, I found out that Kamwelu and his mental wife are heavy believers in witchcraft and killing the kids had something to do with magic, supposed to make him all powerful, untouchable, rich — but you know what?' Paterson shook his head slightly. 'He's not untouchable.' The White Ghost stared into the distance for a second or two.

'So what happened then?' said Paterson.

The White Ghost gave a half laugh and looked him dead in the eye. 'Fuck all. The big brass took the images — for intelligence purposes, you understand,' his voice was heavy with sarcasm, 'and nothing ever happened. No more was ever said.'

The White Ghost rubbed his face, as if trying to cleanse it of the horror that he carried with him every moment of every day.

'What did you do?' Paterson said.

'I kicked up with the brass. Went to my commanding officer, said Kamwelu had to be dealt with. Offered to do it myself, but they refused. Said that that's not how things work. This is Africa, it's political, all that shit. I became a fucking pain in their arse until they decided I was suffering from post-traumatic stress and sent me off for a spot of tea and cuddles with some middle-aged woman with the best of intentions but no idea.' Paterson knew all about that.

'I went off and played the part but did some digging around, found out a lot of things, unsettling things. When I found out that Kamwelu had left the army and was now an ambassador, I knew the bastard was up to something. A different game.'

Paterson looked at him, puzzled. 'Things?' he repeated. 'What sort of things, and how did you find them out?'

The White Ghost eyed him. 'Despite popular belief, Mr P, snipers don't just spend all day sitting in trees or on rooftops. These days we are trained in a number of specialist skills. One of mine is intelligence. I have a number of ways of finding things out about people,' he smiled, 'as I'm sure you're now aware.'

'Fair enough. My apologies,' said Paterson.

'I learned a couple of important things. Despite his behaviour, Kamwelu managed to get very cosy with some high-ranking government official and between them they hatched a plan to steal money, Tanzanian government money, and get it out of the country. Many African countries are corrupt. It runs deep, from top to bottom and there is little anyone can do about it once it takes root.' He looked at Paterson. 'But I'm telling you what you already know.'

* * *

The hunt for Paterson was now in full swing. The helicopter was up and heading toward Westminster Bridge with an ETA of ten minutes. Paterson's description and that of his abductor were being circulated to all units within a fifteen-mile radius, and his car registration had been plugged into the ANPR — the Automatic Number Plate Recognition system — which, if Paterson and the Ghost hadn't been hidden away under the railway arches, might have been their best hope. SCO19 had been informed and were mobile, waiting for the call that would send them tearing across London in pursuit of their colleague. Every uniform on the street was on the lookout.

Johnny Clocks had organised a team to seize the motorbike and was now busy giving instructions to an ARV crew as to Paterson's last known direction. The armed response officers asked if he wanted to jump in with them but he took the view that it would be better to remain where he was on the off chance that Paterson returned.

'There you go, mate. Get that down you.' Clocks turned to see the concerned face of one of the men from outside the pub. He was offering him a polystyrene cup with a lid on it.

'What is it?' said Clocks, eyeing it suspiciously.

'Cup of tea, mate. Reckon you could do with one. Take it, mate. There's nothing wrong with it. Seriously. Just a cup o' tea. No gob in it, I promise. We may not be fond of the old bill but this is different. Can't be having coppers swagged off the street. Get it down you. I've whacked three sugars in it. Good for the shock.'

He offered the cup again, and this time, Clocks took it. He pulled the lid off and thanked the man, his faith in humanity just a little bit restored.

'Cheers, mate,' he said. 'I appreciate it. Listen, what I said earlier. I didn't mean it. I was just, y'know, stressed.'

The man grinned at him. ''Course you did, mate. You've got a job to do and you thought a threat would be the way to go. Done it meself a good few years ago when necessary. Tell you what, though, where the fuck did you come up with "snot gobbling?" Fuckin' brilliant.' And the man turned his back on Clocks and headed over to his little group, chuckling to himself as he went. He couldn't wait to throw that one into the conversation. All his snot-gobbling mates'd be dead impressed.

CHAPTER TEN

Paterson stole a glance at his watch while the White Ghost talked. He guessed he'd been gone ten, fifteen minutes and Clocks would be going frantic. He knew Clocks would have put out an alert, officer missing, but he also knew he wouldn't be found. The White Ghost — Corporal Bailey — clearly knew what he was doing. He'd figured out what to do to kidnap him and get him undercover quickly. What fascinated him was how Bailey had carried out the plan. He figured that Bailey must have known they'd go to Scotland Yard and had most likely followed them, but he couldn't work out how he'd known they would stop for breakfast. Perhaps he hadn't, in which case his knowledge of London, his forethought and his speed once they stopped were astonishing. British Army. Best in the world.

'So, given what you've seen and done so far, what I want to know is why haven't you killed Kamwelu? You clearly intend to do so at some point, so why the wait?' Paterson fixed his gaze on him. If being held captive by a professional executioner holding a gun scared him, he didn't show it. He knew that if Bailey had wanted him dead, he would have done it long before he got him into the car. The fact that he was alive and listening to the man's life story told him he was wanted for some other purpose. He was equally sure it wasn't just to offload his nightmares on him.

'Killing him would be a piece of piss, Mr P. Too easy. I want this bastard and his mad missus to know fear. Real fear. Just like those kids must have felt when they realised what he was going to do to them. Can you imagine it? What they must have felt . . .' His voice trailed off. 'So I set about taking from them. I killed his mother, two sisters, a couple of cousins and his youngest son. He was only fifteen but from what I hear, he was a cruel little bastard just like his father.' Paterson's eyes turned to saucers.

'What?' challenged Bailey. 'Intelligence said he'd already killed a couple of women — after raping them that is. He's no loss to the gene pool, I swear. Anyway, I should have guessed how little it would mean, but Kamwelu really didn't seem to care a shit about them. Didn't bother him at all.' He searched Paterson's face, as if wondering what he made of it all. 'I guess he's a true psychopath, eh? No sympathy, cold, cruel, no remorse, doesn't give a fuck. So I changed tack. I took out Blessing's sister and a couple of aunties. I shot her old grandmother as well. Probably did the old bag a favour. She was so old she couldn't stand up properly.'

'My God,' said Paterson. His earlier reasoning that he was likely safe had turned to anxiety now he knew that Bailey was a stone-cold murderer.

'I wanted them terrified, wanted them to know I could snuff out their miserable lives in an instant. Can you imagine what that's like, Mr Paterson? To live in constant fear that your life will be snuffed out,' he clicked his fingers, 'but never knowing when. Wondering if today is your last day, or if now could be your last moment.' He shook his head. 'Seems the missus got rattled by it. So they ran. Cooked up some scheme with the government to steal a boat load of money and gold and headed over to the UK. Too fucking stupid to realise I'd find them so easily.'

'Europe,' Paterson said. 'The killings in Europe. Your work, I presume?'

Bailey smiled. 'Yep. All me.'

'But . . . but . . .' Paterson struggled to convey his thoughts coherently. 'You shot Babatunde here. He was carrying the body of a child. You knew what he was doing, right?' Bailey nodded. 'So, when you shot those people in Europe, you also knew they were killing kiddies, surely?' Paterson stared at him. 'You let them kill the children.'

'No, no, no. You don't understand. The child had usually already been killed and then brought to the church for some sort of ceremony. I can't always be there when a child is taken. It wasn't always the Kamwelus that killed them either. If I had seen them trying to do that, I would have shot them. Of course I would. I just followed them to whatever church they were going to and took out the man or woman who brought the body out for disposal — and a good few others too, when they came running. I knew that as soon as they found the body, someone would call the police. Police here are pretty quick at responding. All I wanted was for the child's body to be found. Again, I knew the police here would be, shall we say, more efficient than their foreign brothers.' That made sense to Paterson. 'But now it ends,' he finished.

'What does that mean?' said Paterson.

'I know you have all three of them in custody. What's going to happen with them?'

'DI Clocks and I are pressing to keep them in custody. I'm going to charge them with the murder of the child. We've just come from a meeting with the commissioner and he is backing us all the way, despite the diplomatic shit-storm we've stirred up.'

Corporal Bailey nodded, seemingly satisfied with what he was hearing. 'Who was at this meeting?'

'A couple of spooks — standard procedure I've been informed — a rep from the Tanzanian government, someone from the Foreign Office and the deputy commissioner.'

Bailey sat up straight. 'The Foreign Office?' He dug inside his jacket pocket and pulled out an iPhone. He started pressing buttons, called up his images folder and swiped through them quickly.

'Wouldn't be him, would it?' said Bailey, holding the phone up for Paterson to see. Millington.

'Yes, it was,' said Paterson, frowning. 'How come you've got his picture?'

'Because he's been showing up at the Tanzanian Embassy quite a lot, so my best guess is he's involved in this lot somewhere. Likely taking a backhander to help get the money here unhindered. Best you dig around.'

Paterson gave a quiet sigh of relief. Bailey was going to let him go! His mind began to race. He didn't want to believe Bailey's theory about Millington, but it made sense. It explained why he'd been none too supportive at the meeting. 'Hold on. That's a bit of a leap, isn't it? He's a government official, a UK minister. It wouldn't be unusual for him to visit government offices.'

'He always went after eleven at night. Every time. I'd say that was unusual, don't you think?' Bailey slipped the phone back in his pocket and pulled out another one, the one he'd used to call Paterson at the pub.

'I'd love to see them in court, Mr P, but that won't happen. We both know that.'

Paterson looked directly at him. 'I can't promise anything. This is being dealt with at a much higher level than me now. You have to believe that we're trying.'

'I do. I know you are. You're a decent bloke. I also know that the government won't do the right thing. They'll cave. Diplomatic relations will win the day. Kamwelu and certain other beneficiaries of this money will get away scot-free, and the children's cries will go unheard.' He paused. 'Except they won't.'

Paterson's frown deepened. 'Meaning?'

'Meaning I'm going to have to kill all of them.' He sat back in his seat. 'Here's how it's going to work.' Paterson stiffened. Now what was coming? 'You're going to give me the USB key you have in your pocket. The one with the CCTV footage of the boy's murder in the bank.' He gestured with the gun.

Paterson's face tightened. How did Bailey know that footage even existed?

'It's not rocket science, Mr Paterson. I was in the opposite building when you were in the MI room. I watched the whole thing through binos. I saw you take out the USB and put it in your pocket. Right?'

Paterson fumbled around in his inside pocket and pulled out the small green stick. No point in lying to the man. He handed it over to Bailey. 'What are you going to do with it?' he said.

'I have a plan, of sorts, in two parts. First, I already have a large number of documents and photographs, and now this video. I'll be watching it later. The second any one of those three sets foot outside the station, I'll know you failed to keep them in custody. When you fail, and I'm sorry to say you will, I'll send electronic copies of everything I have to a number of news agencies around the world. The video will go up on various news websites. It's not something I wanna do, but I have to. People need to see this shit, to see what's happening to these kids. I'll force this bloody government to act, I'll put pressure on other governments to deal with these witchcraft murders. They poke their noses into other shit — why not this? When it hits the news, the government will go into panic mode. They'll do one of two things. Either they'll do a quick U-turn, defy the diplomats and hang onto them or — and this is the safer bet — they'll spirit them away a bit quick, lie and say that they couldn't hold on to them and then pretend to spend years negotiating to get them back. By which time the fuss will have died down and that will be that. But whatever happens, they're going to have to hold a full public review. It's gotta stop, Mr P. It has to.' Paterson closed his eyes. 'Now this is the bit you won't like, Mr P. You're going to help me.'

'Me?' said Paterson, eyes wide. 'How?'

Bailey handed Paterson the mobile phone. 'Part two of the plan. This phone has one number in it. Mine. You're going to send me a text. Just one. The date, time and place of their flight out of this country. I'll then hand that additional info over to the press and ensure that they're there with their cameras to witness the murderers leaving the country. I'd like to think that given the video they'll just have seen, the press will be out in their droves to see them escape justice, wouldn't you?'

'I guess so,' said Paterson. He sat, turning the phone over in his hands.

'So, to make sure they don't escape justice, when they get on to the tarmac I'll take out all three of them, in full view of the world's media.'

Paterson stared at him. 'Hold on. Let me get this straight. You're asking me to send you a message that will consign three people to their deaths? I know they're the scum of the earth but come on, this is a big ask. I can't live with that.'

'You'll learn to. It's not like you've never killed anyone, is it? And this is different. You're not pulling the trigger this time.'

Paterson's face reddened in anger. 'And if I don't?'

'Thing is, Mr P, you've got yourself a problem now. You're a copper. Believe in the law, an' all that shit. Trouble is, you know what the Kamwelus have done and that they're gonna walk and you won't be able to do fuck all about it. Diplomatic shit. So you're gonna have to stand and wave them off when they get on that plane, knowing they're getting away scot-free with God knows how many murders. And they'll do more, won't they? 'Course they will. Now, I know you don't want that, so the thing is, what do you do? Help me take them out or let them get away to carry on killing?'

Paterson was struck dumb, his mind racing. Bailey was right, of course, but — God. 'I . . . I . . . There has to be some other way.' He was almost pleading.

''Fraid not, Mr P.' Bailey shrugged, his face pained, resigned. 'Tell you what, I can see you're struggling, so let me make it easier for you. If you don't help me, I'll kill Johnny Clocks. Does that help you make up your mind?'

* * *

'Your phone's ringing, sir.' A uniformed policeman broke into Clocks's thoughts.

'Oh, okay. Thanks.' He pulled his phone out of his inside pocket, glanced at the name and hit the answer button. 'Ray!' he shouted. 'Where the fuck are you? Are you alright? Talk to me!' The uniform frowned, hope mixed with concern on his face. Clocks nodded to him and held his thumb up before turning his back on him.

Paterson, behind the wheel of his Bentley, spoke calmly into his hands-free. 'I'm fine, John. Where are you now?'

'Haven't moved. Still outside the pub.' Clocks looked frantically up and down the street for any sign of Paterson.

'Stay there. I'll be with you in a few minutes. Call it in, John. I'm safe and sound.'

Clocks breathed a sigh of relief. As he listened to Paterson's voice, he picked up on an edge to it, more worry than panic, but at least he sounded safe. He turned to the uniform. 'Get the search called off. Stand it down.'

'Will do, guv.'

'Is there an operational commander on scene yet?' Paterson asked.

'Nope. Not yet. One's been assigned and he's on his way, but he's not here yet,' said Clocks. 'Why?'

'They're going to want us debriefed, John. Everything that just happened is going to have to be reported and recorded somewhere, and they'll want to do it immediately.' Paterson's mind was galloping. He needed time. Time to talk to Clocks before he spoke to anyone else. 'Stand him down, John. We're going to debrief the commissioner. No one else. Tell him we're on our way to the Yard now. I have to talk to you first, though. Alone. Things have taken a bit of a turn, and we need to work out a plan before we go talking to anyone. You understand?'

'Not yet, but if you say so, I'll make the call to the commissioner. How long do I tell him we'll be?'

'Tell him we'll be running time from here. In traffic, maybe thirty, forty minutes,' Paterson said.

'Done.' Clocks turned and started barking orders at the uniformed PC.

When Paterson drew up outside the pub, Clocks wrenched the door open and jumped straight in. He took a look at Paterson as he settled himself into his seat. Satisfied to see no blood on the guv'nor, nor any other obvious sign of injury, he said, 'What the fuck happened?'

'Hang on,' said Paterson, and looked out of the windscreen and up into the sky, checking to make sure the helicopter wasn't around. Satisfied, he pulled out and headed back toward the railway arches.

'What's going on, Ray? Where're we going?'

'We have to talk, John, and I want to make sure no one sees or hears us. Railway arches. Nobody there.'

A few minutes later, Paterson drove the car back under the same arch as before, deeper into the shadows, hidden away from prying eyes and ears. He parked up in a large chambered area, killed the engine and got out of the car. Clocks followed, stared at him, searching his face for a clue. He saw nothing but anxiety.

'Couple of things up front,' said Paterson. 'I know exactly who he is now, and I know what his game is. He is, without a doubt, a cold-hearted bastard, though I can't say

I disagree with what he's planning to do. But you and me, we're in shit city.'

Clocks frowned. He was used to being in the shit — occupational hazard for the police, and even more so for policemen like him — but if he was in the shit he wanted it to be of his own making. 'We, Ray?' he said as if the question troubled him. 'Why are *we* in the shit?'

Paterson told him everything he could recall of his conversation with Corporal Bailey up until the last part. He'd get to that soon enough.

Clocks rubbed his face with both hands, digging the heels of his palms into his eyes. Tiredness and stress were taking their toll.

'So? What's the problem? If he wants to kill the wicked bastards, I say we stop looking too hard for him an' let him get on with it. Fuck, I think we should give him a medal.' He thought about that for a second. 'He's probably already got a few for sharpshooting, so how about we get one made up for "killing as many evil fuckers as you can." I'll willingly pin it on him. He sounds like a decent enough chap to me.'

Paterson smiled. Let out a little laugh. 'I don't have a problem with it but,' he sighed, 'he's put me in a situation, John. He's forcing me into helping him.' He explained about the text message and the instructions Bailey had given him.

Clocks breathed out hard. 'Christ. What the fuck are you gonna do? That's aiding and abetting. Big-time prison, Ray, and I seriously doubt I'll be able to wangle you out of that one, 'specially with your previous.' He shook his head. 'The thing is, if you text him, it's always gonna be on his phone. He'll have you by the shorts.'

Then it dawned on Paterson. His face suddenly lit up. 'No, he won't. Think. It's not my phone that's sending the text. It's a phone he gave me. I'll be texting him on a pay 'n' go. If he's killed or captured, what have they got? A message with a day, date, time and place. Anyone could have sent that. There won't be any comeback. He doesn't want there to be. He just wants us to help.'

Clocks looked sceptical. 'But the phone'll have your name in it.'

'So what? What does that prove? He could just as easily have put your name in. Or Young's. Or Elsie the cleaning lady's. It proves nothing.'

Clocks gave a nod. 'Okay, I can see that. Dodgy though. I don't like it. We could just have him nicked, Ray.'

'How we going to do that?'

'Easy. You just drop him a text telling him something's come up, real important like, and you need to meet him urgently. We tuck Lyndsey and the shots out of sight and when he shows, they jump on him and slap the cuffs on or shoot him, up to him.'

'Oh yeah, he'll fall for that one, won't he, John? Fuck me, he's a wicked bastard but he's not stupid. He'll smell it a mile away and then what? I'll tell you. He'll be pissed off big time and we'll both get one in the head. Not for me, if you don't mind. I've gotten quite fond of where my brain is, thanks.'

Clocks shrugged it off. 'Just trying to help.'

'I know. Sorry. Truth is, I've been giving it some thought.'

'And . . .?' Clocks prompted.

'I can't let those animals escape.'

'So what then? What are you saying?'

'Guess I'm all-in. Gonna help him.'

Clocks exhaled, long and hard. 'Fuck, Ray. Fuck.'

Paterson looked over at him. 'Look, this isn't your problem, John. This is on me. My decision. You can walk.'

'What'd you mean, "You can walk?" Think they're not gonna come for me if they find out that you've helped him? 'Course they will.'

Paterson sighed. He was tired, and feeling it.

Clocks was looking agitated, knew this was all kinds of wrong, but felt calm nonetheless. 'To be honest, if you hadn't said you'd help him, I would have done. Not letting 'em go, Ray. They're not gonna kill any more kiddies, not on my watch.'

'You sure, John? We go this way, we're committed. No turning back from it.'

Clocks looked at him. His expression said it was a dumb question he was being asked, and he wasn't sure if he'd heard it right. 'Yes, I'm sure.'

Relief all over his face, Paterson said, 'Thank Christ for that. And anyway, it's not like I have much choice.'

'What'd you mean?' Clocks said.

Should he tell him? He didn't want to worry him, but in the end he figured that if the situation were reversed, Clocks would tell him quick enough.

'When he asked for help, I initially refused. Morals and all that. Said he'd help me make the decision. And he did.'

'How'd he do that then?'

Paterson looked at his friend, dead in the eye. 'Said if I didn't help him, he'd shoot you in the head as an incentive.'

Clocks stiffened. His mouth dropped open. He was picturing what was left of Babatunde's head. He shifted uncomfortably in his seat, looked away, out of the window, faced a blank brick wall. 'Oh, that's fuckin' eighteen carat,' he said. 'There's me thinkin' he's as good as gold, an' it turns out he's a proper bastard after all.'

* * *

Metropolitan Police Commissioner Wallace Young was seated behind his desk, which was the size of a small boat, sipping tea from a bone china cup. He searched the faces of his two officers and struggled to contain the anger and frustration bubbling below the surface. He'd never been one to give in to his emotions and he wasn't about to start now.

Paterson and Clocks related the story of Paterson's kidnapping. Young, meanwhile, breathed in sharply at some of the things they said, and constantly twiddled his thumbs, unaware that he was doing so.

Paterson reached for the tea that Kayleigh had brought in at the very start of the meeting. 'Corporal Bailey desperately wishes to take revenge on Kamwelu, and he's going to do it in spectacular style. If he makes good on his threat, and I see no reason why he wouldn't, then quite shortly he'll be releasing the material he has into the public domain. He'll most certainly make the evening news, sir, and then, at some point he's going to kill them.'

Young rubbed his face. Suddenly he felt the pressure of high office taking its toll on him. He was conscious of the stubble on his chin, reminding him of how long it had been since he'd last slept.

Resigned, he said, 'We'll have to deal with that when it happens.' They'd lost control, and he hated losing control.

'What's the plan with Millington then, sir?' asked Clocks, struggling to fit his finger through the dainty handle of his tea cup.

'Right now, nothing,' said Young. 'Other than the say-so of a weaponised serial killer, we have no evidence whatsoever at this point that he's in bed with a foreign government. I will be making some urgent and discreet enquiries into his background. Clearly you believe he's involved in paving the way for this stolen money to come into the country, and if he is, then, God help us, he must know all about the killing of that young boy.' The CCTV footage came flooding back. Young closed his eyes and sighed heavily. 'If I find out that he's involved, then he will of course be dealt with. Once I have something, I'll let you know. Right now, we're done. You two should get some rest. And don't stop at the pub on the way home, understood?' Both men grinned at him.

'And one other thing, Ray. You need to know — you both need to — that we'll not be able to hold the Kamwelus for much longer. I have had a discussion with the PM, and she has ordered their release. In my response, I politely informed her to go take a flying fuck and that I would not release them until tomorrow, due to ongoing enquiries outside of interview. It didn't go down well, but such is life. To be honest, it's the only way I have of pissing Kamwelu off. We can't interview him or even talk to him now. Fortunately, she acquiesced to my request.' Clocks frowned. He didn't understand. Young picked up on it. 'She has agreed, Mr Clocks. Given her consent.' Clocks's face lit up and he gave a big nod. He hated it when people used big words when it really wasn't necessary.

'This is bollocks, sir,' he said. 'How can they let them go, knowing what they've done? It's just plain wrong.'

'I agree with you, John. The PM is, of course, appalled by their actions but she isn't willing to upset diplomatic relations with the Tanzanians. There are always matters that none of us are party to. It would have world-wide repercussions if we broke off relations. She has had assurances from their government that the Kamwelus will be dealt with accordingly on their return.'

'I don't think the right-thinking world will give a fuck if we do break relations when they watch the tea-time news, sir,' said Clocks. 'I don't think people in this country'll be too impressed at a couple of witch doctor child-killers being allowed to slip the net, diplomats or not. This is going to bite someone in the arse big time.'

Young gave this some thought. 'Maybe. Let's just wait and see what happens. I will of course have to tell her what's about to break. It might change her mind. I don't know. I'd hate to be in her shoes, though.'

Paterson looked up at the ceiling. Ran his fingers through his hair. Scratched his head. His sigh was rather too loud. 'So, if they go, what's the story with Bailey? He wants to kill them. He won't give up.'

Young glanced briefly at Clocks before resting his gaze on Paterson. His hands lay on his desk, fingers interlaced. His face was set. He shook his head slowly. 'I don't know what to tell you boys, other than that a car will collect them tomorrow morning at seven thirty, and they'll be released into the custody of their embassy. I would imagine there'll be some sort of debriefing, interrogation, call it what you like, and then at some stage they'll be put on a flight back to their own country. I'm most upset. Most upset.' He looked Paterson dead in the eye. 'Get some rest, gents. Tomorrow will, I suspect, be quite busy.'

* * *

They stepped into the elevator and Paterson pushed the button for the ground floor. 'Guv,' said Clocks, 'is it me, or did he just do what I think he did?'

'Depends,' said Paterson, watching the floor indicator as they began to descend. Fifth floor. 'If you think Young suspects we've held back some information from him and that he thinks I might have a way to contact Bailey, then yes, he did exactly what you think he did, John. He just gave us the time and date of their release for the benefit of Corporal Bailey. He doesn't want them going free either.'

Clocks had joined in, and had his eyes on the numbers flashing slowly downwards. Third floor. He let out a low whistle. 'Fuckin' hell, that's huge. Are you going to tell him then? Bailey, I mean.'

Paterson threw him a single glance and went straight back to watching the red numbers. They were really quite hypnotic. *Second floor.* He hesitated. *First floor. Ground.* The double door dinged open. 'Yes,' he said, simply. They stepped out into the lobby and Paterson pulled out the phone Bailey had given him. 'He told me I was to contact him with the date, time and place only and only via text. I'm going to call him though. Time for a rethink.'

CHAPTER ELEVEN

Day 4 — Wednesday

Paterson had slept like the dead. He peeled one eye open and squinted at the alarm clock. Seven twenty-five. He rolled over, hit the "off" button, hauled himself up and sat on the edge of his king-size mattress for a minute or two, trying to pull himself together. He put his hands over his eyes and screwed them up tight, looking at the colours and shapes. He stood up, wobbled a bit, steadied himself and hobbled off to the bathroom, leaving the door open. A shower was in order. He caught a quick glimpse of himself in the mirror. A shave wouldn't go amiss either.

'Carrie!' he shouted. No answer. 'Carrie?' Still no answer. He peered into the bedroom at the clock on the wall, and realised she'd be at work by now and had left him sleeping. Thank Christ.

In the shower, he took a quick glance at his little waterproof safe and was tempted to draw off a couple of lines, a livener for the day ahead. Then he remembered the last conversation he'd had with Johnny Clocks as he dropped him off at his house. They had promised each other. No booze and no coke. Clear heads were required for the day to come. While he liked to think Clocks wouldn't have a drink, he couldn't count on it. He, at least, would uphold his end of the deal.

Half an hour or so later, showered, shaved, fully gelled and partly suited, Paterson walked into the bedroom and flicked on the TV. Sky News. His eyes widened. He scrabbled for the remote, and turned the sound up louder than was necessary. 'Christ, he's done it!' he said aloud. He half sat, half fell on the bed. He watched, transfixed, a female newsreader interviewing an expert on child sex offence cases, while the tickertape scrolled across the bottom. Its headline screamed "Breaking News: Sky has been given video of African diplomats killing a child in bizarre witchcraft ritual."

The tickertape scrolled on as the woman news anchor broke away from the expert and told the nation about the dossier they had received, giving its contents and the names of those involved. Paterson listened carefully for a minute or two. No mention was made of any member of the British establishment being involved. Surprise.

The news team suddenly cut away to a shot of the Tanzanian Embassy in London, and then splashed a picture of General Kamwelu's face across the screen. They had chosen well. From the head and shoulders shot, it was clear that Kamwelu was dressed in full military uniform. He wore a stern look on his face. His eyes, set deep into his face, peered out at the world. They were cruel eyes.

Blessing was up next. In a shot taken from her witchcraft curing website, she was mugging happily for the camera, dressed in full church regalia — pink shoes, pink dress and a pink headdress that occupied at least two foot of airspace above her.

Cutting back to the studio, the news anchor was about to launch full flight into the expert. Now that Bailey had started the shit-storm he had promised, there were so many questions the world wanted to ask and have answered. On screen behind the anchor was a large printed image of a document, supposedly "the" document. Paterson knew it wasn't. It occurred to him that the TV executives would be dancing around with the story and being very careful about what images they showed. The internet was a different animal. He knew that Bailey would have uploaded the full CCTV recording to numerous file sharing sites, and by now those images would be viral.

Paterson picked up his phone off the bedside cabinet and checked it for messages. To his surprise there was nothing. He knew that wouldn't be the case for long. He slipped the phone into his trouser pocket and glanced at the clock again: seven fifty-nine. He wandered into the kitchen, lifted the kettle to check it had water in and flicked it on. Tea was required. As he waited for it to boil, he put the telly on. Accustomed as he was to the finer things in life, he had always had a soft spot for a cup of builder's tea. It gave him comfort.

At the top of the hour the headlines ran again, followed by the same photos of Kamwelu and Blessing. He pulled his phone out, put it on the counter next to his cup, and poured the boiling water onto his teabag. He rummaged through the biscuit tin and found a couple of shortcakes. Good for dunking. He checked his watch: 8:04 a.m.

The tickertape suddenly ran a new message. "Breaking News: Reports of a man shot dead outside London police station." Paterson sipped carefully at his steaming tea. His phone rang.

* * *

Within the hour, Paterson and Clocks were standing inside a white tent in the back yard of their own police station. The forensic scene manager stood with them. They stared down at the body of Harold Odonte, minus the top half of its head.

'Found the bullet, Tone?' said Clocks to his old friend. The men had attended many murder scenes together.

Tony Childs, a portly Liverpudlian, knocking on fifty, nodded. His voice was muffled under his white face mask and Paterson had a bit of a job hearing him. Probably would've struggled to understand his accent anyway. 'Yep. Big bugger by all accounts. It's been dug out of the wall and is on its way for analysis.' He scribbled something down on his notepad. 'This one of your diplomats, Timex?'

'Yep. Do we know what happened?' said Clocks.

Childs shook his head. 'Not really. Not yet. Seems he was walking down the steps of the nick, having just been released with some other people. From what I understand, they were all walking towards a limo that was waiting to whisk them off somewhere when the top half of his head disappeared. He dropped like a sack of wet shit. Pandemonium broke out and everyone ran for cover. Can't say I blame them. If I were them, I'd still be running now.'

'Where are the others?' Paterson asked.

'Far as I know, everyone's back inside. SCO19 have been out in force and declared the area safe, but their embassy has instructed that they be kept inside until "strong protective measures can be put in place." Do you know what that means?' Childs asked.

Paterson did. 'Most likely an armoured vehicle with blackout windows and an armed escort from the Met, all the way to their embassy. Just a guess though. Do you know who was with him?'

'General Kamwelu, his missus, a couple of bodyguards, some reps from the embassy and a bod from the Home Office, I think it was.' Paterson and Clocks exchanged a quick glance. 'Sorry, *Foreign* Office.'

Millington again.

With nothing more to do inside the tent, Paterson and Clocks stepped outside, clambered out of their forensic suits and placed them into the brown paper evidence bags a member of the forensics team held open for them. They made their way toward the rear entrance to the station.

'You realise the shit that's gonna go down now, Ray? Diplomatically speaking, I mean.'

'Of course I do. I also know it's going to throw everyone involved into a major panic. You once told me panic was a good thing. People make mistakes then. I imagine that our Mr Millington is panicking so much right now, he'll be shitting through the eye of a needle.'

Clocks grinned at the thought. 'You know what, Ray? You played a blinder there.' Paterson smoothed out his suit and buttoned up his jacket. Grinned. Clocks lowered his voice, looked around him. No one was within earshot. 'Took a risk calling him and telling him.'

'Yep,' said Paterson. He checked his reflection in a window and said, 'Seemed like the only way we were going to get to keep Kamwelu here for a while. I want to talk to him. We can't interrogate the butchers for their crimes, but now they're witnesses to a murder no one can stop us talking to them. I think you're right — Millington's the weak link in all of this. He'll roll over and tell us everything. It'll bring the lot down.'

Clocks's expression became serious. 'You knew Bailey would kill Odonte, am I right?'

Paterson stopped preening. 'Logical choice. He doesn't want to do the Kamwelus until there's TV crews to see. 'S what he said.' He looked down, then back up to Clocks's face. Gave a small shrug and pulled an "Oh dear, how unfortunate but who gives a fuck?" kind of a face. 'Not like he was a good man, was it? Far as I'm concerned, bastard deserved it.'

'No argument from me, Ray.'

* * *

'Mr Mangu,' said Paterson, 'I would strongly advise you to stand aside and let us talk to Benjamin or whatever he's calling himself today.' Paterson stood in the small space that doubled as both waiting and witness room, square on to Mangu, who was busy kicking up a fuss about Paterson and Clocks's presence. Mangu had placed himself between the two policemen and General Kamwelu and Blessing. He was clearly going to be as obstructive as possible. Standing several feet behind Clocks, a couple of uniforms had been briefed to expect trouble. If and when it kicked off, they were to help get any prisoner out of the room.

'You cannot interrogate them. They are under protection. You know this.'

Paterson moved closer, going almost toe-to-toe with Mangu. 'Not going to interrogate them. They're material witnesses in a murder case that I'm investigating, and I'm entitled to question them. Same as you, right? You were there. I'll be questioning you later. Right now, though, you're obstructing my enquiries, which can only end badly for you if you carry on.'

Mangu drew himself upright, extended his chest, held his arms wide. 'What? You think you scare me? You think I am afraid of your silly little show? I know what you are try—'

Paterson punched him hard in the chest, a blow calculated to have just enough force to compress the rib cage and send the heart into an accelerated rhythm but not hard enough to break anything. Done correctly, it induces instant and abject terror in an opponent, as the heart rate suddenly shoots up at a terrifying pace, leaving the recipient thinking that their time has come. Paterson did it correctly.

The shock of the blow registered on Mangu's face and he staggered backwards, clutching his chest. He dropped heavily into a chair next to Blessing, almost missing it and slipping onto the floor. Paterson called the uniforms over. 'Get him seen by a doctor,' he said. 'He'll be fine.'

As the uniforms bundled Mangu out of the room, he turned his attention to Kamwelu.

General Kamwelu stared at him. 'Well done, Mistah Paterson. Most impressive.' He spoke through gritted teeth.

'Shut up, filth. We don't have much time, so I'm not going to waste it listening to you yakking. Let's get something out in the open. I know exactly what you are, what you do and what you've done.' Kamwelu stared impassively, almost uninterested in Paterson. 'And that disgusting thing you call a wife.' He jerked his head round to stare at Blessing. She held his gaze. He turned back to the general.

'Mistah Paterson, please, please, you must try not to get so upset. Those children, they were nothing. Street children. Their parents sell them to us for fifty British pounds. Do you know what that can do for a family?'

Clocks moved fast toward Kamwelu, who saw him coming. 'Go ahead, policeman!' he shouted. 'Go on, hit me. Hit me.'

Johnny Clocks gave him a right hander straight to the mouth that knocked Kamwelu sideways. He yelped as his knuckles connected with Kamwelu's face, and he flapped his hand about. 'Fuckin' hell! 'S like hitting a fuckin' bowling ball. Jesus.'

Kamwelu pulled himself back upright, spat blood from his mouth, and said, 'That is it then, Mistah Clocks. That is all you can do. You can only hit me. You think I am scared of a little punch? If this was my country, you wouldn't be wasting your time with punches but,' he shrugged, 'this is England. You have *rules*.' He spat more blood onto the desk. Snorted. 'Your rules, your laws say you cannot keep us here. You know we'll go. We will leave and you'll have nothing.'

Blessing stood up and moved forward. She waved her arms around, as she had done in the vault. 'God watches over us, policeman. God protects us. God will take us home.'

Johnny Clocks backhanded her, spinning her around. Kamwelu moved to intervene. Paterson slammed his head down onto the desk, and held him there.

'Shut the fuck up, you mad bitch, and don't start all that God bollocks with me,' Clocks said. He shook his hand again. He really would have to stop hitting them. It was far too painful.

Paterson wrenched Kamwelu's head back up, and pulled him into his chair. 'Behave yourself,' he said. Kamwelu sucked his teeth, a sign of disrespect that never failed to aggravate Johnny Clocks.

'Easy, John,' said Paterson. He bent down over Kamwelu and forced one of his hands onto the chair back behind him, and the other onto the desk. He stood over him, cringing a little at the stink of the man's breath. He felt him, just for a second, wince a little. Paterson pulled away from him, sharply, instinctively. 'The fuck have you been eating, butcher boy? Shit? Your breath is diabolical.' He didn't wait for an answer. He moved back in closer, braving the breath. Had to make himself intimidating, crowd him.

'Listen to me closely. I'm not investigating the murder of Odonte. I don't give a flying fuck about him. Or you. Or her. You think you're untouchable? You think your magic shit will save you? Well, listen carefully. Odonte died because of me. Me. I called him. I told him when you would be released. I've joined forces with the White Ghost. I told him when you would leave too.' Sweat broke out on Kamwelu's head. 'For one purpose only. To kill you. And her.' He jerked his head toward a now terrified Blessing.

'I have your money now. I know who helped you, and I'm going to take them next. Do you understand, butcher man? You've lost everything because you killed that boy.'

Kamwelu stared straight ahead. The man who had been responsible for thousands of deaths, who had brutally slain many with his own hands, appeared suddenly anxious.

'Your spirits have left you, Kamwelu. They've deserted you. You know it's true. If it wasn't, would they have let Odonte die? Would they have let me capture you? Take your money? No, you know they wouldn't. The boy you killed in the bank, his life was very important. Not to you, but to the spirits. You had no idea what you were doing when you killed him. You see, butcher man, in death his magic was unleashed. It became stronger. Much stronger. His magic summoned the White Ghost. It summoned us. He joined us together. He made us powerful. And now you have no protection. Your time is coming, Kamwelu. You can't hide behind your diplomatic status. I care nothing for it. You can't hide behind your spirits. They have gone. You've been brought into the light, butcher. To answer for your sins.'

Paterson straightened up abruptly, strode across the room, turned and pointed back at Kamwelu. 'Listen carefully. You will both die on *my* say-so and when I decide, and you'll never know when it's coming. Will you leave my country? Maybe. Will you land safely in yours? Maybe. But death will come for you. When *I* say it will.'

'Mr Clocks,' said Paterson, 'we're done.'

Johnny Clocks grinned and nodded. On the way out, he stabbed his finger at Blessing. 'Oi, you murderin' fat whore. This is what you get for pissing off all them fuckin' mermaids of yours.'

He sucked his teeth and followed Paterson out of the room.

* * *

Paterson and Clocks got back in the car with no real plan in mind. With their two chief suspects immune from prosecution, their investigation was now dead in the water.

Four days into the case and they had the killers, a vault full of stolen money, a possible conspiracy at the highest levels of the British government and a bitter taste in their mouths. They'd lost and they knew it. Their only hope lay in Corporal Bailey.

Helping him had been an easy decision in light of the Kamwelus' imminent departure. It might not have been ethical, but conscience, on the other hand, was a different thing. Theirs were clear. Sometimes you have to do a bad thing in order to do good. The Kamwelus had picked out a small defenceless child, and then dragged that child, scared and alone, halfway across the world for the sole purpose of killing an albino to use in some magic spell.

Paterson wanted to know why the child's parents had given him up. Were they terrified of Kamwelu? Desperate for money, food or medicine? Did they resist? Did they scream? Did they do anything at all? Or did they just hand him over? A little soul, bartered for dollars, with just a teddy for comfort. Paterson knew he was in no position to judge. He had no idea what it was like to be the parent of a child so hungry that its ribs stuck out, or so sick as to be at the point of dying. To see their kid suffering and be unable to give them medicine — medicine that cost pennies in the Western world . . . Perhaps they sold their son to save his siblings, so that at least they would have food or medicine. A heart-breaking, gut-wrenching decision that no parent should ever have to make. He would never know, and it hurt him. It hurt him that the child had still not been identified and that he most likely never would be. So many things about this case were painful.

His phone beeped. Voicemail. Clocks looked out of the window and around the street while Paterson picked up his message. 'It's Commissioner Young,' he said. 'Wants to meet. Seems he's found out something of interest.'

Clocks nodded. 'Where? The Yard?'

'Greenwich Park, apparently,' said Paterson, turning on the ignition. 'In the little café there.'

'Oh,' Clocks said, 'that's different. Don't normally get someone that senior coming outside. They don't like the daylight, any of 'em. Worried they'll turn to dust.'

'Then I guess he has something important for us,' said Paterson, and headed off along Tower Bridge Road.

* * *

The sun streamed in through the small glass window panes, casting shadows across the table. Paterson looked out to the café play area, watching the mums romping with their children, and wondered where his life had gone. Didn't seem that long ago he was a little boy himself, and now, here he was — a big boy, catching those who would harm them. He watched them play for a few seconds longer, then shifted his gaze to Commissioner Young, briefcase in hand, fiddling with the catch on the little swing gate.

Clocks was busy staring at a teenage mum's backside as she leant over to tuck her child into its buggy. He didn't notice Young walk in.

Young, immaculately dressed in a navy suit and tie, spotted them almost immediately. He walked over, sat down and popped the locks on the briefcase. 'Afternoon, gents. Thank you for coming. I'll have a tea please, Inspector.'

Reluctantly, Clocks tore his gaze away from the girl's perfect arse and swung around to face him. 'Sir.' He stood up and went over to the counter.

'This is unusual, sir,' said Paterson. 'Why are we meeting here?'

Young rummaged around in his briefcase and pulled out a manila file. 'Didn't want anyone on my floor knowing what was going on. Told them all I had an impromptu meeting with the PM. I'll wait till DI Clocks returns, and then we'll talk. I've managed to dig up some very interesting information. It's just the tip of the iceberg, mind. I've not had nearly enough time to dig as far as I intend to.'

Clocks was heading back with a brown plastic tray and three Styrofoam cups. He started doling out the cups. Young looked at them and then at Clocks. 'Where's mine?'

Clocks looked slightly confused. 'Sir? You said tea, yes? They're all tea.' He picked up a Styrofoam cup and handed it to Young. A small smile played around Paterson's lips.

'Don't they have cups in this place, man? I like my tea in a bone china cup.'

Clocks recalled their meeting at the Yard. 'Sorry, sir.'

Paterson heard confusion mixed with contempt in those two little words.

Young scowled at the offending cup. 'I didn't work my way up to become the most senior officer in the country, only to be given a cup made out of a recycled nineteen seventies' ceiling tile!' He looked up at Clocks and gave him a broad smile. 'Just winding you up, Mr Clocks. Thought you might like to know I have a sense of humour to go with my big bollocks.'

'Oh, sir. Had me going there for a minute.' Looking around for somewhere to put the tray, Clocks muttered, 'Dick,' under his breath. Finding nowhere, he put it on nice-arse Mum's table and flashed her a grin. She was standing now, and he noted that she also possessed an impressive chest. This was definitely a better venue than New Scotland Yard. He would talk to Paterson about holding future meetings here.

'Sit down, Mr Clocks,' said Young, all his humour gone. He opened up the file and spread out the contents on the table. One photograph and two photocopies. Didn't look like much to Paterson, but it had to be important to drag Young off the fifth floor.

Paterson picked up the photograph. 'What are we looking at, sir?'

Young took a quick sip of his tea and threw a sidelong glance at Clocks, as if to ask if it was really tea he was drinking. 'What do you see, gentlemen?' Paterson put the photo back down on the table, slid it toward Clocks and both men peered at it.

'College photo. Bunch of toffs,' said Clocks and shrugged.

'Looks old, sir,' Paterson said. 'When was it taken?'

'About forty years ago. The men in this photo would be in their early to mid-sixties now. Back then they were just a bunch of students graduating from Cambridge University.'

'I'm guessing you didn't come all the way down here to show us your old college photo, sir, so what are we supposed to be looking at?' Clocks said.

Young tapped a finger on one of the students in the photo. 'Recognise him?'

Paterson and Clocks stared hard at the fresh-faced young man, smiling happily for the camera, pleased with himself for making the grade and now standing poised to embark on a fine career. After a longish pause, Clocks said, 'Is that — Brigadier Harrison?'

Young grinned. 'Well done. It is indeed. And this one?' He tapped at the face of a young man standing in the back row. More silence while they squinted.

Paterson looked up. Stared at Young. 'Millington?' He knew the answer would be yes.

'Correct. We now know that there is a connection between the two of them,' said Young. 'But have a good look and see if you recognise anyone else. Black guy, end of the back row.'

'Harold Odonte? Fucking hell,' Clocks said.

'Yep. Now, one more. See if you can spot him.'

Both men searched the photo. Their eyes darted across each face, up and down and across the rows. Paterson ran his finger across the rows, and Clocks followed it like a cat with a piece of string. And then they saw him. Bottom row, third right. Forty years younger, but it was him alright.

'Fuck me,' said Clocks. 'It's not. It can't be.'

Young sat back. 'It is. Certainly explains a few things, eh? As you can see, the class roll here gives the names of all the pupils in this class. There is no doubt. I have already tasked a small, highly discreet team of officers to carry out extensive background checks into all four men, so we can build a case against them. Because of Millington's involvement, they'll work with MI5. That's a godsend. They can find stuff out a helluva lot quicker than we can. The two spooks who were at the meeting will be detained. Not because they're involved, but because we can't take a chance on the investigation leaking. Their presence was standard procedure, but I'm taking no chances. While this investigation is being carried out, I want you both to carry on as normal. Do what you do and I'll keep you posted as to developments. I expect to be kept informed with regards to your investigation, but I have no doubt at all that you'll hold some stuff back. That's a given, isn't it?' Young wasn't expecting an answer.

'What do we do if we come across him in the meantime?' said Paterson.

'Nothing at all. Be polite and civil. Don't let on.' He turned to Clocks. 'You an' all, Mr Clocks. Polite and civil. Okay?' Clocks pretended to look offended. Young drained his tea. 'John,' he said, 'when the time comes, if you want him, he's yours.'

* * *

'Let's start again, shall we, Mr Harrison?' said Paterson, a pleasant smile on his face. Next to him, Clocks wore a false rictus grin that was designed to aggravate the man. It appeared to be working, although Harrison kept his cool. He chose to ignore Clocks entirely and focused on the younger, but more mature, senior officer. But he knew Clocks was there. He could feel his eyes on him.

They were sitting in Harrison's office, having driven there straight from Greenwich Park.

'I'm going to tell you what we know. We know you lied to us first time around. We know you lied about the gun, about the shooter — who he is and what he's up to. Corporal Liam Bailey, aka the White Ghost. We know he's one of yours. We know he's a top-level sniper, responsible for killing a large number of people. We also know that he's on the run from the army because of what appears to be a mental breakdown manifested in his overriding desire to kill one General Kamwelu, late of the Tanzanian Army. We know that Kamwelu is now an ambassador for the Tanzanian government and we have good reason to believe that he has colluded with officials within our government to steal an extremely large quantity of money. Money which is housed in a private bank, whose owner Bailey shot dead on the steps of my police station earlier today. That's not been confirmed as yet but trust me, the lack of a skull indicates that Bailey fired the shot. Now we can keep dancing around each other, sir, or we can work together to stop Corporal Bailey and bring him to justice. No point lying any more. I just want your help.'

Harrison listened intently, chin resting on his steepled fingers. After a moment or two of rising anger, he turned to Clocks, who was still grinning like a corpse. 'You need to grow up, officer. Your undisciplined behaviour is a damn disgrace to the police service.' He turned to Paterson. 'You're his senior officer — you should bloody well bring him under control.'

Paterson frowned. 'You'd think, wouldn't you? Thing is, sir, you don't control DI Clocks, you merely wind him up, point him in the right direction and get out of the fucking way. His behaviour is all part of his uniqueness.'

Eager to join in, Clocks said to Harrison, 'Sorry, sir. Don't mean to upset you. I was told to show you respect, but I struggle to do so with people who lie, particularly when murder is involved. Best I can do is smile. Take it or leave it. I don't give a tiny rat's arse. *Sir.*'

Harrison's face turned puce and he balled his fists. Never in his life had anyone treated him with such disrespect, and it was all he could do to contain himself. If Clocks had been a soldier, things would not be going too well for him right now.

'John,' said Paterson, firm, trying to recover the situation. Clocks's rictus grin immediately gave way to a more sombre expression.

Paterson scratched the side of his head and smoothed his hair down. 'The thing is, sir, I also know Bailey's plan.'

Harrison turned away from Clocks and stared at Paterson. He breathed deeply, trying to regain his composure. 'And how would you know what he plans to do, Superintendent?'

'He kidnapped me yesterday. At gunpoint. That's how I came to know all about him and why he's doing what he's doing.' Paterson sat back in his chair. For now at least, he had piqued Harrison's interest and drawn him off Clocks.

Harrison gave this some thought. 'He kidnapped you? Why would he do that?'

'He wanted to know where we, the police, were with regards to our investigation into him. During our conversation he told me that he'd been watching us through a window and he relieved me of a USB stick containing images of Kamwelu and his wife murdering and then dismembering a small child. You no doubt know by now that Bailey has sent out a load of information in the form of documents, photos and the video of the child's murder to the international news outlets. It's been playing on a continuous loop on the TV and will no doubt run for a long while yet. Thing is, it's caused a huge uproar in the public both here and abroad, and the whole issue of diplomatic immunity is now in doubt. I believe that he's done this partly to inform the world of the Kamwelus' atrocities, but also to distract us all from his real purpose — that is, killing them both.'

Harrison's eyes narrowed. 'Why are you bringing this to me, Mr Paterson? What do you think I can help you with?'

'We have to stop him, don't we? Somehow. Now, since he's one of yours, sir, I thought it likely you would know how he thinks. We don't. It pains me to say it, but he's way out of our league.' Harrison straightened slightly — pride. 'I'm hoping you might try dropping the games now, and work with us to capture him.'

'And if I don't?'

Paterson wasn't expecting that answer. Clocks frowned. Neither was he.

Paterson sighed, thought quickly. 'We'll bring you in for obstructing police in the execution of their duty. Just so you know, you're not above the law.'

Harrison eyeballed Paterson, thought of pushing it. Decided not to. 'How long do we have?'

Paterson smiled. 'Not long, sir. They're in custody at the moment. Because of the information that's been released, we've been given special permission to question them on the murders and the money. Kamwelu's a tough old bastard, though, and he won't crack too easily — neither will she, I suspect — but once it sinks in that he can't hide behind his diplomatic status, I think he'll start talking. Once we've got that information, they'll be released back into the wild, onto a plane and homeward bound, and we can start making arrests. He clearly had contacts in this country — Odonte for one. Once we start digging, we'll find the others and there *will* have been others. Matter of time.'

'Has he named anybody yet?' Harrison asked.

'No. As I said, he's a tough old bird.'

'Did Bailey give you any information as to when he intends to fulfil his mission?'

Paterson shrugged. 'No. He got information from me at the business end of a gun. I didn't have that same leverage.'

'Fair point, Mr Paterson,' Harrison said. 'Now we know what he's up to—'

'You've always known what he's up to,' Clocks interrupted, still determined to crank the old boy up. 'He wants to kill them, and while I personally don't have a problem with that, they're still criminals and our job is to nick them for it. That's what we'll do.'

Harrison's eyes flashed with anger. 'Now we know what he's up to,' he repeated, 'I'll instruct an intelligence unit to consider every possible scenario whereby he's likely to carry out his threat. Once I have credible intelligence, I'll ensure that you're informed, so that we can work together.'

Paterson smiled. It looked like Harrison had gone for it. 'Thank you, sir. But we need to be quick if we're to stop Bailey killing them both. So, rather than wait for you to contact us, I'm requesting that two of my officers, John Miller and Abbi Okonkwo, are attached to your unit. They can report to me directly at the end of each day.'

Harrison bristled. 'No. I'm sorry, Mr Paterson, but this is a matter for the military, and I do not want anybody, police officers included, being privy to our intelligence methods. I'm sure you understand.'

Before Paterson could speak, Clocks dived in. 'I don't. No. It was looking to me like we were all gonna play nicely together, but now you won't let the new kids come into the sandpit with you. What's that all about?'

Paterson looked at Harrison. Clocks did have a point but as usual, he'd been slightly less delicate than he would have been in putting it across.

Harrison rose from his chair, signalling that the meeting was now at an end. 'I'll have someone show you the way out, gentlemen. Have your people report at the main gates at nine tomorrow morning. But they are not to interfere. Understood, Mr Paterson?'

'Understood, Mr Harrison, and thank you,' said Paterson, and shook his hand.

Clocks didn't offer his. Didn't see much point. 'Where's the door gone, Mr Harrison? I can't find it anywhere.'

* * *

They drove out of the barrack gates and headed off toward Charlton under a sky as black as Newgate's knocker. Johnny Clocks knew from experience that the traffic through Greenwich was likely to be heavy, and directed Paterson to cut across Blackheath. From there, they could cut back up through the side streets to Deptford, Rotherhithe and on to Tower Bridge. It wasn't the most direct route but Clocks thought it'd be better in the long run.

'You think he's on to us?' said Clocks.

Paterson shrugged. 'He's not stupid, John. He knows we've figured out Kamwelu's game. He knows that the money is in our possession now, so he's not going to see any of it. None of them will. It's all over from that point of view. So it's self-preservation time now. Harrison will be wondering if Kamwelu's already grassed him up and our little visit today was just a ruse to put our people in on the pretext of a joint operation — when the real aim is to find out what he's going to do next. Whichever way, he'll be cooking up a plan to take out Kamwelu himself just in case Bailey fails, and a second plan to take out Bailey too.'

'Sounds like this is gonna be fun. What's the real point of putting Miller and Abbi in?'

'Just to tune him up a bit. Rattle him. He knows Miller's ex-army and can smell military bullshit a mile away. Harrison has to give them some kind of access, otherwise we'll get suspicious, which, in turn, might lead to us arresting him. Basically, it's a bit of a head-fuck for him all round. He might have been a bloody good soldier once but what's his psychological warfare like, eh?' Paterson took his eyes off the road and turned them to Clocks.

'Guess we'll find out. You think Miller and Abbi will be safe?'

'Don't see why not. Harrison will just stick them in with a bunch of analysts to keep them out of the way. Don't see how they'll get hurt shut away in an office drinking tea all day.'

Paterson pulled up at a red light and scrolled through the phonebook on his centre console.

'Who we calling?' said Clocks, watching the lights. 'Amber, guv.'

As Paterson pulled away, Clocks read the name on the console. 'Billy Kingston! What the hell are you up to, Ray?'

'We need some help, John. He's about the only person we can trust at the—'

The familiar voice of ex-Inspector Kingston boomed out of the speaker.

Billy Kingston had had to retire from active service with SCO19 after Adam Walker threw him off the walkway of Tower Bridge, smashing up his back and legs when he hit the river. Commissioner Young had seen fit to bring him back part-time in a consultative role. Few people had Kingston's experience, and Young wasn't a man to waste resources.

After that night, Paterson spent some considerable time mending fences with Kingston. The burden of guilt hung heavy on him, and he made sure that Kingston had the very best care, whatever the cost. It was most likely through Paterson's financial intervention that Kingston was as mobile as he was. It was nothing to be proud of and nothing for Kingston to be grateful for.

Paterson could never talk to the man without seeing the events of that night play out in his head like a movie on a screen. He'd gone to meet Walker on the walkways of Tower Bridge — Walker had chosen the venue, aware of

Paterson's fear of heights. The movie flickered and ran. He remembered overpowering the crew of an armed response vehicle, taking their guns and entering the building. He remembered the showdown. The fight, the chase, shooting at Walker. Chasing him out onto the roof of the walkways, and the fear that gripped him as the wind and the height struck home. Kingston and Clocks running through the stairway door, both armed.

Shot and beaten, Adam Walker surrendered to Kingston. He knew Kingston was a straight player, and that if he surrendered, Kingston would protect him. And he did. Kingston told Paterson to stand down. He wouldn't. He moved toward his injured prey until Kingston stood between them. Paterson was determined to get his revenge on Walker for all the harm he'd done, all the people he'd killed. His friend, Dave Jordan, Peter Reichenbach, the girls he'd made use of, and his wife. Out of all the women Paterson had been with, Lisa was the only one he'd ever truly loved. He'd lost her twice — first, because he couldn't keep his dick under control and slept with Lisa's sister. That cost him his marriage. The second time, he'd slept with Walker's wife. That cost him her life.

Paterson told Kingston to stay out of the way and when he refused, Paterson took a wild, angry swing at him and missed. Kingston ducked, danced away, turned his back but was just close enough to Walker for Walker to grab him and press a scalpel to his throat. Faced with the situation, Paterson had no option but to do as Walker said and throw his weapon into the river. Now they were both disarmed, Walker had no further use for Kingston. Casually, like a man who tosses away a cigarette butt, he dragged Kingston backward and over the side. He fell until he plunged into the river a hundred and sixty feet below.

'Mr Paterson. Unexpected. Can't say it's a pleasure though. What can I do you for?'

'Look, Bill, tell me to go fuck myself if you like, but I need your help. *We* need your help. Me and Clocks. He's with me now.'

Silence.

'Is it to do with that poor little kid?' Kingston said at length.

'Yes, it is. We can't do this without you.'

'Well, screw you, Paterson. I can't really say no, can I? Best you come over then.' And Kingston hung up.

CHAPTER TWELVE

Some days were better than others for Kingston. Today was a bad back day. He shuffled down the hallway of his bungalow like a man in his nineties, shouting at that arsehole Clocks to take his bloody finger off the doorbell.

Clocks put his mouth to the letterbox. 'Come on, Bill, don't sod about. Sky's as black as yer 'at out here. It's gonna piss down any second. What's taking yer so long?'

Kingston thought about slowing down even more just to piss him off, but realised this meeting would then take up the best part of the day. He didn't want that. The sooner they got in, the sooner they'd be off. As it was, it took him a good two or three minutes to get to the door.

As he pulled on the door it scraped the carpet, reminding him that he still needed to get a chippy in to lift it a half inch. One of a thousand jobs he could no longer do himself.

It had been a few months since they'd last met up, and Kingston looked drawn. Paterson guessed it was because he was pushing himself at work, probably too hard, to show that he could still hold his own. Men like

Billy Kingston never complained, and a mere crunched-up back wasn't going to set him off.

'Johnny Clocks.' Kingston looked at the man's beaming face, which he hadn't seen for the best part of a year. 'You don't change, do you? Still a knob.'

Clocks started to let himself in. 'That's Inspector knob to you, civvy boy. Some things do change, you know.'

Kingston let Clocks sidle past. 'I heard. All I can say is the bloody job's gone to rack and ruin.' Clocks's laugh grew fainter as he moved away.

'That happened years ago. Didn't need any help from me. Where's the kitchen? I'll put the kettle on. I'll die of fuckin' thirst if I have to wait for you, Ironside.'

Kingston shook his head, smiled, and turned back to Paterson who was still standing anxiously outside, one foot on the top step. 'Come in, Ray,' Kingston said coolly. 'Go through to the kitchen.'

Head lowered, Paterson nodded and made his way into the hallway. He turned back to see Kingston close the door and stagger slightly as he turned around. There were things he wished he'd done differently that night. Swinging at Billy Kingston was one of them. Killing Adam Walker wasn't, but it had cost Kingston dearly and Paterson would always regret that.

'He's got a point, I suppose,' Kingston said, waving a hand toward the kitchen. 'Takes me ages to get going. I can't tell you how many parcel deliveries I've missed. Bastards won't wait.'

'I'm sorry—'

'Yeah, I know. Leave it, Ray. What's done is done. Let's get a cup of tea off DI knob-head, and you can tell me what's going on.'

They made their way into the kitchen, where Clocks was standing with his back to them rifling through the overhead cupboards to find the cups. He pulled out three big mugs and set them down on the counter. 'Got any biscuits, Bill?'

'Got a warrant, Inspector?'

'Don't need one for biscuit searches, Bill. You should know that.'

Tea made, biscuits found, they filled Kingston in on events so far.

'Sounds like a busy ol' week,' said Kingston, dunking a Hobnob into his mug and watching to make sure it didn't drop into his tea. 'What exactly do you want from me?'

'We know that Corporal Bailey, or the White Ghost, is going to take out the Kamwelus. So does Harrison. We told him so, but we didn't tell him where. We're going to. So, I'm thinking that to protect himself, Harrison will want to take out Bailey. I think he'll let Bailey do the Kamwelus first, then have his boys take him out straight after the shooting. Bit of a double whammy really. He's not sure how much Bailey knows. If he has him killed, it will ensure two things — Bailey, if he does know anything, will never be able to tell anyone if he's dead and it will also stop him from coming after Harrison, once the Kamwelus have been taken care of.'

Kingston dunked again, crammed the remainder of the soggy biscuit into his mouth and spat out a few crumbs as he spoke. 'Once again, then, what do you want from me?'

'We want you to put a team together, Bill,' said Clocks, putting his cup into the washing-up bowl. 'Gotta be on the hush-hush though. Off the books.' Kingston's eyes narrowed. 'Can't risk it getting back to anyone. Bailey will tell us where he intends to shoot from. Our man Miller will plant the suggestion in Harrison's little command unit and they, in turn, will work out a way to take Bailey out. We want your boys to ambush his.'

'Seems an odd way of doing things,' said Kingston. 'Why don't you just nick this Harrison bloke?'

'We thought of that, but this way we can build an even stronger case against him — conspiracy to commit murder. Don't know if it will stick or if it will even work, but it's better than nothing.'

Billy Kingston pulled himself up off his stool, put both hands on his lower back and stretched. Paterson caught the grimace. 'Let me be clear on something. You're asking me to put together an unauthorised firearms team whose job will be to stand by and allow a sniper to kill two people in front of the world's press and then move in to arrest the soldier or soldiers sent in to kill him. Is that about right?'

'Yep,' said Clocks. 'Sounds about right.'

'Okay, I've got that bit. But what about this White Ghost? Once he's shot those two bastards, what's the plan for him? How do we nick him?'

Paterson and Clocks exchanged a quick glance. Clocks coughed. 'Right. Here's where it gets a bit suspect.'

'Oh really? Just this bit?' said Kingston.

'Thing is, Bill, we don't want him nicked.'

There was a long silence. Kingston looked back and forth between the two of them, trying to work out if they were being serious. From the look on their faces, they were.

'Why the fuck not? What's he to you?' Kingston said.

'Nothing, Bill,' said Paterson. 'But he's doing the right thing. He'll leave the country and keep trying to hurt these animals. Plus, and here's the kicker, if we don't help, he'll probably kill us both. Certainly John, anyways. One in the head. Told me he would.'

'Alright,' said Clocks. 'Don't need to sound so fuckin' cheerful about it.'

Kingston couldn't help smiling. 'Imagine. DI Johnny No-head. Not like you'll miss it though, John. You've never had much use out of it, have you?' Clocks gave him the finger.

'And when I'm questioned by Professional Standards, how do I explain what we were doing there?'

'You and your boys were out on a training exercise when you got a call from me,' said Paterson. 'Asking for help.'

'Why would you call *me*?'

Paterson thought fast. 'We got a tip-off that someone was seen with a gun heading to the rooftop. We thought it might be Bailey.'

'Why not use the armed officers already on the ground?'

'There's your answer,' said Paterson. 'Already ground assigned. Protecting the Kamwelus. Couldn't spare the manpower and wouldn't have got any further units together in time. No time to call it in officially. I called you up because I know you go training with your team on a regular basis. I took a chance on you being close to the scene.'

'Why didn't we stop Bailey?' Kingston said.

'Nobody knew for sure that he was there,' Paterson said. 'Call said a gunman. Could have been anybody, could have been bollocks. I asked you to check it out for me.'

'You sent a team to check it out, your boys heard a shot, rushed upstairs and found the soldier, or soldiers maybe. They get nicked, end of. So why don't we nick Bailey?' Kingston was beginning to think that it might work.

'Bailey will be long gone, maybe he'll go hide, or get off the roof, or . . . maybe he gets killed. If he is killed, then we can definitely have the soldiers and Harrison nicked. If he's gone, then he's gone. Your boys can say in all honesty that they never knew of his existence until they saw the news on the telly about the Kamwelus' deaths. Too late then.'

'And has this been given the nod from higher up, or are you two pulling a stroke?'

Paterson and Clocks glanced at each other. 'Well, technically we're pulling a stroke, Bill,' said Clocks, 'but we've had an unofficial nod from upstairs.'

'Have you now?' said Kingston, far from convinced. 'I'm just not happy about letting two people get shot, or about letting the shooter get away. This is way too big an ask, boys. Way too big.'

'We know it is, Bill,' said Clocks. 'We're sorry to have to ask, but these ain't people. They're bastards. Dirty, vicious, no-good motherfuckin', evil, child-murdering scum-of-the-fuckin'-earth bastards who have no right to be breathing the same air as human beings.' He chucked a USB onto the counter. 'While you're giving it your consideration, take a look at this video. Fire up your laptop after we've gone, and when you're done looking at it, I'll bet you a pound to a pinch of shit you're gonna wanna pull on your leg irons and go do 'em yourself. If, after watching it, you still don't wanna help, fair enough. We'll think of something else, mate.'

Billy Kingston peered into the biscuit barrel, took out the last Hobnob and said, 'Put the kettle back on for me, Ray, and shut the door on your way out.'

* * *

Nestled deep in the heart of London, the India Club, an old established gentlemen's club founded in the eighteen-hundreds, was the closest Harrison would ever get to a home. It was a place where old soldiers went, not to die but to live again, reminiscing on former glories, and battlefields they had known. It was a remnant of a different era, when Britain was still an empire and held sway over nearly a quarter of the globe. Membership was strictly vetted, and the club had somehow managed to hold onto its policy of excluding women.

Brigadier Montague Harrison settled back into an old leather armchair, warming his large glass of brandy in his hand. The chair was positioned close to the window, giving him just enough of a view of the outside to be interesting but far enough back so that he'd remain unseen. Opposite him, sipping at a whiskey, sat his old friend, Nigel Millington. Millington's tired and pinched face clearly showed all the wear and tear of a man in his mid-sixties who has been under considerable stress. He fidgeted in his chair, uncomfortable in surroundings that were every bit as familiar to him as they were to Harrison. Every few seconds his eyes darted to the hefty oak door, as if he were expecting someone — Paterson or Clocks most likely — to come barging through and arrest him.

Harrison noted the slight tremor in Millington's hands and wondered if it was a sign of fear or the early onset of the Parkinson's that his old friend had recently been diagnosed with. He hoped it was only the latter. Millington wasn't cut out for extreme pressure. Harrison felt nothing but contempt for a man who crumbled under fire.

At Cambridge, the four of them had been inseparable. They studied together, drank together. Dreamed together. Big dreams. And all of them had succeeded in their chosen fields. While two of them had made careers out of conflict, Millington was more comfortable away from the line of fire, working quietly in the shadows and rising high within the ranks of the Foreign Office, until he became the Minister of State for African Affairs.

'How do we deal with it?' asked Millington.

Harrison eyed him over the rim of his glass. 'I've given it considerable thought. It shouldn't be that difficult to handle, if we keep our nerve.'

Millington took a deep breath. 'By "we," you mean me, don't you?'

'Hmm.' Harrison took a large gulp. 'Look, Bailey's out there. We know he wants to kill the general and his wife, so we let him. Simple as that. We can't allow them to go back to Africa because I don't trust the bastard to keep his mouth shut. He's lost the money — we've all lost the money — and Benjamin has nothing to lose now. If his back's to the wall, and it will be when he gets there, he might decide to drag us all down with him. What have their people said to you about it?'

Millington paused. 'The person I spoke to was very, er, upset. They don't know if the general was just unlucky to have met with Paterson, or whether he's double-crossed them and kept all the money for himself. I assured my contact that there's no doubt that the money's in the custody of the police following the arrest of Harry, but that didn't seem to placate him all that much. They're not certain they can trust us. They want Kamwelu back badly. For, ah, questioning, shall we say. We both know that claiming diplomatic immunity is just an excuse to get them out. They'll torture him to find out what happened and once they've finished with him, he'll be dead. Her too. The last thing they want is for the world to know that their government has been complicit in stealing the country's own money.'

Harrison snorted and took another mouthful. 'I'd like to say win-win then, but we still can't rule out the possibility that he'll talk — or that he already has. Either way, I say we let Bailey carry on.' He put his glass down, and sighed. 'Paterson and Clocks,' he said after a second or two. 'Is it possible that they're working with Bailey?'

Millington, always careful to speak only after considered thought, stared into the distance. 'At the meeting, both men were extremely angry when they were informed that the Kamwelus would have to be released. Inspector Clocks was particularly agitated, and somewhat verbal.'

Harrison shot him a look. 'Man has no discipline. A few years in the army would have done him good. Give me—'

'To answer your question,' Millington interrupted, 'I really don't know. I doubt it, but how else would Corporal Bailey have known when the Kamwelus would be released from custody?'

'Bailey is a highly trained soldier. He knew where they were being held. He would have watched and waited, for days if necessary. It doesn't mean the police tipped him off.' Harrison went over to the window, stood to one side, and peered out into the street. He had his back to Millington. 'What does concern me is whether or not Benjamin has already told them of our involvement.'

Millington frowned. The thought hadn't properly occurred to him. 'But if he has, why haven't they come for us?'

Harrison shrugged. He was tired of it all, and wishing he'd never gotten involved in Millington's schemes all those years ago. He was promised easy money, and easy it was. More so if you had no conscience.

'I don't know. Can't trust any of them. Coppers are devious bastards by nature.' He stood, his back still turned, talking out to the street. 'Anyway, whatever happens, I have a plan. Corporal Bailey will be dealt with. Once he has taken care of Benjamin, I have a loyal man who'll eliminate him.'

'And how will he do that?'

'Simple,' said Harrison. 'Once we know which airport they are leaving from, my man will take up position. He'll know how Bailey will choose his vantage point and will intercept him after the hits. Then it's "Goodnight, Corporal Bailey." We need to finish this business, and tie up all the loose ends.'

Lost in thought, Millington ran a hand across his face. 'I still can't believe Harry's gone,' he murmured. 'I really did like him. Always so kind . . .' He caught Harrison staring at him, felt his face grow warm. 'To me, anyway.'

'Kind? What on earth is wrong with you?' said Harrison, marching back to his chair. Millington said nothing. 'He was an off-the-chart psychopath. Always was. You know that. Christ, I still remember the day he bit off Roger Wilkes's ear playing rugby. Bloody well enjoyed it too. Saw it in his eyes. He laughed as he spat it out. Remember? You must remember. Took six policemen to arrest him after he put the first three on the ground. That's when I knew, without a doubt, that he was mental. Did you ever once stop to wonder why they're both so bloody vicious? Did you never read their files? Benjamin and Harold were brothers. Dirt poor, hugely violent parents, beat them day in, day out. Just think. You both share a tiny hut with your little sister. You, Harry, spend your formative years watching your crazy brother violently rape her, night after night, week after week, year after year. It must do something to you, no? Of course it does. You really should have read their files, Nigel.' Harrison walked further into the room, back toward the shadows.

'Aged fourteen, Benjamin, a big boy now, a soldier, takes a wife. And guess who little wifey is? His ten-year-old kid sister. What was her name again?' He snapped his fingers in the air. 'Oh yes, Blessing. So the question now is — how did Harry get so rich? While Benjamin is off rampaging across Africa, his shit-poor brother, whom he left in their little dusty village in the arse end of Africa ends up becoming the owner of a bank. How does he do it? He probably couldn't even spell "bank" before he paid his way into Cambridge. The answer, of course, is that he stole it — *they* stole it. They robbed, and they killed. Between them, they killed anything that crawled across the face of the earth if it happened to have what they wanted.'

He turned to face Millington, about to speak again. Instead, he showered him in blood and brains as Corporal Bailey's shot punched through his head.

CHAPTER THIRTEEN

'Took him a while to get going,' said DS Miller, 'but once he started screaming, he never stopped until security came rushing in. They found Millington still in his chair, covered in snot and gore with his eyes screwed tight shut. Bloke didn't want to look. Couldn't take in what had just happened. Pissed himself an' all.'

Paterson, only half listening, was looking down at the near headless body on the floor. From the way it looked to him, Brigadier Harrison had just dropped. Straight down. Sandbagged, while his head splattered over Millington. Harrison had obviously gotten careless. Stood in the wrong place.

Paterson turned to look out of the window, wondering where Bailey had fired from. Didn't really matter too much at the moment. Ballistics could sort it out later.

Clocks wandered into the room and looked down at Harrison. 'Fuckin' hell. That looks soddin' painful.' He cast his eyes around the room, looked at the splatter, looked back at Harrison again. He shuddered, remembering what Paterson had said — that Bailey would shoot him if Paterson didn't help. Thank fuck Paterson had said he would.

'Miller,' he said, 'do me a favour. Go and grab a couple of coffees and meet us out in the street. We won't be long. Bit lively, fella. Good man.' Turning to Paterson, he missed John Miller's one-finger salute.

As soon as Miller had gone, Clocks said quietly, 'Did you know he was gonna do this?'

'No. Of course not.' Paterson shrugged. 'I'm not surprised though.'

'Me neither,' said Clocks. 'Suppose that's what happens when you get in bed with the Devil. One of his little angels, archangels or whatever the fuck they're called, is gonna screw you up the arse till it hurts.'

Paterson seemed to think about this. 'I'd have thought it would hurt straight away.'

'S'what I've been told,' Clocks said.

'Who told you that? Your boyfriend?' Paterson grinned. Wind-up time.

Clocks looked embarrassed. 'Fuck off, Ray. You know what I meant.'

'Do I?' said Paterson, grinning all over his face now.

Clocks glared at him — hard. 'Don't even start on that one.'

Paterson let it go. This probably wasn't the best time for wind-ups. Chris Sharpe, today's crime scene manager, was waiting at the door in his white paper suit and staring at them impatiently.

Paterson nodded and raised his index finger to indicate that he should wait.

'You gonna call him?' said Clocks, Paterson's teasing forgotten.

'I'll have to, won't I?' He pointed to the chair that Millington had taken his brains shower in. 'Why didn't he take them both out, John? Would have been a piece of piss for him.'

'He's fuckin' around again. Enjoying himself, I guess. He probably got more fun out of seeing the look on Millington's face and hearing him scream like a crowning mum.'

'A what?' said Paterson. 'You don't get crowning mums, John. Babies do the crowning, not the mums.'

'Do they? Whatever,' said Clocks. 'So, to carry on with what I was sayin', I was flicking through the telly programmes, an' I caught a bit of *One Born Every Minute*. Me and Lyndsey were having our dinner at the time, and she wanted to watch it. Fair enough, I thought. I'll give it a go, me being the new man and all. Honest, Ray, I nearly met me dinner on the way out.' He pointed at Harrison. 'Looked like an upside-down version of him. Only nowhere near as pretty.'

Paterson shook his head slowly, in despair. 'Anyway, moving on, we need to find out what Bailey's up to. And we need to nick Millington now, find out the full extent of his involvement and see if he'll really drop our man in the shit.'

Chris Sharpe's voice sounded across the room. 'Gentlemen, you're not supposed to be in here yet. Have you even signed in?'

Paterson's finger went up again.

''Course he will,' said Clocks. 'He must know we've figured it all out by now, so if he thinks he can deal himself a shorter sentence he'll grass him up like a shot. Besides, he's just seen another one of his bffs' heads do a David Copperfield. He's gotta be thinking that he's next on the list. He might think that if he talks, helps us out, we can get him into protective and then Bailey won't be able to nut him too.'

'Gentlemen. Please!' said Sharpe. 'Can't you do this outside?'

Clocks spun around. 'Oh, fer . . . Just fuckin' jog on, will yer? We're thinkin' here, mate. Proper police work. Go and fingerprint yer arse or something until we're done.'

'Oh, you're a funny one. What? You think this is the only murder in town? I've got to finish up here and deal with a dead girl cut to ribbons.'

Paterson turned sharply. 'Where?'

'Over near Dulwich way. Take me ages to get through the traffic.'

'Not our problem, Ray. Not our patch,' Clocks said.

Paterson nodded. 'Well take a seat then, and wait till rush hour's over.' Clocks said as he turned back to Paterson, missing his second one-finger salute of the day.

Paterson set off toward the door. 'We need to go talk to Millington now. Find out what the true story is before Bailey tops him too. Nothing further to gain from standing around here, is there?'

Clocks followed. He couldn't resist a last dig at Sharpe, by now almost dancing with impatience. 'There's the dead body, there.' He pointed to Harrison. 'Most of his head is running down the wall — there.' He pointed to the back wall. 'I'm no expert, but I reckon it was a bullet that did for him and he is what we call dead. Very. There you go, you don't need your little dusty brush and sellotape now. I've gone and figured it all out for you, helped you beat the traffic. If you set off now, you should be in Dulwich in no time. You're welcome.'

The two men glared at each other, all the way through Clocks's passage out and down the stairs.

'John,' Paterson said. 'We really, *really* have to work on your people skills.'

* * *

Huddled in the back of the ambulance and shivering violently, Nigel Millington sat wrapped in a blood-red blanket over the top of a silver aluminium sheet. Beside him, a young female paramedic sat busying herself with some electronic gadgetry. She'd placed a dark grey band around his bicep and a clip on his finger to monitor his blood pressure. She talked to him in calm, even tones, aware that the trembling was a natural and healthy way of the body releasing excess adrenaline. Physically he would be fine. She wasn't sure about the mental side of things.

'Mr Millington.' Paterson stood in the middle of the doorway, blocking out the light. Clocks peered over his shoulder. Millington ignored them and carried on trembling. 'Nigel!' Paterson snapped.

Millington started. He turned to the voice, and looked at Paterson with uncomprehending eyes. 'Mr Pat . . . Pate . . . Paterson. My God. Dear God.'

'Rough old day, eh?' Paterson said. He looked at the paramedic, a striking blonde who couldn't have been more than twenty-five if she was a day. Her name badge said "Hannah Kline." He automatically clocked the absence of a ring on her finger — single. Old habits die hard. A year or so ago, Paterson would have already had her name and number, and she'd likely have been out on a date with him that same evening. His life was different now. A little bit.

'Can I have a quick five minutes with him, please?' he asked.

She looked up, noted his looks, knew his type at once, pushed down the sudden flush like a professional. 'Sorry? Who are you, please?'

'Detective Superintendent Paterson.' He fished out his warrant card and held it up for her to see.

She looked at the card and raised an eyebrow, unimpressed. 'I'm sorry, Superintendent, but this man is in severe shock. I need to monitor him for a while. We'll be taking him to Charing Cross Hospital in a minute. You can talk to him there, once he's been checked over.' She went back to her work.

'I appreciate that. I understand. Miss, do you think it would make any difference if I told you that this man is suspected of being involved in a number of child murders and the dismemberment of those children for monetary gain?'

Hannah Kline stopped what she was doing and looked up. Paterson had a look on his face somewhere between amusement and deadly serious. She got up out of her seat, and he was somewhat taken aback to see that she was at least five foot ten, five foot eleven tall and had to duck her head as she moved toward him.

'Take your time, Mr Paterson,' she said, and jumped down onto the ground. 'I'll be up front pretending to write some notes.' Paterson gave her a wry grin and mouthed 'thank you' as she passed him. Clocks stood there, awestruck by this Amazonian beauty. In his sexist opinion, she really should be a swimwear model.

Paterson climbed into the ambulance and dropped onto the seat Hannah had vacated. Once she'd let herself into the front of the ambulance, Clocks tore himself away, climbed in after Paterson and slammed the door shut behind him.

Millington eyed them both. 'Mr Paterson. Mr . . . Mr Clocks. Please. You . . . You have to help me.'

Clocks sat down on the end of the stretcher bed and stared at him. 'Oh, jog on, mate,' he said, his voice cold, hard. 'We don't have to do fuck all.'

'Please . . . He's going to kill me, I know he is.'

Paterson leaned in and looked Millington in the eye. 'I know he is. He told me.'

Millington's eyes went wide. He let out a loud, involuntary sob and trembled even more violently. He looked to Paterson, to Clocks, seeking a shred of compassion in their faces. He saw nothing but disdain.

'You . . . can't. You're police.' He saw it was hopeless, and tears welled in his eyes.

'Not right now we're not, Nige.' Clocks moved closer. Leaned into him. Millington put his head down, unable to face Clocks.

'Right now we're a couple of right 'orrible cunts that don't give a fuck about you one way or the other. You're a despicable piece of no-good shit, and this is your payback.

You brought this on yourself. You and your greed. No one can help you now, not even your mates in MI5 who, by the way, are doing a good job of digging up all the dirt on you.'

'We know what's gone on,' Paterson said. 'We know your involvement. You and your band of schoolmates. We're building a case against you all, so be assured that if you're lucky, very lucky, you might just be able to go to prison for the rest of your life. Understand?'

Millington nodded furiously. He understood alright. The tears began falling now, he was convulsed with sobs. Clocks could swear his teeth were chattering. 'Please, please. Protect me. Please.'

'Listen. Even if we wanted to, and bein' 'onest, we don't, how the hell do you think we're gonna protect you from a man who can shoot the bollocks off a fly from two postcodes away?' Clocks said. Paterson shrugged. Clocks had made a good point as usual.

'So,' Paterson said, 'before whatever happens, happens, you need to understand this. When you're released from the hospital, you'll be taken to Tower Bridge Police Station where you'll be formally interviewed. When that recorder starts going, you are going to give an account of the whole of this little adventure you've all cooked up and you're going to give us the full names of everyone involved and their exact role in it. I want everything. I want to know how long you've been on the take, how much money you, along with the rest of 'em, have made. You're going to tell me all about your hidden bank accounts, as well as where all their money's going. I want to know how many murders you've been involved in. How many innocent people have died because of you and that mad bastard Kamwelu and his evil wife. You're going to spill your fucking guts, Millington. Understand?'

Millington nodded and gave a weak grin. Part of him was relieved.

'In return, you will be released, to return at a later date to be formally charged. That's only because I want you in the back of the car when the Kamwelus get to the airport,' Paterson said.

Millington stared at him, genuinely perplexed. 'Why?'

'Because I want you to watch. I want you to see the whole fucking thing come apart, and for you to watch the Kamwelus die.' Paterson grinned briefly, enjoying the prospect. 'If you don't play ball, then I'll also make sure all your assets are grabbed through the courts. Cars, boats, properties — the lot.'

Millington caught his breath, struggled to breathe. 'My wife! Not the house. Please . . .'

'Fuck, yeah,' said Clocks. ''Specially the house, you fucker. We'll kick your missus out onto the street, and you'll have to live with that for however long you've got left. Your kids'll love you for it. Time to pay for your sins, Mr Millington. Everybody gets hurt, eh?' Paterson and Clocks got up and headed to the ambulance door.

Millington watched them, and a wave of despair washed over him. 'Mr Paterson!' he called. Paterson stopped. Clocks, now out in the street, put his head back inside.

'What?' Paterson said.

'What can I do? To say sorry, I mean. I'm so, so sorry . . . Please help me. I'm so scared.'

Paterson turned away and jumped down. He turned back around and stared hard at this snivelling wreck, all swaddled in red and silver. A man who wanted mercy, called for help but gave none himself.

'What you're feeling now, Millington, is a tiny fraction of what that poor little boy must have felt. The fear. The terror. You allowed that to happen. You turned a blind eye. You allowed them all to suffer because of your greed, and now you're getting a taste of it. Not nice, is it?'

Millington looked away. 'Please, please God . . .'

Clocks spat on the ground.

Paterson took a deep breath. 'No such thing as God, Millington. If there was, I don't see how he'd permit scum like you to walk the earth, or allow this to happen to children.' He shook his head, despairing. 'But, on the off chance that there is a God, then at least he's setting it right now. You asked me what you can do, Millington.' He began to close the doors. 'What you can do is give the statement, confess everything, and hope Bailey takes you quickly.' Paterson slammed both doors and walked away, followed by the sound of a dead man's anguished howl.

* * *

'It's tomorrow. Nine a.m. London City Airport,' Paterson was saying. 'I don't know if you're familiar with it, but you'll only have a very small window available to you.' He and Clocks were seated at the back of a small café just off Tower Bridge Road. Opposite them, Corporal Bailey was listening to Paterson carefully, attentive to any sign of a problem — from them or elsewhere. He held a mug of hot tea in one hand and in the other, a Glock 19 pistol resting carefully on his lap and hidden from view. Both were weapons that he could make use of, should it become necessary.

'They'll be brought in under armed escort,' Paterson continued, 'and taken into the airport. Once inside, they will then be ushered through the airport and out onto the tarmac. It's no distance at all from the airport concourse to the private jet, maybe forty-odd metres. They'll be up the steps and gone before you know it.'

Bailey's eyes darted toward the young girl who was headed toward their table with two plates. Assessed her. No threat. He leaned forward slightly to ensure she wouldn't spot the gun and looked back to Paterson and Clocks.

Linda, the waitress, had been trying not to stare at Bailey and finding it difficult. It wasn't every day you got someone so very white come into the café. 'Who's got the all-day full English?' She turned to Clocks almost instinctively. He looked the sort. Clocks pointed at the table in front of him and she set the plate down. She put the other plate down in front of Paterson. 'Scrambled egg on wholemeal toast for you.'

'You sure you don't want anything, love?' she said to Bailey, giving herself the chance to have a proper stare at him. He gave her a faint smile and shook his head. From her apron pocket, she took out two sets of cutlery wrapped in napkins and went off back to the counter.

'Fine,' said Bailey. 'You let me worry about the logistics.' He took a sip of his tea. 'Where's Millington?'

'He's in protective custody. He gave us everything. We have more than enough to prosecute him and put him away for the rest of his life.' Paterson cut himself a piece of egg and toast and ate, savouring it as if it was some sort of haute cuisine dish. He'd lost all memory of when he had last eaten and would likely have swallowed shoe leather if it was all they'd had on offer.

Clocks looked toward the counter, trying to catch the waitress's eye. 'Soppy cow's forgot the fried bread,' he said, and turned back to his grub with a sigh.

'Protective custody? That's a laugh,' said Bailey. 'You can't protect him if I want him. We all know that.'

'I know,' said Paterson. 'But it's a gesture.'

Clocks stopped shovelling food into his mouth for a second. 'Look, mate, I know you're doing the world a favour and all that, but here's a question for you.' He cut off a bit of sausage, dipped it in his egg, popped it in his mouth and started to chew, without taking his eyes off Bailey.

'Go on, Mr Clocks,' said Bailey.

'Ray here told me that if he hadn't said yes to helping you, you'd have shot me. Is that right?'

Bailey smiled. 'It is. Problem with that?'

The little muscles around Clocks's eyes twitched. He swallowed his food. 'Fuckin' right there's a problem, mate. I take exception to some fucked up little Rambo threatening to hide in a tree and shoot me in the back of the nut.'

Bailey's eyes narrowed. 'Mr Clocks. Don't make the mistake of getting all mouthy with me. I said what I had to, to get Paterson to cooperate. You were leverage. I didn't want to shoot you but I would have, quite happily. Don't take it personally. Eat your breakfast.'

Clocks started forward. 'What? Don't take it fuckin' personal?'

Bailey moved back quickly, defensive, his gun hand moving upward.

'John!' said Paterson. His arm shot across Clocks's chest. 'Pack it in. Don't be a fucking idiot. Let it go.'

Clocks eased off. This was a fight he would most certainly lose and in this case, discretion was definitely the better part of valour.

'Okay,' said Paterson. 'Now we've cleared the air a little bit, let me ask you a question. Why did you kill Harrison?'

Bailey took a sip of tea. 'He was one of the officers I went to after that night in the hut. Remember? The one with the upside-down kids? He wasn't having any of it. Gave it all the cultural bullshit. The "none of our business" bullshit. When I started digging, doing my homework, he flashed up on the radar. He was at the embassy with Millington, and it didn't take a genius to figure out they were pals. He was bound to be in on it. Was he in on it?' He shrugged. 'Doesn't matter. He had to go. Plus the fact that the dirty bastard was planning to have me shot. No choice really.'

'Well, so you know, that bit might still be on,' said Paterson. 'Just because Harrison is dead doesn't mean his boys won't still be coming after you. Perhaps even more so now.'

Bailey shrugged again. 'I know. Their problem.'

'Let us have Millington,' said Paterson. 'It'll be good if the public see that the police are doing their job and putting people as high up in the government as him in prison. Restores their confidence in us.'

'Maybe,' said Bailey. 'I'll think about it.' He drained his mug and set it down on the table. 'Why not Heathrow? Or Gatwick?'

'Sorry?' asked Paterson. 'Oh — security. City Airport will be much easier to contain than the bigger ones. Less ground for the security teams to cover. Fewer people milling around. The usual.'

Clocks was ploughing through his breakfast like an express train. He put his knife and fork down and slugged back his tea. 'So, what's the score then? What happens when you've killed 'em both? You'll be leaving, I s'pose?'

Bailey stared off into the distance. 'That's the gist of it, yes. I'm not going to hang around here, am I? I'll have the army chasing me still, and your lot so no, I won't be staying. Talking of being chased, what's happening tomorrow? Have you managed to swing it so that Harrison's boys get taken down?'

'Certainly hope so,' said Paterson. 'We have someone willing to help, and I trust him. He's a good man, knows his way around a scenario. Everything will be good.'

'I hope so,' said Bailey. 'Though Billy Kingston is a bit of a wreck now, thanks to you. Maybe his game is off.'

Paterson stared at him. 'How the hell did you know that?'

'Not difficult, Mr P. You'll have had to go off the books on this one. Couldn't take it to the current SCO19 team because there's not a single operational who'd condone what we're doing, and you wouldn't take a chance on roping in people you don't know with something this big. Plus the fact that you don't know if you could contain it, keep it in-house. Who to trust, eh? They might have arrested you on a conspiracy charge, so that really only left Billy Kingston. He would be the only one who might give it some thought. Clearly, he has.'

'Billy's game is far from off,' Paterson said. 'I trust him with your life.'

Bailey pulled out his mobile phone. Snorted. 'Seems now I'm the one who don't really have a choice, do I?' Not bothering with an answer, he called up Google maps and typed in London City Airport. With forefinger and thumb, he pinch-zoomed until he got to where he wanted. 'Harrison's boy will be working out where I'm likely to shoot from. Looking at this, he'll conclude there are at least five places I can use. For that, he'll have to recruit a small kill-squad to station themselves around all the possible sites.' He stared at the screen. 'Let's make this easy. I'll be on top of the Travelodge. Feed it back to your people on the inside so they can drip it out to someone. Tell Kingston to have his boys hidden away on standby. Once they know my shot point they'll send one, maybe two men. As soon as Harrison's team are in place, Kingston's boys should be able to take them out easy.'

'Sounds like a plan,' said Paterson.

'Best I can come up with for now,' Bailey said. He slipped the phone back into his pocket and stood up. He suddenly stopped and looked at the two detectives. 'Why are you both doing this? Why are you helping me?'

'Cause you threatened to kill me,' said Clocks.

'No. There's more to it than that. You'd have found a way around that somehow. You could have set me up today, had firearms officers swarm all over this place to take me down. But you haven't. So why?'

Paterson sighed. 'You're the only way we have to make them pay.'

'Gentlemen,' said Bailey as he slid out from behind the table. 'I'll be in touch. Breakfast is on you, Mr P.'

CHAPTER FOURTEEN

Temperatures had taken a sharp dive overnight and London, at four in the morning, was decidedly cold. It was still dark and below him, the cityscape would glitter for another hour or so before it faded with the dawn.

Flat on his belly, Corporal Bailey inched over the cold concrete of the Travelodge roof. On his back, in a reverse fitted harness, was a MOLLE tactical assault pack that contained enough equipment to keep him alive for months should it prove necessary. It also doubled as a support for his rifle. He wondered if Harrison's man was already somewhere out there in the dark, watching him. He knew he was taking a gamble on the man not deploying a sniper like himself to take him out, but he figured that Harrison would most likely have sent someone in for a close-up kill. That way he'd be certain that the job had been done. For the first time in his life, Bailey was afraid. At least if he were sniped he wouldn't know a damn thing about it.

He reached the edge of the building and peered over a ledge toward the airport. The position of the planes on the tarmac in relation to the exit from the main hallway troubled him. Google satellite photos had their uses but they could never give a true picture. Whoever had picked this place as an extraction point had chosen well, for it was almost impossible to get a clean shot.

He set up LISA, slipped off his pack and pulled out a roll of thick nylon rope. Bent double, he duck-walked over to one of the mobile phone masts and secured the line around one of the stanchions before tying it to himself. He tested it a few times and lay flat once more. He checked his scope, made a few minor adjustments and pulled out two pistols from his vest. He laid them carefully on the ground, one on each side of him, at roughly shoulder height.

At eight o'clock, his watch beeped. He silenced it and pulled out his mobile phone. He scrolled through his list of contacts and stopped at "BBC News." He pressed "call."

After a couple of rings a disinterested man on the news desk answered the phone. 'Hello. BBC News. How can I help?'

'Listen to me carefully. I am known as the White Ghost. I have already released information to the press and into the public domain. Ambassador Kamwelu and his wife Blessing will not stand trial for their crimes. In exactly one hour they will arrive at London City Airport to be flown out to the safety of their own country under diplomatic protection. This information has not been made public at this time because of the outcry and protests it would provoke. Instead, the British government have chosen to remove them quietly and deal with the fallout later. Enquiries will be dragged out, taking years, by which time people will have forgotten what they did. You already know the crimes this man and his wife have committed. If you want to get the scoop and be the only news organisation to record the cowardly actions of our corrupt government, I would suggest you get a television crew and a reporter to the departure hall at precisely eight fifty-eight.

If they arrive any earlier, the government will get wind of it and call the transfer off or redirect. Do you understand?'

'Er, yes.' The disinterested man had suddenly perked up and Bailey could hear him scribbling something down. 'How do I know you are this "White Ghost" fella, and not some hoax caller?'

'You don't. And I don't have the time to waste in convincing you otherwise. If you're not interested, fine. I'll find another news agency that is. So I'd recommend you get someone down there. Their departure must be recorded. The government cannot be allowed to get away with this.' Bailey hung up. It was up to them now. He scrolled through his contacts. Reuters next. Then Sky News. And CNN — that was a good one.

He gave them all the "scoop." At least one crew would be enterprising enough to get themselves out onto the tarmac at the right time, even if just on the off chance.

He lifted the rifle and peered through the scope.

* * *

At exactly 8:58, the first of several vans skidded to a halt outside the main concourse of London City Airport. Corporal Bailey watched through his binoculars as the crews decamped and frantically grabbed at their equipment. The "talent" were hastily patting their wind-blown hair into place and preparing themselves to tell the world a story about which they knew very little. Cameramen were busy swinging hand-held cameras over their shoulders and carrying out their tests. "Breaking News" scrolls would soon be rolling across the nation's TV screens.

Bailey smiled. Full house. They had all turned up, looking to get the exclusive. Well, they'd get a whole lot more than they expected. Much more.

A few minutes later two police motorcycles, followed by a blacked-out, black-all-over Range Rover, roared to a halt outside the airport. In the back of the heavily armoured vehicle sat Kamwelu, Blessing and Mr Mangu from the embassy. A very nervous Nigel Millington hunched deeper into a corner, trying his best to keep away from the windows, blacked-out or not. Behind them was an SCO19 crew, fully kitted up and ready to go. Paterson and Clocks brought up the rear in the BMW.

'Looks like he's got himself the audience he wanted,' said Paterson. He took in the scene. News vans everywhere, reporters all over the place, some crowding the Kamwelus' car, several already inside the main hall. Many would be desperately trying to get tarmac side. They were more of a distraction. ITV were already in position outside on the banks of the Thames, looking toward the airport. They should have a clear and unobstructed view of the boarding party, and would get the definitive film for any ensuing enquiry.

Paterson got out of the car and was immediately recognised by one of the reporters, who made a beeline for him. Clocks jumped out the other side, and scowled at the approaching reporter, who kept coming, microphone in hand. His cameraman ran after him.

'Detective Superintendent Paterson! Mr Paterson!' the reporter called. He stopped short in front of him. 'Peter Burson, BBC. Is it true that Ambassador Kamwelu and his wife are being freed from police custody and allowed to return to Africa?'

'As you can see, I'm a busy man, Mr Burson. I have no comment. Call the press office,' Paterson said. He side-stepped the reporter and headed off toward the Kamwelus' car. Burson, who was a seasoned reporter, wasn't about to give up.

He and the cameraman followed the two detectives. 'Detective Paterson. The BBC have reliable information that the Kamwelus are to be released and deported under diplomatic immunity. Is this tr—?'

There was a loud clattering, and shouts rose from behind him. He and Paterson turned at the same time, startled at the noise. Sprawled on the pavement lay the cameraman. His camera was a couple of feet beyond.

DI Clocks was walking past, glancing down at him with a satisfied look on his face. 'Dunno what happened to him,' he said. 'Bloke just seemed to fall over.' Paterson grinned. Burson was furious. The cameraman let out a torrent of filthy abuse at Clocks, who carried on walking. Clocks looked briefly back at him. 'You need to lay off the drink, fella. Seems to make you a bit wobbly. And foul-mouthed.'

* * *

The Range Rover had mounted the pavement and parked close to one of the sliding doors, ready for its occupants to make a swift exit into the relative safety of the main hall. SCO19 had surrounded the vehicle and were swing-pointing their machine guns into the air, looking to the rooftops. These were not Kingston's men.

Billy Kingston, having watched the film of the boy's horrific death in the vault, couldn't bring himself to stand by and do nothing. He was involved now, as Paterson and Clocks had known he would be. They'd been counting on it.

He'd deployed a team of plain-clothed firearms officers into the Travelodge, and two of them were already in position in a hallway, one floor down from the roof. They were watching the elevator numbers. Their task was to wait for the call, and watch the lift go past them to the top. They would then creep out and up the stairway, where they would hopefully arrest the would-be assassin before he could get to Bailey.

The team in the foyer had easily spotted their target on his way in. Crew-cut, strong, no-nonsense bearing, moving fast and with purpose. A man with a mission. He might be a good soldier, but he was piss-poor at undercover work. He even patted his breast pocket while he waited for the lift. As soon as the doors closed, the shout went up on the radio — 'Target is go.'

The back door of the Range Rover flew open and as quickly as they could manage, Benjamin and Blessing stumbled out and into the airport building. Three SCO19 officers escorted — or rather pulled them into a waiting room and away from the news teams that were scrabbling for a comment and trying desperately to film them. Mangu and Millington followed quickly behind. Once the Kamwelus were out of sight, the reporters went back to broadcasting events live to the nation.

Out on the tarmac, final preparations were underway in the privately chartered Lear jet. The boarding steps were now in place. Paterson and Clocks looked around the hall. A camera crew were pleading to be let out onto the tarmac and being sternly repulsed by airport security. An armed police officer shouted to them to stand aside and not to obstruct the doorway. From the tone of his voice, it was clear that he wasn't going to put up with shit from anyone.

On the roof, Bailey readied himself. He could sense Harrison's man waiting, and his mind was working overtime. So many things to think of. So much activity below. He knew he had a very limited window of time. The man behind bothered him. Could he trust Paterson? Could he trust Kingston? He had to. Up to a point. He didn't have time to deal with the problem now. He took a deep breath, settled himself down, drew the rifle in closer to his shoulder, steadied it on the rucksack. *Whatever happens, happens*, he told himself. He pulled back the slide-action bolt on the rifle, chambered the Magnum bullet and aimed. It would soon be over.

Inside the waiting room, a SCO19 officer was struggling to fit a Kevlar vest over Benjamin's bloated stomach and failing miserably. Blessing was a lost cause. In the end, the lady officer attending to her decided that there was no way of closing it and instructed her to hold it shut, as tight as she could. In truth, the protective clothing was no more than a gesture. This type of vest would no more stop a round of that velocity and calibre than a half-pound tub of Flora Light.

It was a pointless exercise anyway, as Bailey always went for the head. Everybody knew that. Even if the Kamwelus' heads were wrapped three sheets deep in Kevlar, the force of a Mag bullet from the Lisa would still be like a hit to the side of a head with a wrecking ball, causing instant death at best and serious brain damage at worst — the kind that leaves you wishing you *were* dead.

Paterson was standing with Clocks by the doors leading out to the tarmac. He calculated the distance from the doors to the stairs of the Lear. 'John, he won't get them both.'

Clocks took his eyes away from the stewardess standing at the door of the plane. 'Just what I was thinking. They're not going to bring them out together, are they? Too risky. They know that if Bailey is here, then it's one or the other.' He lowered his voice. 'He's going to have to make a choice, irrespective of who comes out first. Fat bastard number one or fat bastard number two. What'd you reckon, Ray? Fiver says he lets Benjamin live.'

Paterson looked perplexed. 'Why? He hates him with a vengeance.'

'Exactly. If he kills his old woman, then Benjamin is going to throw a thrombie just on the strength of seeing his missus lose her head.' Paterson grimaced. 'The thing is, he can then keep going after Benjamin, keep dangling death in front of him. Benjamin is going to have to live with the fact that's she's dead. He might be able to handle it — callous bastard that he is — who knows how he'll take it? But whichever what way, he's going to be handling a big old dose of twenty-four-seven anxiety for his own life.'

An armed officer appeared in the doorway of the plane and moved the stewardess back inside, telling her to go to the back of the plane and wait. A police dog handler

— explosives — emerged and hustled his dog down the steps. The officer on the plane touched his throat mic and spoke.

The waiting room doors burst open. Two gunmen led the entourage out toward the tarmac, shouting, 'Clear the way! Move!' Behind them more SCO19 watched the entrance doors. On the concourse, five more SCO19 held their ground, crouching, their SIG MCXs moving in wide arcs as they strained to see any sign of anything or anyone out of the ordinary. Paterson and Clocks moved rapidly out onto the concourse, careful to pick where they stood. The staircase was quite steep and not particularly wide. It was the obvious choice for Bailey when he took his shot.

SCO19 stopped the group at the doorway. Blessing was up first. The gunman looked at her. Her eyes were full of nothing but terror and tears.

Paterson froze, gripped by a panic that suddenly and unexpectedly flooded his brain. *Supposing Bailey misses? Supposing he kills a police officer? Supposing he kills me? Or Clocks? He threatened to. What the fuck am I doing? I'm allowing Bailey to murder someone. I've helped Bailey commit murder. Ah, Jesus . . . Jesus Christ . . . I have to stop—*

A loud crack rang out and reverberated around the hall. Everyone ducked, and turned sharply toward the noise. Somehow, instinctively, they all knew what it was. A shooter among them.

* * *

Benjamin Kamwelu lay face up on the floor, staring at the ceiling. There was a neat hole in the side of his head, and a pool of blood started to seep out from underneath him. Blessing screamed. It was the most blood-curdling of screams, tearing right through the soul. The sound of pure, unadulterated anguish. Apparently she was capable of feeling after all.

'Drop the gun! Drop the fucking gun! Do it! Do it now!' SCO19 were back in the game and screaming orders.

Cameramen, torn between their personal safety and the chance of a Pulitzer award, composed themselves and hoisted their rigs onto their shoulders.

Nigel Millington peered out through the glass doors and caught sight of Ray Paterson staring at him, his mouth gaping open. Their eyes locked for a moment or two. Millington turned away. He saw all the guns pointing at him, the faces of the men shouting at him with their mouths moving, but heard only the humming in his ears. He pulled the trigger again, putting two bullets into Kamwelu's stricken torso, before something punched hard into his own chest. For a brief second, he saw the ceiling flash into his field of vision, and then he died.

'Stay back!' shouted the SCO19 officer who'd put him down. Shocked, the reporters and unarmed police did as they were told. Several SCO19 officers moved closer, surrounding his body. One kicked Millington's Walther P99 just out of reach. The officer crouched, put his fingers on Millington's carotid artery and pronounced him "neutralised." Someone else would pronounce him dead.

'What the fuck?' said Johnny Clocks. He pushed his hands through his hair, held it back, a look of genuine shock on his face. 'Why did he . . .?'

'Go. Now!' the officer in charge of SCO19 barked at his team. 'Get her moving.' *Big mistake*. The sensible thing to do would have been to get her back into the waiting room and then contain it, but adrenaline and the fear of another possible shooter do funny things to a man, however much experience he has.

In the midst of all the confusion, Blessing had dropped to her knees, screaming, babbling, wailing. Two officers struggled to lift her dead weight. Finally, they managed to haul her to her feet and back onto the concourse.

* * *

Bailey, looking through his scope, could see that something was wrong. Inside the terminal, the cops were screaming, waving their arms about, looking back into the airport.

Something had gone *very* wrong in there.

He breathed deeply, and watched the movements of the people below. What had started out as a simple, professional hand-over had descended into an undisciplined shambles. He knew they would pick the ball up soon, but right now something inside the hall was still distracting them, and until it was under control, their thinking would be fuzzy.

He watched.

* * *

Blessing burst out of the hall onto the tarmac, arms waving, in a stumbling run toward the Lear. The SCO19 officers tried to catch her and hold her back, keep her head down but she was determined to run. She reached the steps and began an ungainly climb. Her foot slipped on one of the steps and she fell hard, smashing her face against the metal. Her mouth gushing with blood, she hauled herself up, steadied herself and looked up, just for a second. It was long enough for Bailey to take her.

It took the SCO19 officers a moment or two to realise what had happened as Blessing, minus most of her head, slithered down the stairway and beached on the tarmac. They began screaming instructions to one another, guns moving wildly around, looking for the shooter. Frozen to the spot, Paterson and Clocks looked toward the Travelodge and saw nothing there.

* * *

Corporal Bailey moved fast. He dropped the rifle, rolled onto his back, snatched up the Glocks and aimed toward the fire-exit door just as it opened slightly. Harrison's man coming for him. He had no time to aim properly, no time to steady himself. He fired just as the soldier stepped out onto the roof. The bullets went wide, and smashed into the concrete wall above the soldier's head, making him duck before he crouched and rolled.

The two plain-clothes SCO19 officers, guns drawn, chequered baseball caps and armbands on, began to run up to the roof. No need for stealth now, their man was in play. The sound of shots from above brought them to a walk.

The soldier rolled himself to a kneeling position, found the man who'd shot at him dead ahead and raised his weapon two-handed. Bailey was already half up on his feet, crouching low and running toward the edge of the building. The soldier got off two rounds, double taps, then watched in disbelief as Bailey launched himself off the roof. He saw the rope, and realised Bailey was about to run the building, abseiling down.

He picked himself up and began to run toward the fire exit when the door suddenly burst open and the first SCO19 emerged, gun held out high in front of him in a two-handed grip.

'Armed poli—'

The soldier fired instinctively, two sharp cracks. He had no idea who was coming through the door, and didn't particularly care. The policeman went down, hard, onto his back. As he landed, his colleague scrambled back down three or four stairs, crouched low and waited.

The soldier ran into the doorway. He stood, silhouetted against the sky, and the waiting policeman, without warning, opened up with his SIG, punching the soldier back out through the door a lot faster than he came in.

Satisfied that the soldier was no longer a threat, the officer eased his way up the stairs toward his colleague. He was relieved to find him alive, his Kevlar vest having done its job against small arms fire. The soldier really should have worn his.

* * *

On the airport concourse, Paterson and Clocks looked on in amazement as the tiny figure of Corporal Liam Bailey jumped off the roof and plummeted toward the ground until his body abruptly jerked a few times before bouncing him feet first onto the wall. And then he was running, literally, down the wall.

'For the love of God,' said Paterson. 'Do you see this, John?'

Clocks was standing stock-still, mouth open, staring at the running man. In the space of maybe twenty seconds, Bailey had sniped and hit a moving target, shot at an assassin, jumped off a building and was now fleeing the scene. Down a wall. The side of a building. 'I see it, guv, but I'm fucked if I believe it.' And then Bailey was gone. Out of sight, behind a treeline, he quickly unhooked himself and sprinted away. He was safe.

By ten past nine the news services had updated themselves and were busy scrolling the story to the nation — "Breaking News: Woman shot dead at London City Airport. Two other people are believed to have been injured in bungled police operation."

'You can always rely on the news boys to get it arse upwards,' said Clocks, reading out the ticker to Paterson. He finished watching the news on the BBC app and looked up from his phone. 'What do we do now?'

Paterson took a deep breath. 'Our job. We're murder squad, John. Let's get it under control. You take the outside.' Paterson headed back into the hall and started barking orders to the officers there. 'Get away from the body. Clear the area. Now! Who fired on the dead man?'

The shooter, a man in his thirties, came out of his reverie. 'Sir,' he snapped.

'Waiting room. Surrender your weapons to your inspector. Talk to no one.' Paterson yelled at the TV crews to get out. 'Crime scene. Contamination. Do it now or be arrested.' He continued to bark as he took control of a very messy crime scene.

By ten o'clock, both scenes were as preserved as they were ever going to be. Paterson had drafted in his entire team, and some more from a neighbouring borough, to help out. Everyone had to be interviewed, everyone brought in, and the men in white suits needed to do their job.

Paterson walked out onto the tarmac, gingerly holding two paper cups by the rim, full of nuclear hot tea. He handed one to Clocks. 'Well, this is a clusterfuck of epic proportions, isn't it?'

'Ain't it just,' said Clocks, blowing on his tea before risking a sip. Nope. Scalding. He put it down on the ground. 'What the fuck happened with Millington? Why the hell did he tap Kamwelu?'

Paterson gave it some thought, glanced toward the Travelodge again. 'Don't know. I guess he was scared. Maybe he wanted to be buried with his head intact. Or maybe he grew a last-minute conscience. You know, a sudden epiphany. Didn't have the balls to top himself so went suicide-by-cop. I dunno.' He glanced over at Blessing's body, sprawled face up — except she had no face. And very little head, come to that. A SOCO man was busying himself around her, treading carefully.

Paterson rubbed his face. A true bastard of a first week back at work. He sniffed, pinched his nose, sniffed again. 'At least they got served,' he said. He gestured toward Blessing with his cup. 'And good fucking riddance to the pair of them.'

'By my reckoning,' said Clocks, 'that's a straight flush — Odonte, Harrison, Millington and the Kamwelus. All gone bye-byes.'

'Except we're still one adrift. We need to get this wrapped up.' Paterson glanced at his watch and pulled out his phone. 'DI Clarke from Deptford is going to handle things here for a while.' He pressed his phone to his ear.

'We need to report in to Mr Young. He's going to want an urgent update. I expect the PM will be bending his ear something chronic by now.' He drained his tea, a feat that perplexed Clocks who could only just manage a few sips without it taking the roof of his mouth off.

'Sir,' Paterson said into the phone. 'We need to brief you on events at the Kamwelus' transfer. You're no doubt aware of what's happened.' He listened. 'Okay. We're on our way in to see you now.'

CHAPTER FIFTEEN

Day 5 — Thursday

At nine thirty the next morning, Commissioner Young was seated behind his vast desk, having just finished his third phone call of the day. Everybody wanted a piece of him and the pressure was on. The Home Office wanted an urgent meeting to discuss the investigation. They seemed concerned, but really all they wanted was to cover their own backsides and figure out a way to publicly distance themselves from Millington. Damage limitation was now the order of the day.

The Department of Professional Standards, the Met's anti-corruption unit known as DOS, had called with their findings so far. They had discussed an allegation of GBH against DI Clocks along with other allegations that DS Paterson had stamped on a man's face and also violently assaulted a member of the Tanzanian Embassy in the course of his official duties. Unlikely that one would fly, as the only witnesses to it were now dead. Clocks's complaint, maybe. Still, he'd wriggled out of worse.

And now Young had just finished up with the Prime Minister, an amiable enough but serious conversation in which she had demanded a full face-to-face briefing at midday. He explained that there was a matter of extreme importance that he had to attend to and that it ought not to be delayed, but it cut no ice. The information that Bailey had leaked, plus the news footage that had come out of yesterday's events, had left the government in a seriously embarrassing position and the PM was not best pleased. Statements had to be made. Blame had to be laid. Politicians must be made to wriggle.

Wallace Young took off his glasses, pinched the bridge of his nose and rubbed his eyes. Today was all set to be another long one. Interesting, but long. He poured himself a large medicinal Scotch and sat back in his chair, momentarily captivated by tiny dust motes floating lazily in a solid wedge of light that slanted through his window.

A sharp rap on the door brought him back to earth, and he shot a glance at his watch. Two minutes late. He could wear that.

'Come!' he called. Deputy Commissioner Watson strode in, and shut the door behind him. 'Morning, Tony,' said Young. 'Come in. Take a seat.'

Watson sat down and put his briefcase beside him. 'Bit early for that, isn't it, sir?' He nodded toward the drink.

Young gave him a look and a faint smile. 'You'd think. I've been up pretty much all night sorting out the shit-storm that hit us yesterday. I'm tired and just a tad grumpy, so best you don't fret about my breakfast beverage, Tony.'

Watson shrugged. 'What's the order of the day then, Wallace? What's our priority?'

Young scratched the back of his neck. 'I met with Paterson and Clocks yesterday, just briefly, and they brought me up to speed. However, they were needed on scene so we didn't get into too much detail. Paterson described it as a, er, "clusterfuck," and I have to say, I agree with him. Sounds like it all got away from SCO19 but in fairness, it's too early to start playing the blame game. We have a lot to look at.' He took another sip of his drink. 'This business with Millington — totally out of left field. No one saw that coming.'

Watson stiffened slightly. 'Has this bloody sniper been found yet? For Chrissakes, why haven't those two clowns Paterson and Clocks got him yet? They know who he is. Rumour is they've been feeding him info. Set this whole thing up.' He shifted about in his chair, agitated. 'They need to be brought in and bloody well questioned by DOS.'

Young frowned and held his hand up. 'They will be. Professional Standards are on their way in to see them now.'

'Good job too,' said Watson.

Young ignored him and carried on. 'They will have to give statements about what's happened, of course. We all will. They know that. Before that, though, we have a meeting with them.'

'What?' said Watson.

'They're coming in. Thought it would be useful if we all spoke together. So you know what's going on. Bring you up to speed.'

'I don't trust them, sir. They're both bad lots. Clocks is an insubordinate thug, a football hooligan with a badge. And Paterson? Incompetent at best and a bloody murderer at worst.'

Young squinted, eyes hard, cold. 'Careful, Tony. Clocks has his . . . drawbacks, I'll accept that, but after a full investigation the CPS decided that Paterson had no case to answer. I've spoken to him at length and I'm satisfied with his version of events. That's the end of it. Don't forget, it was my decision to bring Paterson back to the team and from what I can see of this case, they've done their level best given the circumstances and how quickly everything has moved. In my opinion, they are both bloody good coppers.'

'With respect, sir, I don't think it was your best move, bringing him back. They've both continued to bring the force into disrepute. They've acted in defiance of diplomatic agreements between countries.' Watson was visibly angry now, barely holding himself in check.

Young shook his head, disappointed to the last. 'They are police officers first and foremost. They did what they believed to be right, irrespective of any agreement.'

'Well sometimes, sir, we can't always do the right thing. Sometimes we have to do just what we're told.'

Young downed his whiskey, grimaced and shook his head as the liquid burned a path to his gullet. He leaned across his desk. 'Let me give you some advice, Tony. We've known each other for some years now. We don't always see eye to eye and sometimes that's not a bad thing. Checks and balances and all that. But you might want to reconsider your tone when you speak to me. Bear in mind that I'm your bloody senior officer and not some subordinate copper you can throw your weight at. Clear?' Their eyes locked. Watson was first to blink. 'Good,' said Young. 'Now, when they arrive, you would do well to listen and treat them both with respect. Especially Clocks, as he is not too fond of senior officers at the best of times and, from the short conversation we had, right now he is seriously stressed and edgy.'

Watson looked incredulous. 'Are you serious? Are you sitting there saying that DI Clocks might actually assault me?'

'He might, yes. That's why you might not want to get too uppity with him. He can be tricky to control.'

'For God's sake, Wallace. You're the bloody Commissioner of Police! You can't honestly be saying that you'd just sit back and allow a junior rank to assault your deputy commissioner.'

'I didn't say he would, or that I'd let him, or that I would sit back. I said to be careful how you speak to him. Fair warning.' Watson shook his head in disbelief.

There was a sharp rap at the door and Watson sat bolt upright. He turned to look at the door as Young called them in. Paterson and Clocks strode into the office, said their good mornings and took up seats on either side of Watson. It made him uneasy.

Young reached into a drawer, pulled out a plain brown folder and dropped it on his desk. 'Gentlemen, thank you for coming. I know you had a bloody rough day yesterday. Been a bit frantic here too.' He gave them a smile, offered and poured them a drink each, asked Watson again. He accepted.

'Okay, gents. Skipping the bits we already know — airport related and all that – tell me everything you've found out over the last week.'

For the next few minutes, Paterson recounted all that had happened — the shooting of Babatunde, the discovery of the child's torso, the meeting with Kamwelu when he was calling himself Atewojaye then Abimbola. His meetings with Harrison, Millington, and Odonte. How they'd all been killed one by one. His kidnapping by the White Ghost, formerly known as Corporal Liam Bailey. The video showing Blessing's beheading and subsequent dismemberment of the boy. Right up until the airport bloodbath. DI Clocks sat in silence, giving the occasional nod at salient points. When he'd finished, Paterson took a big slug of his whiskey, screwed up his face and set down the glass. Watson eyed him up and down, looked across at Clocks, caught Clocks grinning at him.

'I want to thank you for your support in this matter, sir,' Paterson said to Young. 'Your assistance has been of great help, and I want to thank you for the investigation you ran in the background on my behalf.'

Watson looked perplexed. 'Wallace? What's going on? What investigation? Why wasn't I informed?'

Young looked down his nose at his deputy, over the top of his glasses. 'I needed to keep this one tight, Tony. Very tight. Some information came to light early on in this case and I needed to get some background checks done very quickly. I had to get the PM's authority, which wasn't a problem when I outlined the facts to her. I really don't know why people think she can be awkward. She was quite delightful.' He opened the folder and spread out some papers. They seemed to be financial records, details of telephone calls, copies of cheques, bank statements and a number of photographs. These were face down. Young flipped a few of them over and spread them out. Head and shoulder shots of Odonte, Millington and Harrison.

'Here's what we know so far,' said Young. 'We were quite fortunate in that Millington was in such a senior position within the government. I was able to gain access to an awful lot of information extremely quickly via the intelligence services. They got onto it like a hungry dog with a bone.' He moved his finger along the spread photos.

'These three are all known to one another.'

'How exactly?' said Watson. He looked at the photos, frowning.

'I'll get to that,' said Young. 'Bear with me. These three, along with General Benjamin Kamwelu and his wife Blessing, conspired with unknown officials within the Tanzanian government to steal and subsequently launder just under a billion pounds of government money. We think this was a double whammy in so much as the Tanzanians could then claim that they'd been the victims of a very audacious and complex robbery involving Kamwelu. They would subsequently make pleas featuring a looming doomsday scenario for their country's economy, and various governments world-wide would assist by making up the lost money. It being Africa, Western governments would be queuing up to chuck money at them, not wanting to be accused of failing to help such an impoverished country. There would be a puppet investigation, nothing would come of it and certain people would subsequently live extremely comfortable lives on the proceeds.'

He stopped to look at Watson, to see if he was following. Watson was still looking at the photos, tapping the one of Millington for some reason.

'The stolen gold and money would have been washed by then,' Paterson chimed in. 'No trace of it, if anyone was to look.'

'We also,' continued Young, 'found out that Benjamin and Odonte are blood brothers and that Benjamin married their kid sister Blessing when she was just a child. Ten, I think she was.'

Clocks leaned forward. 'The whole family were seriously fucked up.' Watson drew back from Clocks's intrusion into his space. 'That's hillbilly shit, that is.' Clocks smiled, mostly to himself. 'African hillbillies.'

Young picked it back up. 'We're still putting it together, but we think that Millington was the brains behind the whole job. Not just this one. There were a lot of others, all in Tanzania, all involving theft, all involving murder and, of course, all involving the murder of small children to satisfy the Kamwelus' belief in witchcraft. Millington knew of this and turned a blind eye in exchange for mountains of cash. Then he had the mother of all brainwaves. His position as Minister of State for Africa gave him access to some very powerful people who could be, shall we say, greased to overlook Kamwelu's atrocities. We think he reached out to some government officials and explained that if Kamwelu was pardoned, or whatever the equivalent is over there, and made an ambassador for his country, he would be able to travel freely and, since his brother happened to own a bank, it would be easy to remove some of the government's money, put it on a plane and bring it over here to be laundered.'

Paterson pointed to the shot of Harrison. 'Harrison's job was to keep Kamwelu from running up against any sort of military intervention while he was in Tanzania. They couldn't afford to have him killed or arrested. Of course, none of them could have foreseen Corporal Bailey's righteous intervention. Once he found out that Bailey had a bee in his bonnet and an insatiable desire to kill the Kamwelus, Harrison spent a lot of resources trying to track him down and have him eliminated but we all know that didn't go according to plan either.' Watson lifted his head, looked at Paterson and nodded. 'We do know for a fact that Harrison sent someone to kill Bailey on that rooftop yesterday. The soldier he sent shot a policeman, who, fortunately, is fine, but was not so fortunate himself. He's got more holes in him than a colander.' Clocks grinned at the mental image of the soldier pissing out blood from various holes in his body.

Young straightened his back to get the stiffness out. 'So, that's what we do know. But what we don't know for sure,' he stared at Watson, 'is what *your* role was.'

Watson stiffened. 'What? What are you . . .?' He couldn't finish the sentence. A rabbit caught in the headlights, he looked around at all three of them. All were staring straight back at him, their faces cold. Hard. Clocks, though, had a hint of a smile on his. Just a hint.

A deathly silence fell over the room. Everyone waited for the accused to speak. He didn't. Couldn't. A sudden sound, like a double tap from a hand pistol, startled Watson into jumping. Paterson had popped the two locks on his briefcase. He raised the lid, pulled out a single photo and dropped it onto the desk in front of the startled Watson. The Cambridge class photo. 'Is there a reason why you didn't tell us you were at Cambridge with this lot of murdering bastards?' he said, his tone even, calm. Watson said nothing. 'It is quite important, don't you think?' said Paterson. 'The Deputy Commissioner of the

Metropolitan Police failing to disclose his relationship with three people involved in theft and murder.'

Watson turned to Paterson, tried to hold his gaze. Failed. 'I . . . it was a long time ago. I didn't realise at first. I . . .'

'You sayin' you didn't recognise Kamwelu and Odonte in the vault video? You sat an' watched it with the rest of us. Their faces were pretty clear,' said Clocks, who was beginning to get antsy. 'How could you not recognise 'em? Summink wrong with your eyes?'

'Valid question,' said Young to Watson. 'Answer it.'

'I was . . . was concerned that if I had, had mentioned it, you would think that I was—'

'More bent than a bag of pretzels going round a bendy road on a bendy bus?' Clocks chimed in. 'Fuckin' right we do.'

Watson took his chance, a pitiful one. 'How dare you, Clocks!' He rounded on him, his chair went back a bit too fast. Clocks shifted his position. 'I'm the bloody deputy commissioner, not some two-bit thug you think you can frighten. Don't you dare make such accusations! You're suspended. Now!' That made Clocks and Paterson laugh. Clocks gave him the hand gesture — tosser.

Young's face was dark as thunder. 'Stop being an arsehole, Watson. Clocks will put you down in a heartbeat and he'll have my full backing,' he said. 'I warned you about being careful.' The two men glared at each other. 'So, moving on, and please stop me if I go wrong anywhere, we think that your role in this job was to monitor the situation, the money and boy's arrival, and to ensure there was no police interference either then or on the money's subsequent onward journey to the bank. Once you heard about the murder of Babatunde, you figured Bailey was here too and so you started to monitor HOLMES and other systems. We know you did, so don't waste time trying to deny it — digital fingerprints and all that — and you would have watched Paterson and

Clocks's investigation unfold. That's why you kept wanting to suspend Clocks, so as to throw a spanner in the works long enough for the money to be washed and the investigation disrupted. You thought everything would be fine once Kamwelu played the diplomat card. They'd all disappear into the sunset and that would be that. Got pretty pissed when these two decided to play go-fuck-yourselves. Weren't expecting that, were you?'

Young rubbed his face and put his hands together behind his head. 'That about right, isn't it?'

Watson shook his head slowly, the reality of the situation sinking in.

'Thanks to the efforts of the intelligence and security services,' said Young, 'I have solid evidence that you were involved in the scheme to launder stolen money from the Tanzanian government. I have bank statements — not your legitimate ones, but the others you thought you'd hidden. The ones with far too much money in them, even for someone on your salary.' He pushed the copies across to Watson. 'The deposits go back several years. Now I know why you kept going to Africa on your holidays. I also have your phone records. They show a number of calls to Millington and Harrison over the past few weeks. We have three calls to Odonte in the first two days after the Kamwelus landed. I would imagine you were checking to ensure the money had arrived safely.'

Watson snapped out of his reverie. 'Sir. If I can just—'

'Shut up, Watson. Don't bloody well interrupt me,' said Young. 'I have at least fifteen calls made by Millington to you. The idiot used his government-issue phone.' He rolled his eyes and shook his head. 'What fascinates me is that he didn't know his calls were being recorded. Standard practice.'

Paterson took another slug of whiskey, rolled the remainder around the glass and drained it off. 'Though it's possible he did know they would come to light at some point. In light of his actions at the airport yesterday, perhaps he did grow a conscience over this one, some time ago. Maybe subconsciously he wanted them found and all of you brought down.' He put the glass down. 'But I guess we'll never know now, will we?'

'I have audio copies of those calls,' Young said. 'All of them have been transcribed. I had your house, office and car bugged for good measure. Those recordings make for interesting listening. In short, you're going away for a very, very long time, you filthy bastard.'

Watson sat still, breathing heavily, his heart going like a trip hammer. He glanced across at the window. Saw the office blocks outside. He knew he was five floors up, and for a split-second pictured himself running and jumping through, glass shattering everywhere, and plummeting the five floors to crash onto the pavement below. Wishful thinking. He remembered the window was made of armoured glass and felt more than a bit disappointed, even though, in his heart, he knew he didn't have the balls.

Wallace Young pushed the heels of his palms into his eyes and exhaled loudly. 'Y'know, I could understand you doing it for money,' he pushed his chair back and stood up, his temper rising, 'but what I can't get my head around is that you allowed them to murder a child. A child. No more than, what, six? They fucking cut him to pieces just because of some voodoo shit. Some bloody money spell to help make sure you all got your cash. What the fuck is wrong with you? You have kids yourself.' He swallowed hard, his face dark with rage. Never a good sign in a man like Young.

Watson stood up slowly, trembling. His voice shook. 'Let me explain, let me . . .' Paterson and Clocks stood up. Oh, come *on,* thought Clocks, make a run for it. Please.

Young moved around the desk and stood over Watson. 'You have no explanation. None. You were sworn to uphold the law. In my book, there's nothing worse in this world than a bent copper. You coward. Fuck you to hell. You're lucky that Bailey never shot you. Damn pity he didn't bother. Would've saved us all the time and trouble of putting you in prison, you worthless piece of shit.'

'Sir, I . . . let me . . . please!'

'Don't bother, Watson. Tell it to Professional Standards. They might give a shit.' Young looked across at Clocks. 'Inspector,' he said, 'as I promised, he's all yours. Get him out of my fucking office. He stinks. Arrest him for—'

'No!' said Watson, squaring up to Clocks, much to the junior officer's delight.

Young went on, overriding Watson's pleas. He had warned him. 'Perverting the course of justice, conspiracy to steal, conspiracy to handle stolen goods and money, conspiracy to murder, murder, suspected involvement in a number of child murders . . . I could go on. Oh, plus of course bringing the Metropolitan Police service into disrepute.'

Watson turned to him, eyes wide, unable to take in what was being said, his world gone to rat-shit. Clocks touched his arm. *You are under arrest.*

Watson reacted. He snatched his arm away, turned back to Clocks and drew his arm back to throw a punch at him. Commissioner Young moved fast. He smacked Watson full in the face, breaking his nose and sending him backwards over a couple of chairs, where he clattered onto the carpet.

Paterson and Clocks stood stock-still, taken aback. 'That's for the boy,' Young said, and walked round his desk to look down at the fallen man. He spat on Watson. Paterson noticed that Commissioner Young didn't shake his hand out the way people do when they've hit someone hard. He didn't seem to have felt any pain. The man might be cracking on age-wise, but a fighter was a fighter. 'Get it out of here,' said Young, and turned his back.

Clocks bent down and pulled Watson up by the lapels, struggling to hold him upright. 'C'mon, scum. Time to go meet those nice boys from Pro Standards. They've got a shitload to talk to you about.' He hooked his shoulder under Watson's armpit and took his weight. Watson's head wobbled, and there was blood in his mouth, his teeth red with it. He tried to focus and babbled incoherently. Clocks grinned. 'Don't forget to tell them how slippery Mr Young's big thick carpet is. You might be able to have a claim-up.'

CHAPTER SIXTEEN

Almost done now. From the building opposite, Corporal Liam Bailey looked across at Commissioner Young's office and watched the scene play out. The butt of the rifle felt like an old friend, warm and comfortable against his cheek. He peered through the scope and for a moment or two, toyed with the idea of killing Deputy Commissioner Watson. He swung the gun around, found Paterson, then Clocks. *No. Not them.* They were the good guys.

Paterson had asked him to spare Millington. He wanted to arrest him, and show the world that even the establishment could be brought to book. It was a good idea, one he'd been happy to go along with until the gutless bastard went and got himself topped by the Bill. Bailey wasn't overly upset by his demise, but felt for Paterson. Guy just couldn't catch a break.

He dropped his finger from the guard, rested it against the trigger, curled his finger around it. Took a breath.

He could see Watson getting angry. He was on his feet now. Looked like he was shouting at Johnny Clocks. From the limited interaction Bailey had had with Clocks, even he knew that wasn't the best idea. A broad grin spread across his face while he watched Young chin Watson, saw him sprawl back amongst the chairs. Wasn't expecting that. *Good on yer, Pops.*

He watched Clocks haul him up, and the grin faded. *Move aside, Mr C, move aside. You can't have Millington now, Mr Paterson, but you can have this one.* A bit damaged, though.

He squeezed the trigger.

One moment Johnny Clocks was holding DC Watson up, the next the man seemed to spasm violently and jerk away, collapsing with a god-awful scream of agony. Clocks froze. Paterson and Young jumped back instinctively. Bailey's shot had hit Watson smack on the kneecap, severing his leg and dropping him to the ground. The man on the floor kept screaming, his face a mask of agony, shock and fear.

'John!' shouted Paterson. 'Get down! Get down!' Paterson had rolled himself against the wall. 'C'mon. Move!'

Dazed, Clocks glanced over to the window, saw the hole, the broken glass. He looked back at Watson. 'Fuckin' hell!' he shouted, dropped to a crouch, rolled under the window and crawled toward Paterson.

Young found the panic button under his desk. Within seconds, two AFOs burst into the room, weapons free. Young shouted to them, 'Get down! Shooter outside.' They dropped down, one frantically shouting into his radio, the other trying to drag Watson to safety. Every pull only increased the man's agony and his screams grew more frantic until finally he passed out.

The firearms officers crawled toward the window and scanned the area for the shot venue, barking into the radio. Several more firearms officers — always present in New Scotland Yard — tore through the foyer, out into the street and into the building opposite. SCO19 were mobile and very close.

Bailey was long gone.

He stood on the pavement outside the Yard, his baseball cap pulled down over his eyes, and watched the officers race into the building he had just left. He hailed a passing cab and politely asked to be taken to Gatwick.

As the cab pulled away, the driver, in typical London cabbie style, tried to start up a conversation. It made his job a bit more pleasant. 'Looks like something's gone pear shaped over there, mate. They're all tooled up to the nines. Someone's going to get a bloody good hiding. Wouldn't like to be on the end of that lot when they catch him.'

Bailey looked out of the window, a faint smile on his face. 'Me neither. Can we just go, please? I really don't like guns.'

* * *

Johnny Clocks took his dunny hat off and wiped his forehead with his handkerchief. He was dressed in a pair of khaki cut-offs, a cheesecloth shirt held together by a single button and a pair of flip-flops.

'Jesus, Ray. How do these people *do* this fuckin' heat every day? I'm sweatin' me bollocks off.' He wiped the back of his neck and pulled his collar out, flapping it to get a bit of a breeze going.

Paterson smiled. 'It's Africa, John. Normal for them.'

'I'm bloody well dyin' here.'

'Just think of the suntan you'll get.'

'Bloody skin cancer is what I'll get, more like.'

Paterson smiled and turned when he heard a woman call his name. His smile grew into a big grin as Abbi Okonkwo came running toward him. It had been eight months since she'd quit the force to take up a post in Africa, six since she'd left England. Six months since he'd last seen her.

Paterson had mentioned that he was looking for someone to run the place he was putting together, and she'd jumped at it. She quit there and then, absolutely determined to help stamp out the ritual child abuse enacted in the name of witchcraft. And what better place to start than Africa? At the heart of it all. Paterson had always known she was a smart cookie, dedicated and ambitious, but he was astonished by what she'd achieved since she arrived. She'd been a good cop but she was a better humanitarian, a tireless fighter for the safety of these kids. Raising both funds and awareness of the problem, she had somehow enlisted the help of pop and movie stars, and even governments, to her cause.

Abbi threw herself into his arms and he swung her around. 'Ray! How are you? It's so good to see you. I've missed you.'

'I'm good, Ab, I'm good. It's good to see you too, hun. I've missed you.' He looked into her eyes. She was a good choice. 'Love what you've done with the place.'

She laughed and broke away from him. 'John,' she said, just as happy to see Clocks. 'Good to see you. Why, gosh, I've missed you most of all, Scarecrow.'

He smiled back. ''Ello, babe,' he said, completely missing the reference to the *Wizard of Oz* and the brainless Scarecrow. 'How you been? Coping with this heat? Fuckin' doing me in.'

Abbi laughed at him. 'This? This is autumn. Wait until the summer comes around and it turns hot.' He looked horrified, and she threw him a wink. 'Come on in, let's get out of the sun.' She grabbed Paterson's hand and they headed off toward a large yellowish building at the back of the compound. Clocks followed on behind as they weaved their way through the groups of young children playing happily in the dirt yard. Most of them were albino. She greeted a few adults, parents and carers, waved, smiled and then they were inside. The change in temperature hit them like an arctic breeze. Air-conditioning ramped to the max.

'Oh, thank you, Jesus,' said Clocks, making a beeline for the machine. He ripped open the one-button shirt and let the ice-cold air hit his sweat dampened chest. 'Oh, God. This is better than sex, I swear.'

Abbi raised an eyebrow and strolled over to the fridge, a brand-new big American job. 'What? I hope you're not still doing that. Has someone been letting you do that to them? Not Lyndsey, surely? She must know what you're like by now. Damn it. I left explicit instructions to all the women within ten miles of you to give you a swerve if you came sniffing around.' She gave him a broad smile. He gave her the finger from each hand. And a smile to match hers.

She pulled out three cold beers, opened them, handed them out and then took a seat. Paterson joined her. Clocks refused to leave the air con.

'How's Miller?' said Paterson.

Abbi swigged her beer. 'Yeah, he's good. He's meeting some bigwigs to try and squeeze some money out of them.' Shortly after Abbi quit the force, DS John Miller had gone too, and followed her out to Africa. Apparently being thrown together in amongst Harrison's unit had brought them a lot closer together than either could ever have expected. They'd been married in a local ceremony and were now working together to set the world to rights. No one saw that coming. 'He'll be back this evening. He's dying to catch up with the pair of you.'

Paterson clinked his bottle against hers. 'Me too. I like him.'

'Trial's over then?' she said, her expression serious now. 'What happened to him?'

Paterson took a swig of beer, breathed in sharp, the cold hitting the heat from his gullet. 'You haven't heard?'

'Not much telly here, Ray.' She waved a hand around the room.

'Watson pulled a lifer.' Abbi's eyebrows shot up. 'Judge has insisted that he be detained without hope of early release.'

'Bloody hell,' she said. 'That's a shocker. Thought the establishment would've helped him out. A few years and out.'

'Nope. Not this time. He's appealed, of course, but it won't do him any good. Second highest ranking police officer in the Met. Huge betrayal of his office, of the people. Judge was damned angry. Saw the Kamwelu video and nearly passed out. Six of the jury actually did and the other six chucked up, and then passed out. All getting counselling now.' He chuckled at the memory. 'Not going to be easy for him. A one-legged bent copper in prison. Bailey made sure he'd suffer for his sins.'

She smiled. 'Serves the bastard right.'

'Oi, Abs,' shouted Clocks. 'That fucker nearly took my head off when he shot Watson. Frightened the shit out of me.'

Abbi laughed. 'I'll bet he did, John. Never mind, you're all rufty-tufty, aren't you? You'll get over it.'

'I dunno, Abs. You don't get over a thing like that. Terrible. Gives me nightmares still.' He drifted off somewhere before coming back with a grin. 'At least that's what I tell the psychiatrist bird. Should be able to get a few quid compo out of that if they think I've got that PTSD bollocks that everyone raves about.'

The door opened and a large man walked in. He was in his mid- to late fifties and wore glasses. He looked at Clocks with some amusement as the man himself looked over his shoulder, still hogging the air conditioner, refusing to give it up.

'Peter,' Abbi said to the man, evidently pleased to see him. 'Come, come. This is Mr Paterson, the owner.'

Peter Ako, the compound's chief medical officer, strode across the room, his hand outstretched, a warm, sincere smile on his face. 'Mr Paterson. It is a pleasure to meet you. Thank you, thank you.' He pumped Paterson's hand up and down furiously.

Paterson grinned, a bit embarrassed. 'Good to meet you too, Peter. Abbi tells me you've been doing some wonderful work here. I'm very grateful to you.'

'No. It is I who am grateful to you. You have helped so many with your generous gift. Gifts, that is.'

'It's okay,' said Paterson. He looked across at Abbi. 'Glad I could help.'

She cocked her head to one side, smiled at Paterson again. 'You really have done a wonderful thing, Ray. This compound will help to save the lives of many children. It gives them and their families a safe place to be, away from the witch doctors, people like Kamwelu. They'll be much safer now, and it's down to you.' She gave him a look. 'And your money.'

'Yes, Mr Paterson,' said Peter. He looked at Paterson almost reverently, still not quite able to believe that a single man had paid for a fortified compound to be built, and staffed with doctors, nurses and teachers. The armed guards were a necessary evil, but they ensured the children's safety. 'Your kindness is beyond compare. Thank you again.'

Clocks, cooling off his back now, shouted across to the group. 'Abbi! The gold statue of him should be here on Monday. Make sure you bang it up in the middle of the square where everyone can worship it. Three times a day. He's got quite used to that. Had one put in his office back home.' Grinning, Paterson gave him the finger.

'And thank you for giving us Abbi,' Peter went on. 'She is a most wonderful woman. Her business skills are second to none.' He beamed at his co-director and made for the door. He had work to do. Medical stuff. He shook Paterson's hand, then Clocks's, then went out.

'We're working closely with the government, Ray, and a number of protection charities and awareness groups. The government had already outlawed witch doctors before all this happened but, like I said, you'll never totally stop it. Never.'

Paterson drained his beer and asked Abbi for another before taking a seat next to a big floor-standing fan.

Clearly he wasn't going to be getting any of the air con anytime soon.

Re-fuelled, Paterson said, 'Did you find out about the boy? Who he was? Where he came from?' He took a big swig.

Abbi looked at him, lowered her head a bit. 'Yes. I did. I tracked down his village. Spoke to people, witnesses.' She took a deep breath. 'His name was William Chikawe . . .' Her voice trailed off.

Paterson rubbed his chin. 'Go on. What happened?'

Abbi took a sip from her bottle, and pressed the cool glass against her neck. 'William's mother was down by the river, washing the family's clothes, when she saw Kamwelu and a gang of men, heavily armed, heading toward her village. It's a small one — maybe sixty, eighty people, no more than that. She knew why they were coming. Knew it would happen one day. She ran, raised the alarm. Hid William — or thought she had done.' Abbi breathed in. 'Blessing was with them, strutting around like she was some kind of fucking princess.' Paterson frowned. 'Anyway, they fired their guns into the air, terrifying the villagers, ordered everyone to be rounded up and dragged into the middle of the village. Kamwelu was shouting that they were there for something special, a boy with skin lighter than that of a white man. The child was of great importance, he said. They must bring him out. If they didn't, there would be consequences. To their credit, nobody gave him up. They all denied having seen such a boy until Kamwelu, seriously pissed off now, hacked one guy in the neck with his machete. He almost killed him, then left him lying in the dirt, bleeding like a pig. They started talking then, pointing to the boy's parents. Kamwelu thanked them and, to show his appreciation, killed the wounded man. A single shot. His men raided the parents' home and came out with the boy.'

'What did the parents do, Ab?' said Paterson, distressed.

'They knew what was in store for them. Dad tried to fight them, to get his boy back, but got himself stabbed to death, right in front of his wife and child. Evil bastards. Evil.' She sniffed, swiped her nose with the back of her hand. Paterson noticed her eyes. Big, brown, full of sorrow. Abbi's voice dropped lower. 'Know what Blessing did?' Paterson shook his head. 'Stood by. Watched and laughed, fucking laughed, as Kamwelu raped the boy's mum. Right there on the ground, in the dirt.' She choked. 'She fought back though, Ray. She really tried.'

Paterson remembered. 'The plaster on Kamwelu's face. She do that?'

'Yeah, I think so,' Abbi said. 'Raked his face with her nails. Guess she figured she had nothing left to lose, so she might as well inflict some damage on him. Anyway, that wasn't the worst of it.'

Paterson stared at her. *More? Jesus wept.*

'When he'd finished, the troops took a turn each and when they'd finished, Blessing . . .' She stopped and rubbed her face, wiped at the tears that were falling freely now. 'Blessing rammed a crucifix into her vagina. Raped her with it, hard. Went into some kind of fucking trance. Witnesses said there was blood everywhere . . . so much.' Speechless, Paterson looked up to the heavens, more convinced than ever that God was just a fairy tale. 'And as the coup de grace, she ordered the mother to be necklaced. Know what that is?' He shook his head, not really wanting to know.

'It's when they put a petrol-soaked tyre around your neck and set fire to it. Blessing herself lit it up.' Abbi let that sink in. 'As they left, they torched the village.' She lifted the bottle, drank deep, finished it. She was quiet for a minute or two. 'One more thing, Ray. You know William had a little teddy bear?' Paterson's eyes were overflowing now. 'His mum and dad worked for a month to get the money together for that. It was William's birthday that day. He was five years old.'

CHAPTER SEVENTEEN

Liam Bailey lay in the tall grass, flat on his stomach. The harsh African sun beat down on him mercilessly. The heat burned his back, his legs, and under his hat, a ring of sweat soaked the headband.

Within the next twenty minutes the sun would be at its zenith. The heat didn't particularly bother him. He'd operated in worse conditions. Besides, he was busy. He had his bottle of water and his rifle. That was all he needed. And he had a witch doctor.

He followed the man through his telescopic sight, watching him carefully. Bailey noticed he was carrying a small bundle and looking altogether too pleased with himself. He estimated him to be about a quarter of a mile away.

Corporal Bailey checked the wind direction.

Took a deep breath.

Calmed himself.

And squeezed the trigger.

THE END

Thank you for reading this book. If you enjoyed it please leave feedback on Amazon, and if there is anything we missed or you have a question about then please get in touch. The author and publishing team appreciate your feedback and time reading this book.

DETECTIVE RAY PATERSON BOOKS
Book 1: THEIR LAST WORDS
Book 2: THE LOST CHILDREN

LOOK OUT FOR STEVE PARKER'S NEXT BOOK
COMING SOON

Printed in Great Britain
by Amazon

54419747R00154